Surveillance

Ghost Targets, Volume 1

Aaron Pogue

Published by Masked Fox Productions, 2010.

This is a work of fiction. Similarities to real people, places, or events are entirely coincidental.

SURVEILLANCE

First edition. October 12, 2010.

Copyright © 2010 Aaron Pogue.

ISBN: 978-1499735901

Written by Aaron Pogue.

Also by Aaron Pogue

A Consortium of Worlds
A Consortium of Worlds No. 1
A Consortium of Worlds No. 2

A Dragonswarm Short Story
Remnant
From Embers

Auric's Valiants
Notes from a Thief
Auric and the Wolf

Ghost Targets
Surveillance
Expectation
Restraint
Camouflage

The Dragonprince's Arrows
A Darkness in the East

The Dragonprince's Legacy
Taming Fire
The Dragonswarm
The Dragonprince's Heir
The Original Dragonprince Trilogy

Unstressed Syllables Presents
Turn Your Story into an eBook: Easy Self-Publishing with Draft2Digital.com

Watch for more at AaronPogue.com.

This one's for Trish.

Katie's biggest fan. And mine, too.

Prologue

It was easier than he ever would have imagined, wringing a woman's neck. Cleaner than using a gun or knife, certainly. She struggled, but she was a slip of a thing and he still had the strength of a younger man. With his hand crushing her windpipe she couldn't scream, and he could see in her wide blue eyes that she was too terrified to cry. For that he was grateful. It made everything easier, after all.

He waited in the frantic silence. At last she stopped thrashing, but he waited still for the angry throb of her pulse to die away under his thumb before he let her go. Then he left her body where it fell, on the dense gray pile carpet half-hidden behind a giant fake potted plant, and made his way back through the empty offices to the elevators.

When the doors rumbled open, he paid no mind to the sign hanging at eye level, an ornate curl that declared, "Hathor knows what you've done." He stepped into the car and turned his back on it to push the button for the lobby. When the doors closed, they made another sign in matching font, "...but Helen knows what you need."

He ignored the marketing slogan, as he had on the way up. His hands, so sure a moment ago, were shaking now. He looked down at them in bemused curiosity, but his mind drifted on to other things. All in all, he thought, it had gone fairly well. Not the evening he had been hoping for, but not as bad as it could have been. All things considered. As the numbers ticked down, it did occur to him that he probably hadn't needed to kill her, but she'd surprised him and he'd gone on first instincts.

A loud ding sounded before the doors buzzed open, and he stepped into the foyer. Out of old habit he nodded to the receptionist on his way out. Across the marble floor, he pushed through the big plate glass doors and stepped out into the night, darker already than it ever got back home but not nearly so chill as he would have expected.

His car was still waiting for him by the curb. Another lucky break. He pulled the door open, and as he was climbing in he thought once more about the sign hanging in the elevator. "Hathor knows what you've done." The door fell heavily shut behind him, *clunk-tk*, and the reality of it finally struck him.

He'd killed a girl. He had committed a crime in front of God and everybody. He sank deeper into his seat and pressed the heels of his hands against his eyes. He took a deep breath.

Why did he feel so calm? Was this shock? Or had he simply made the wisest choice in a difficult situation? He shook his head, because it didn't matter. Panic or not, he was in trouble. He knew that much. He took another breath.

"I know you're listening," he said. He was surprised his voice didn't tremble. He took some confidence from that. "And I need your help. I need the record changed. I need that not to have happened. Please." He winced at the word. It always made him feel small. But he caught his breath and pressed on. "Please. Fix this for me."

He waited a moment in silence, head bowed, hoping for some answer. None came. Still, his heart felt a little lighter. There was never any answer, but he was always listening. Everything would be all right.

He let his head fall back, until he was staring up out the rear window at the massive looming edifice of the database service's office building glowing in the night. "Take me to the airport," he said to his driver. "Make it quick." He felt the wash of motion carrying him away from his sin. Overhead, the streetlights became a percussion and then a blur, and the noise of the city outside faded to a hum.

He sighed, and let his mind wander. Nothing to worry about at all.

1. Ghosts

Katie was a woman in her mid-thirties, dangerously close to her late thirties, with long, straight black hair, and a pixie face with a grin that could still turn heads. She wasn't grinning now, though. Yesterday she had been the top detective in her department. Today she was late, first day on a new job, and there was no excuse for it. She darted into the elevator just before the doors fell closed. An older man built like a linebacker smiled down at her as she straightened her clothes—half sympathetic, half amused—and her heart stopped as a voice whispered in her ear, "Rick Goodall, Department Head, FBI Ghost Targets." Her boss. She blanched, and his smile widened as he extended a hand.

"Good morning, Katie Pratt. I'm glad you could make it."

She fought down a blush and cleared her throat. It was no good making up excuses, so she just said, "Thank you, sir."

He laughed. "Call me Rick. And I mean it, Pratt. I'm glad to have you with us. You have a hell of a record."

She shrugged. It was true, but she knew that wasn't enough. "I've always wanted to work for the Bureau. Since I was a little girl. For me, this opportunity—"

"For all of us, Pratt." He turned to stare at the burnished steel doors, freeing Katie from his laughing gaze. He went on. "It's a fine department. You probably know that already, but we get the real action." He glanced at her, measuring. "We're the only ones left doing real police work. I'm showing my age, saying that, but I think you know what I mean. Your old man—"

"Yeah," she said, then blushed again. "I mean, 'yes, sir.' I know exactly what you mean."

He chuckled. "I told you to call me Rick." The doors whispered open, and he waved her out ahead of him.

The landing served only one office, sealed off wall-to-wall with floor-to-ceiling glass doors that had the words "Ghost Targets" frosted into them at eye level. The receptionist by the door looked like an old intercom panel—ancient technology. The courthouse back in Brooklyn was using tiny, almost invisible microphones and just relaying video feedback directly to people's handhelds. She'd gotten used to that. Most places these days had sleek pedestal monitors that fed directly off the ambient local audio (for a small fee to Hathor). This one looked like it was just a panel mic, probably connected to a local computer running voice recognition code in some back corner of the office. With all the other fanciness of the building, it surprised her.

The department head paid no mind. He stepped up to the sealed doors and said, "It's me, and Katie Pratt with me."

Katie called out a tentative "Hi!" just in case, because she'd worked with old equipment before. Still, she felt a little silly, especially when Rick turned that laughing gaze back to her as the doors slid open.

"Come on, Pratt."

The office beyond felt so much like the one she'd left behind that a sudden homesickness stabbed at her. She'd only been away a day, it was silly, but her stomach knotted and for a moment she couldn't move. The office was mostly given over to an open floor plan with desks back-to-back along the walls and a handful in a cluster in the center of the floor. They'd always referred to that as the "bullpen." Just like home, there was too much clutter for a modern office, but she knew how that happened. There were also the busy, serious faces at the desks, and laughing conversations at the water cooler and in the break room there to her left.

She spotted three conference rooms that could work as interrogation rooms (or maybe the other way around, up here), and the lights were on in one of them as a handful of agents discussed something on the full-table display—and Katie suspected it was even odds whether they were looking over a new break in an important case, or the latest fantasy football numbers. This time of day, on a Monday, she'd put her money on football.

This place still looked just like home. But none of the faces were familiar, and the ones that turned to her as she followed Rick to his office were the serious desk faces, not the friendly water cooler ones. She hated that. She hated being new. She hated being alone.

Rick didn't notice. He never slowed his step, and she had to hurry to catch up with him as he pulled open his office door and held it for her. She took one of the plush chairs, her back to the window on the familiar office all full of strangers. His desk was neat, bare except for three matching framed photos, all turned away from her, a notepad, a black pen, and a coffee mug. About half of the pages had been torn from the notepad, leaving only a clean, unmarred page staring up at the ceiling. She'd never seen a notepad like that on a person's desk. Certainly not on a cop's. There were always half a dozen pages folded over the top, and scribbles on the exposed page from passing thoughts and phone messages as often as meeting minutes and memoranda. This page was pristine, its spent, soiled brethren nowhere in sight. It fascinated her.

Then a moment later something else struck her. The desktop wasn't a monitor. Just stained mahogany, with a real grain finer than anything a screensaver could fake. That surprised her enough that her eyes jerked to his, just as he sank into his plush leather office chair. He smiled at the questions plain on her face.

"I have a handheld in a desk drawer somewhere. I work mostly with voice notes, though, and just keep track of it all in my head. After all, the work we're doing...the computers don't do us much good anyway."

She sighed and shook her head. "You know," she said, "it really irritates me when anyone can read me like that."

"It should," he said. "Bad news for a cop. But go easy on yourself, it's your first day. And you are *not* the first new recruit to sit in that chair."

She shrugged and put on a rueful grin, but in her head she was cursing her foolishness. There was no reason for any of this to take her by surprise. She'd known for weeks what she was getting into. Mr. Goodall sat on his throne, safe behind the expanse of his bare mahogany desk, and waited for her to take control of herself. She *knew* that was what he was doing, and it only irked her the more.

"Fine," she said. She sat up straight and muted her headset with a deft flick of her wrist, just as she would have done taking the witness stand. She knew how a cop behaved, and it wasn't like a scared little girl. She met her boss's eyes levelly. "In the elevator, you said you do real police work here. Did you mean that?" He chuckled and spread his hands, but she pushed on. "My dad was a cop, and that was all I ever wanted to be. But by the time I got into the Academy, it was already more about search engines than search and seizure. You know what I mean?"

This time he nodded, and he was paying attention. For the first time since she'd met him, he wasn't laughing at her. He was weighing her, and that was perfectly fine by Katie. She had nothing to hide. "I've always tried to do my best, but this right here—*this* is what I want to do. Maybe there's not a lot of police work left to do, but I know for a fact there are still perps slipping through the cracks, and I'd rather be out there on the streets, chasing them down, than sitting behind a computer screen connecting the dots."

He waited a moment in silence, then rocked back in his chair, considering her. "You could have said that on your application, Katie."

"Frankly, Rick, I wasn't auditioning for the job. It was the right place for my career, and I was the right candidate. I've been connecting the dots for twelve years now, and that was an easy one. What I want to know from you...." She realized her tone was challenging, demanding, and she almost blushed and dropped it. But he had invited her to be blunt, and she needed this answer. Without it, she might as well go home. "Mr. Goodall. Rick. I need you to tell me the truth. Were *you* auditioning for me? Or were you telling it straight? What should I really expect out of this job?"

He leaned forward, his elbows falling onto his desk with a solid *thump*, and he couldn't quite fight off the grin as he said, "Pratt...why don't you let me show you?" He jumped to his feet, strode across the room, and heaved the door open before Katie was even on her feet. He beckoned, and stepped out into the bullpen. He caught the arm of an agent hurrying past, and said, "Katie, this is Reed. He's my second-in-command around here. Best agent I've got." He ignored Reed's modest shrug and asked him bluntly, "What have we got working?"

Reed was tall, a lithe leopard where Rick was the sturdy bulldog. He was also young, barely thirty and that put him almost ten years under everyone else she'd seen in the department. Katie measured him in one glance, and was ready to write him off as a college pretty-boy when his eyes met hers— emerald green and packing a punch. She saw intelligence in this fellow's eyes, coupled with a remarkable depth.

In this case, with just a glance at Katie, Reed obviously understood what his boss was asking for. "Phillips is in Cincinnati," he said.

Rick frowned. "That's the burglaries, yeah? No, I don't think—"

"Go ahead," Reed said. "It's good for a laugh, if nothing else." He frowned, thinking, and that penetrating gaze flicked to Katie's eyes again. She thought she saw the hint of a smile as he said, "I'll see if there's anything we can show her on the SS case."

"I like where your head's at." Rick turned to Katie and jerked his head toward an empty desk. "We'll use Phillips's spot. You know how to use HaRRE?" He pronounced it "hare," as everyone at her old precinct had.

She nodded. "Doesn't everyone?"

"You'd be surprised." He grabbed an extra chair, and waved her to the one front and center at Phillips's desk. "Take the wheel. Case file 60452, real-time stream." He checked his watch, then heaved himself back to his feet. "Actually, we've probably got ten to twenty. I'm going to grab a coffee. You need anything?"

She shook her head absently, her attention all on the desktop monitor. This guy used plugins she'd never heard of, and it was in her nature to snoop. Rick noticed that and chuckled as he left her to it.

It only took her a moment to pull up the case file she needed, and the real-time stream was dedicated to a shady dispensary in a run-down part of town. The software built a full 3-D environment out of available information. She panned the camera to get a good view of the street, but it was mostly deserted. She saw an elderly couple haggling over some jewelry in a shop across the way, and a drunk lounging against a storefront halfway to the next corner. In the other direction, she saw nobody.

She maneuvered into the shop as though she were controlling a character in a game and found a couple strung-out clients sitting around an invisible table, watching the invisible TV suspended in one corner of the room. The proprietor behind the counter was a weaselly little man with a pencil mustache. She checked all their names, pulled up records out of habit, and wondered idly if these guys were worth protecting.

She pulled up the dispensary's menu, and nodded when it confirmed her suspicions. Heroin and meth available without so much as a membership. She checked the shop's license and it was in good shape. She pulled up the credentials on its last auditor, too, and he seemed clean. Still...even with the regulation, even with all the surveillance, heavy drug stores like this had a bad habit of attracting trouble from their clientele.

Rick sank down in the chair next to her, and she knew he was evaluating her. No problem there. HaRRE always made her feel unsettled—fake environments with flat white interiors and missing all the little touches of humanity. Mostly it showed just the people, lifelike avatars moving around in vacant corridors. Some people had expensive enough possessions that they warranted tracking, and those appeared in the rendered environment, but they usually only emphasized the lack of any other props. In a way, she hated HaRRE, but she was as good at using the system as anyone she knew. She turned on the audio on the stoners, but they weren't saying anything she wanted to hear. It was clear they weren't expecting any excitement.

She glanced to Rick. He shrugged. "We've got a ninety-four percent likelihood this place is the next target. If you'll move back out into the street, I can show you—" She activated a macro and the camera moved to focus on Phillips, waiting in an unmarked car two blocks down. He said, "Good. Okay, if you'll zoom out...." She pulled the camera back, outside the car, and as soon as he pointed she panned around to find four local police cruisers just around the corner.

She nodded. "I've been on a raid like this."

"I know," he said. He glanced at his watch, then spoke into his headset. "Phillips, we good?"

She got the camera back inside the car in time to hear Phillips answer, "—ny minute now, boss-man. Should be...there."

He pointed with a jerky, dreamlike motion that was worse than everything else about HaRRE. There were enough points of reference that the system could reconstruct pretty much anything in range of a camera or microphone, but human motion sometimes stuttered just outside of normal, and that was eerie. She'd logged thousands of hours in the system, but it still creeped her out, especially when the audio was so perfectly clear.

Rick said, "You're getting video, yeah? Save that for me. I've got a new recruit looking over your shoulder."

Phillips waved and said, "Good to meet you, Katie. This one should be fun."

She changed her camera angle away from him just as he climbed out of his car. She could hear him passing orders to his backup as he sprinted up to the nearest corner, and she flew on ahead of him. The street was empty, but even as the thought crossed her mind, she heard Phillips say, "That's them! Move! Move! Move!"

Confused, she zipped down the street, but it was still empty. Then she saw what they were after. Ten feet from the dispensary's door, five handguns appeared suspended in the air. These were the ghosts the task force was named after, invisible gunmen within the otherwise perfect surveillance system, their weapons the only hint of their existence within the simulated environment. Those weapons danced a frenetic line through the air, rushing toward the drugist's open door.

She hit a quick key and the camera returned to the inside. One of the HaRRE plugins on this desktop isolated the drawn weapons and wrapped them in a red glow, then drew a faint red line along their predicted trajectories. Two of the lines disappeared into the store's clients, moving with them as they shrank away in terror and cowered on the floor. The other three were all fixed on the store's proprietor behind the counter.

Katie couldn't help herself. She whispered softly, "Oh, that is cool!"

Rick wasn't so easily distracted. He scanned the scene and said, "Okay Phillips, nobody's watching the door. You're good to go."

Even as he gave the all clear, Katie saw one of the guns jerk twice, and the infostream on the edge of the screen flooded with data about the gunshot. The proprietor disappeared behind his counter, and Katie didn't know if he'd been shot or simply dropped out of sight. The gun that had been fired clattered onto an invisible table, though, leaving her no idea where the ghostly gunman had gone.

Irritated, she reached for the control to turn on video overlay—usually more trouble than it was worth—but Rick restrained her with a light touch on her hand. "In due time," he said. "Watch."

Phillips arrived just then, bursting onto the scene with a squad of police behind him. They flooded the room. She could see the officers fighting, wrestling with empty air, falling from phantom punches. Two of the gunmen had time to respond. Katie watched helplessly as the trajectory traces whipped around to bury themselves in police uniforms. One of them dropped a police officer, but the other flew wide, smashing a hole in the wall by the door.

HaRRE helped her keep track of it all, but the whole scene lasted only a heartbeat, maybe two, before the room fell still. When it was done, the perpetrators' guns lay discarded and police officers knelt in position, restraining assailants she still couldn't see. Katie said, "Okay, I get it. They're ghosts. But—"

Rick only nodded toward the screen. "Watch."

It was Phillips who crossed the room in two quick steps and kicked something, hard, and then she heard his voice quite clearly—the first audio from HaRRE since he'd given the order to move out.

"What's your name, kid?"

"Bite me!" from one of the ghosts, and an instant later a young man appeared on the ground at Phillips's feet, clearly restrained by one of the other police officers. HaRRE identified him as Bryce Leightner, and off to the left of the real-time stream a frame showed his police record. She wasn't interested in that, though.

Another of the ghosts barked, "Dammit, keep quiet!" and almost immediately resolved on frame. Keith Brown. There were two more, and Phillips couldn't elicit vocal responses from them, but he pulled something from his pocket (some artifact invisible to HaRRE) and pointed it at one of the other ghosts. Then he said, "Eighty-seven says this kid is Leo Benedict, Rick."

Rick leaned across Katie to pull up the police records on the other two. He scrolled through them in a flash, and said, "Yeah, we've got a known associate Leo. Plug him in."

Phillips did something with his invisible object, and the third ghost resolved. Katie said, "What's he using? A camera?"

Rick laughed. "No, we have good video of the site. This is better. He's got a biometric scanner that uses lasers to read facial contours. It's about ten percent behind the standard vocal predictions, but we're usually operating on more than hunches anyway, so it's good enough." He nodded to the display, where the fourth ghost was now unmasked. "And that one is Garrett Brown. He'd be the ringleader, as we suspected. Scanner got him right away."

"That's impressive," Katie said, but Rick held up a hand.

Into his headset, he said, "Good work, Phillips. EMT is on the way for the wounded. What's our bodycount?"

Phillips shook his head. "Nobody's dying today. These kids were sloppy."

Phillips couldn't have known that with the same certainty the software provided Katie, but he seemed satisfied with his hunch. He glanced at an invisible watch, and said casually, "I'm going to clean up and head home. You got the rest of this, boss?"

"I'll put Craig on it," Rick said. "See you in the morning." Then he turned to Katie. "You were saying?"

She took a breath, trying to decide where to start. "I've seen people go ghost before," she finally said. "Sometimes the mics lose track, I know, that's just a limitation of the technology. But it's never for that long. How did they do it?" She looked back at their avatars, and raised an eyebrow. "These guys don't look too high tech."

"No," Rick said. "They went old school. Garrett knows more than he should about how the system works. He hatched the idea in juvie, then went mute for a couple months after he got out." Rick reached across her again, stopped the real-time stream in HaRRE and skipped backward several minutes, to the point when she had first returned to the building's interior.

"Anybody can go off the grid if they don't wear a watch and don't say a word," he said, "but that never lasts long. These guys came up with another plan." She saw Rick reaching for the "source audio" option and braced herself for the ugly barks of the burglars' guns, the screams of the strung-out clients. She was all too familiar with the sounds of violence, but she was entirely unprepared for the cacophony that hit her as soon as he activated the audio.

A blaring roar of urban music came from the speakers, so deafening every head in the office turned toward Phillips's desk before Katie could adjust the volume. It didn't stop until the perps were subdued and Phillips took his mighty kick. Katie said, "So, what, they—"

"Boomboxes," Rick said. "Sometimes street noise is enough to make the ghosts you mentioned. There was a time when turning up a radio so loud it could be heard two blocks away might seem like a foolish plan for someone intending to commit a crime. These days it borders on genius. If you wanted to run the stream backward, you could probably find two or three of the ghosts positively identified on a cross-town bus ten minutes back. Something like that. They all got together at some rendezvous, pumped up the volume, and moved completely undetected for four or five blocks to storm this little shop."

He shut off the source audio again. "Of course, HaRRE suppresses any noise that it can't positively identify, and it couldn't map the motions of the kids onto any identity model, so they just got filtered out, like the couch, and the potted plant in the corner, and the family cat. That's where we get our ghosts."

He turned off the HaRRE simulation and loaded a newly-filed report from Phillips, scanning the contents absently.

He kept speaking. "Those kids were clever, in a way, but it was a gimmick. Garrett was already associated with the comments he'd made in juvie, so I think Hathor and Jurisprudence had him pegged at about seventy-eight percent. If they'd stopped after their second job, they could have caught a jury trial and probably gotten off clean. Cops brought us in to put faces on them."

"That's just lazy." Katie shook her head. "They didn't need FBI for this. Yeah, they blinded HaRRE, but I would have just pulled up source video and gotten a good look at them. Hell, I could have turned on source audio, figured out their MO before my ears stopped ringing, and then I could have nabbed them next time they turned up the noise."

Rick closed the report he'd been reading and turned to Katie. "That's why we hired you," he said. "Besides, it's not *all* like that. What we really do is track discrepancies. Not active ghosts like these, most of the time, but after-the-fact ghosts. The people rich or powerful enough to get their records erased are far more dangerous than the kids who figure out how to hide from the cameras for an hour at a time. It *looks* the same in HaRRE, but it's far more sinister."

"How do they do it?" she said.

He frowned. "At the end of the day, it's another service the Aggregators sell, just like everything else. They're the ones keeping the data, and there's nothing to stop them misplacing a bit or two if the price is right. Reed!" He waited a moment for an answer on his headset, then asked, "You got anything to show her?" He nodded twice, then snapped his fingers as he climbed to his feet. "Come on," he said. "I'll show you what that looks like."

She followed him across the bullpen to the conference room she'd noticed earlier. Either she'd been wrong, or the football stats had been put away. The long conference table was divided into six monitors, and Rick led her right to the first one, where

Reed stood poring over a database report from a ritzy restaurant in Richmond, four days old. He gave her a glance out of the corner of his eye, then moved aside to give her room at the monitor. She scanned it for a while, but saw nothing interesting. She could tell Rick and Reed were waiting for her analysis, so she said, "Looks harmless. What's this?"

Reed answered her. "This is an event report submitted to us by the Secret Service." He hesitated, probably wondering how much background she needed, and when she gave him a blank look, he filled in. "Secret Service has a list of keywords that they pay Hathor to track for them. On this night, in the main dining hall of this restaurant, someone carried on a six- to nine-minute conversation that ran eleven percent over the confidence threshold for the subject, 'presidential assassination.' I have *never* handled a Secret Service request higher than one or two percent above confidence, and those ones and twos were all dead on. So this is serious stuff."

She nodded, her eyes locked on the monitor now, and even knowing what to look for she saw nothing. "Can you play the audio?"

Rick chuckled, dark and sarcastic. "We *can*," he said. "But it would do no good. Hathor has access to seven mics in the room, not counting the dozens of private headsets, but—would you believe it—there's gaps in the audio archive wherever the conversation might have taken place."

"Then how did the Secret Service—"

"That's the thing," Rick said, his easy grin now twisted into a sneer. "It's all Hathor's audio. Even the pickup from the private headsets belongs to Hathor. The Secret Service has a standing order, so as soon as the language filter threw up a match, they got a red flag from Hathor. It took them seventeen minutes to respond to it, on a Thursday night at nine forty-four local, and by then the audio was 'unavailable for technical reasons.' It was available again the following morning, but already scrubbed clean."

"And the video?"

"Not just the video," Reed said, his frustration showing through. "Whole identities. Someone—more than one someone, actually—came to this restaurant, sat down at one of three apparently empty tables, and had a six- to nine-minute conspiracy, then disappeared from history. GPS records, voice ID, video and audio footage, all of it scrubbed clean far enough back in time and space that we can't figure out better than single-digit percentages who might have been on a trajectory to that empty table. Anyone within miles of the place who fell outside of Hathor's attention for a window of less than two hours could, conceivably, be our guys. That's people at home in bed, hell, anyone who went to a movie at the right time could show up as a suspect."

She tapped the screen. "This is last Thursday night. Friday was the holiday, so you can't have been looking at this long—"

Reed snorted, and caught a sharp look from Rick for it. He shrugged defensively. "Friday wasn't a holiday here," he said. "The president's life is on the line, and we're the only people in the world who can figure it out. Rick called me up at…what was it, a little after midnight?" Rick shrugged, leaving Reed enough leash to tell the story how he wanted. Reed nodded. "I think that's right, and we were here all night. Been here ever since, and most of the others worked through the weekend on it, too." He smirked. "I hope you're not coming here with hopes of a twenty-hour work-week dancing in your head."

She didn't bother answering that. Nobody on the force worked a twenty-hour week, and she knew he knew that. She wasn't interested in first-day teasing, though. Her attention was all on this new world, this new approach to law enforcement. She stared at the columns in the Hathor report. She was familiar with those reports, but they'd never tried to hide anything from her before. She saw the second and third monitors had HaRRE simulations on them, and another one was playing security camera footage. While Katie was looking over them something must have caught Reed's eye because he moved to the fifth monitor and started typing up notes. She realized with a start that he looked as bewildered by it all as she felt.

Rick gave her plenty of time to take it in, then said, "We're not just connecting the dots up here, Katie. This is the real police work."

2. Ms. Linson

Rick held up a finger, a look in his eyes that said someone was talking in his headset. A moment later he said, "Thanks, Craig. Can you put that on monitor six in CF1? Thanks. And look in on Phillips's Cincinnati case and clear up the paperwork for him, would you? Thanks." He reached up and muted his headset, then gathered Katie up with his eyes and led her around the end of the table to the last monitor in the back corner, just as a case file appeared on it.

"We just got this one in." He scanned the details tab of the case file, brows coming down in thought, then flicked rapidly through the other pages, including a handful of crime-scene stills. Then he flipped back to the front page and stepped aside, ceding his place to Katie. "Homicide in Little Rock," he said, almost offhand. "I think I'll let you cut your teeth on that, if you feel up to it. Everyone I have in town is going full-speed-ahead on the assassination threat."

Katie nodded. "I'll be happy to get on it, sir—"

"I knew you would," Rick said, almost cutting her off, and she had to dredge up the courage to finish the thought.

"It's just, I don't know how."

Rick tilted his head, considering her for a moment. She was acutely aware of Reed right behind her, tapping away on his notes, and she wished for a moment he hadn't heard her pitiful admission. The jarring force of Rick's hand falling on her shoulder drove the thought from her mind. He'd clearly meant it as a friendly gesture, because he caught her eyes with his eyebrows raised, his face tilted forward until it almost touched her forehead. "Pratt, you listen to me. What we do here, the *core* of what we do here, is police work. Same as you've been doing all your life, same as your old man did before you. In the end, it all comes down to figuring out which people were where, and when. For the most part, Hathor has made that easy."

"Yes, sir, but—"

He spoke over her, undeterred. "But we can't *trust* Hathor, Pratt. Everyone else in the damn world trusts Hathor. Fine. The cameras see everything, the mics hear everything. Every time somebody orders a pizza or tracks down an old friend, they fall a little bit more in love with the databases. That's all well and good, but it doesn't do *us* any favors. Because Hathor owns it all. If we could see the raw input, if we could see every read and write to the database before the company monkeyed with it.... I don't care how many lines of printout we'd have to scroll through, Pratt, we could catch every criminal in the world with that kind of power. I swear it. And that data exists. There are people who *have* that level of access, but we don't."

He stepped back but held her eye. "But we get by. We are tasked with tracking down the information Hathor won't give us, and we have our little tricks. It's the kind of police work you used to see on TV, maybe. Mostly, it's just knowing the right people to talk to, the right places to look for smudges or inconsistencies. It's all stuff I can teach you, Pratt—"

Just then Reed, eyes fixed on the HaRRE playback on monitor two, waved absently to catch Rick's attention and then tapped something he'd just written on monitor five. Rick held up a finger, "Just a sec," he said and stepped around Katie to look at it. Rick reached to his headset and said, "Craig, I need you to take a look at this. Process Reed's notes on monitor five, and bring up case file 22120 on six. Send in Dean and Simmons and...dammit. Who else is here? Well, push this whole case file to Phillips's handheld and let him know he's going to be active as soon as he touches down." He turned to monitor six, looking for the case file he'd requested from Craig, and found Katie still standing there. He blinked.

"I'm sorry, Katie. What I was saying...at the heart of it, even if we use slightly different tools, it's the same thing you've been doing all your life. You may not be able to trust Hathor, but you can still trust your instincts." He glanced over his shoulder at the monitor, then looked back to her with frustration in his eyes. "This case over here is bigger than any of us. You've got to understand that. I'll teach you everything you need to know, once we get this settled. Meantime, grab a desk out there, and start feeling your way around. You'll catch on pretty quick." The look in his eyes said he was sorry, but saving the president was more important than training the new girl, and right now she was in his way. She stepped aside and squeezed against the wall to let the senior agents get by.

Dismissed. She left the conference room with a clenched jaw and balled fists. She had a murder case to work. Her first day on the job, and he'd given her a homicide. That was something. Some guidance would have been nice, but there was a victim out there demanding justice, and Katie was the cop on the job. She headed toward an empty desk in the back corner against the outer wall, beneath a window with a view of the Washington Monument. She could tell from its cleanliness that it was available. On her way across the bullpen, she turned on her headset and said, "Craig? Is that right? Give me the Little Rock homicide case file on desk..." She tapped the blank desktop and the monitor sprang to life. She found an identifier in the lower right-hand corner. "Desk twelve. Thanks."

The case file appeared on the desktop immediately, and she breathed a sigh of relief. If she had access to the secretary, she could get *something* done. She opened it up, the same pages Rick had flipped through so quickly before, but it wasn't the same case file form she'd used at home. She looked through the various tabs, then started over at the top of page one, reading everything carefully.

Her victim was Janeane Linson, twenty-one and plain. Blonde hair, blue eyes, five-five, lived in an apartment in North Little Rock. Katie interrupted her reading to figure out how to request a financial report using the bureau's system, and got lost in the process for half an hour. It was much more powerful than anything they'd had back home, but with that always came complexity. She figured it out quickly enough, though, and blinked in surprise when she got the report back immediately. The bureau was making direct queries through Midas into the main database. Fascinating.

She tucked the financial report to one side, and went back to the case file. Linson was a Junior Administrative Officer for Pellincorp, a major Aggregator, which also ran a minor database service called Helen. Katie pulled up corporate details on Pellincorp for casual reading later, then discovered in the case file that Linson had been found dead in her office. That brought the company right back into the spotlight.

The victim had been found early that morning, but Hathor's last positive ID on her had been Thursday night, late. Her fingers kept twitching toward the HaRRE launcher, but she always made it a point to read through the full police report first. That would matter even more here, where HaRRE could lie. She shook her head at the thought and read on.

It was a strangulation. Video footage showed her dead before midnight on Thursday, but there was nothing on the actual event. Still, bruising was clear on her throat, and the overturned chair was enough to show there had been a struggle. There were no obvious suspects. Ms. Linson was single, and Hathor showed no signs of romantic involvement in the last six months. Katie made a note to look into possible romantic links anyway. After all, Hathor could be lying to her. Same for the financial report, really. If Hathor could be bought out, Midas certainly could, too.

She thought back to the report Reed had been reviewing for the Secret Service. The only evidence they had to go on, and it specifically showed a record of nothing illegal happening. And someone had tampered with the audio and video feeds to hide it. Her dad would have gone after Hathor for that alone. Hell, he *did*, back when Hathor was just Total Awareness Monitoring Systems, a partner of AT&T—back when judges issued search warrants against corporations, and no one even knew what an "aggregator" was. Her dad had chased TAMS right into the newspapers. Then Congress had gotten involved, and her dad had gotten retired just in time to attend her graduation from the Academy.

She sighed and rubbed her eyes. This case wouldn't be like that. Rick hadn't handed her a Secret Service case. She leaned back over the case file, reading on. She forced herself through her ritual, reading every page of the case file, then glanced at her watch. One-twenty already. She glanced at the HaRRE launcher, and shook her head. "Lunch first," she said out loud, then blinked in surprise. Rick was standing at her left hand, towering over her.

"I was thinking the same thing," he said, grinning at the surprise on her face. "If you're okay with a sandwich, the cafeteria downstairs does a good one."

"Do they make a decent grilled turkey, mayo?" she asked. He nodded and she said, "Sounds great, then." She swiped a hand across her desk to hide the monitor display. "Craig, save my workspace. Desk twelve." Then she darted off after Rick, through the frosted glass doors and down the long elevator ride.

As soon as they stepped into the cafeteria she spotted Dean, Simmons, and Reed all waiting at a table. Reed frowned at Katie until Rick clapped him on the shoulder and said, "She was still plugging away at her desk. Be right back. Don't start without me."

He led her across to the counter at the head of the room, and as she approached a server caught her eye and said, "You had the grilled turkey?"

She said, "Midas—" but Rick cut her off with a hand on her arm.

"Craig, pick up Katie's lunch, would you?" The server just waited for a green light acknowledging that someone had paid, then slid the tray across to Katie with a smile. She grabbed a glass and helped herself to some Coke, then turned to find Rick waiting just behind her.

"Prices are reasonable. Feel free to put your lunches here on the government tab. If you go off-site, you're on your own."

"Fair enough," she said with a smile. "We're sitting over there?"

He nodded and let her lead the way. As soon as he settled down beside her, though, Dean leaned across the table and said, "Canvas still isn't turning up anything, but we may have a lead on a private voice recording."

Rick shook his head. "No good. I spotted that Friday, but the timing is iffy and nothing on the consumer market would get us usable feed from six tables away in a busy restaurant. I still think our best bet is tourist photos taken outside the restaurant during our window."

Dean and Simmons groaned at that. Reed said, "I told you." He turned to Rick. "Phillips checked in ten minutes ago and he's willing to reinterview the other patrons, but you're talking serious overtime. He's already pushing a regular week from the time he clocked Saturday and Sunday."

Rick snorted. "Bullshit. The new girl had his case solved before her ears stopped ringing. Phillips can kiss my ass if he thinks I'm paying for a weekend playing with his nieces in Cincinnati." The others laughed, but an instant later they were back into their case. Katie listened intently, trying her best to keep up, but half of it was beyond her, and they never slowed for a breath. She'd barely finished her sandwich before Rick pushed back from his place, folded his untouched sandwich back into its wax paper wrapper, and rose to head upstairs.

While the others took their cue and started gathering their things, Katie caught at Rick's sleeve. "Umm...hey, could you help me out for a sec? I still don't know exactly—"

He patted her lightly on the shoulder and smiled. "Take it easy, kid. It's your first day. No one is expecting miracles. Just nose around and try to get a feel for our system. I'll assign someone to train you up as soon as we get a break in the big one."

And that was it. He turned away, and the others rose from their places to follow him out the door toward the elevators. Katie was left alone, frustrated and helpless, watching them leave.

Almost alone. She took control of herself, then turned back to the table to grab her trash, and nearly jumped when she found Reed still seated across from her. He was watching her with a frown, and now he nodded wordlessly to her seat, and she sank back down at the table.

"What's up?" he said.

Katie glanced at her watch, then took a deep breath and let it out. "I appreciate the confidence Rick's put in me," she said. "And I realize it's just my first day. I do. But I don't even know where to begin with this case. And I understand all too well that time is short when it comes to something like this."

He clasped his hands on the table between them, leaned on his elbows, and took a deep breath. "What we do...." He trailed off, thinking and shook his head. "Listen.... What we do isn't the same as what you did in Brooklyn. Jurisprudence has got most of the world tied up nice and neat right now—way better than anything we ever had before—and the people are happy with that." He leaned back, never releasing her eyes from his hard green gaze. "I can't tell you the victim's family is going to be okay with that murderer getting away, but most of the world will never care. Most of Little Rock, even, takes comfort knowing that's probably the only bastard in town who'll go free all year."

"Yes, but *I* care. And he's not going to go free—"

Reed shrugged. "Chances are good he will, because you're right. Time is short, and you don't know what you're doing here. And everyone who does is too busy."

She bit her lip against an angry retort. "Okay," she said. "So why are you still sitting here?"

"Because I can't really get started until Phillips shows up, anyway, and because I'll be saving us all a lot of time if I can make you see things as they are. Rick's got a big heart, so he's not going to tell you this, but you've got to leave him the hell alone. You're small potatoes."

She didn't hit him. "Maybe I am," she said, fighting to keep her cool. "But the case isn't. It's a homicide."

He shrugged again. "That's the only reason we're looking at it at all. Listen, these cases aren't open-and-shut like the stuff you're used to. Put that kind of work out of your mind. It's days and weeks and often months of grueling research to put the truth together, when Hathor isn't there to do it for you. Sometimes—most of the time, really—it can't be done at all. There's a sitting senator down the street who assaulted four different women in the time I've been on this team, and we can't pin a thing on him. Everybody knows he did it. Everybody but Hathor. Hell, that dude in Seattle killed his wife and dumped her in the ocean, you know the one—"

She frowned. "The programmer?"

"Network architect, but yeah. See? That's my point. You know he did it, I know he did it, but two of our best guys put in six months trying to find some way to prove it to Hathor, and the links just kept getting thinner and thinner until there were no dots left to connect. Rick eventually had to pull us off it, because there was other work to do."

She shook her head. "I don't understand."

"Nobody's asking for Sherlock Holmes anymore. That's what I'm telling you. The law still allows for court trials, but try finding a judge who's willing to spend the time. There's barely a district attorney left who's even willing to try it. The system does a job that's good enough, as far as everyone else is concerned." He took a deep breath and let it out slowly. "I disagree. That's why I work here. But we have to take what we can get. Nobody's throwing money at our department, and every time Rick has tried to get Congress to give us more powers, they've taken them away instead. Right now, we just don't have enough bodies on the payroll to work this Little Rock case. That's the fact of it."

"And, at the same time," Katie said, waving a hand toward the elevators, "you've been handed an opportunity to do something Congress won't ignore. If you can put a stop to this assassination attempt—"

Reed's eyes narrowed. "Yeah," he said, measuring her. "That would be a big deal." He pushed to his feet, eyes lingering on her face, and nodded. "Glad you can see the truth of it. Maybe you'll make it here after all."

She understood, but she didn't feel much better. Reed didn't bother offering her a pep talk, either. He tossed his trash in the bin on the way out, and left her there as the others had. She waited until she knew he'd had time to catch an elevator, then finally rose put away her tray before heading upstairs after him. By the time she got back into the office Reed was back in Conference Room One with Rick and the rest of his team, leaving her alone with the corpse of Ms. Linson.

She returned to her desk, and pulled up the case file report again. She couldn't rule out jealous lovers or financial disputes, but there was nothing surface-level to suggest those. She found a custom query tool for Hathor called "Conversation Analysis: Victim," and ran that, just to see what happened. It came back with an empty results string after about four minutes that could as easily have been her mistake as any actual cover-up. She didn't know how to use this stuff.

Hippocrates gave her an overview of the victim's recent health, and she was clean on any sort of illicit substance. The Automated Coroner's Report said there was nothing presenting or hereditary that would aggravate with a strangling. She rolled her eyes at the thought and pushed away from her desk. Another hour burned, and her most useful tools were trying to figure out if she should be looking for signs of anemia in a homicide victim. The camera stills were perfectly clear. Bulging eyes, dark purple bruises on the throat: the girl had been choked out. Katie was floundering.

There was too much information. She knew that was part of it. She'd never had direct query access to Hippocrates and Midas and Shopper and CV before. She was overwhelmed with data, and at the same time doubting every bit of it. She didn't know how to sort it all, or where the cuts had been made.

So she took a deep breath. Then she decided that wasn't enough and she went to get a drink of water at the cooler. No one said a word to her as she crossed the bullpen—too busy with their tasks—but she felt better by the time she got back to her desk. She brushed all her open database reports off to the side, opened up the case file report, and launched HaRRE. Hathor Real-time Rendering Engine. The real-time stream on Linson's case file showed the empty office Katie had seen in the still photos, although she only knew it by the dimensions. The corpse was as invisible as the furniture.

For the second time today (and the second time this year) she reached for the video source. The rendered environment disappeared, replaced by a roving camera view, and she saw that her invisible corpse was gone. Someone had taken care of the body, and neatened the room while they were at it. The disturbed chair was righted, tucked neatly behind the empty desk. Other than that, the room was empty.

She switched off the source video and went back to the rendered environment, rolling back in time until she saw the cleaners working in the room. Earlier still, she saw the coroners arrive, walking backward, and deposit Ms. Linson's body in a corner behind the plant. Nine in the morning, and she increased the rewind speed. She saw the cleaning girl pop her head into the office at seven, just a blip, and she could imagine the scream, but it was muted while the footage reversed. She thought about playing it back then, listening in on the conversations that followed the discovery, but she squashed the idea as more morbid curiosity than professional interest. The murderers wouldn't give themselves away over the coffeepot.

She still hadn't seen why the local police requested FBI assistance, either. She increased the rewind speed again, watched the clock fly backward as nothing else changed. Empty white room, still corpse in the corner, facedown and forgotten.

Then the screen went black, for just an instant, and it took a moment for that to register. After that, there was no corpse in the corner, but Ms. Linson moved out from behind her desk, walking jerkily backward around the room, examining invisible paintings on the wall, checking her watch and the invisible clock on the wall, and then back out into the reception area where she was just barely visible in the environment. Katie paused the stream, switched it back to play, but forty minutes had passed in the footage in the time it took her to react.

She skipped ahead half of that, putting the victim back in the corner office, and watched once again as she moved nervously about the room. She twitched and jittered, her body position snapping up to reality every time the roaming security camera drifted back to focus on her. Katie just sat back, watching for any clue. She turned on audio, and heard the disjointed, off-key singing of a girl listening to loud music over her headset. It was like hearing someone in the next room singing in the shower. She searched up the necessary keywords to overlay the audio from the victim's headset just in time to watch Ms. Linson reach up and mute it. Out in the lobby, the elevator dinged.

Katie moved the camera toward the lobby, but a moment later the screen went black. She sat back, stunned. That's what she had seen before. She played it forward, and the scene stayed black. Bizarre. Lighting in HaRRE was entirely artificial, independent of real world light sources. She switched to source video, and found it blindingly white. Remembering the Cincinnati kids, she turned the volume down low, then switched on source audio. A solid hum came from her speakers, droning and useless. She switched it back off, turned off the white source video, and dropped back into the darkness that had swallowed HaRRE.

There was, predictably, no reconstructed audio. This was why Ghost Targets had gotten the case file, of course. Someone had come to see Ms. Linson, after hours, and she'd been waiting impatiently for her guest to show up. She'd been nervous, but she hadn't seemed scared. So Katie had that to go on, at least. Whoever had attacked the victim had had an appointment.

She paused HaRRE and ran a check through Ms. Linson's secretary, but there was no official appointment any time on Friday. That could have been cleaned, or it could have been an unofficial appointment. Anything untoward—whether a romantic liaison or a drug deal gone bad—would have been off the record anyway. She started to run a search on the building's receptionist, but shook her head. That was connecting the dots. That was the easy stuff. Even with the weird blackout, local cops would've nabbed the killer if he was in the records. The building sure looked empty. It wouldn't have taken long to check out everyone on the premises, even without a clear ID on the killer.

She sped up the playback, and waited four minutes real-time for the lights to come back on in the imaginary world of HaRRE. For Ms. Linson, it was over half an hour, and now she was a quiet rag doll in the back corner. She made a note of the exact time on the blackout, then skipped back to just before it. She waited for the ding of the elevator, then paused and zoomed the camera out into the foyer. The doors were already opening, just a crack, but the HaRRE camera could go wherever she wanted it to. She stepped into the elevator, but it was empty.

Of course it was empty. That would have been too easy. Ghosted like the conspirators in the Richmond restaurant. Like the kids in Cincinnati. He was there, frozen, in the spacious elevator car with her, but she couldn't see him. He'd been erased. It irked her, and she wondered at the difference between this empty space and the inky blackness that came later. What exactly had happened here?

She ran time backward and rode down to the ground floor with the killer. She slipped off the elevator and waited. The big plate glass doors swung open, and she knew her killer had just walked backward out through them, but still there was no one. How far back in time had they cleaned? She moved the camera outside, scanned the curbside. Every car with a license was registered and tracked in the system, but a car could be erased as easily as a body. There were none curbside. She paused the scenario, a moment before the murderer entered the building, and zoomed to the parking lots outside. One sad little Hyundai stood beneath a light post in the very middle of the lot, but a quick search showed it to be the victim's.

Even in the sterilized environment, Katie could still clearly imagine the real world it depicted. Already well past sunset, the car would be huddled in a silvery pool of streetlight, a hundred yards from the door of the nearly-empty building. The girl had picked that spot for a reason. Katie sighed and hit a quick key to take her back to the office where Ms. Linson had died. She switched to source video, paused in time with the rendered world, and saw the timid little girl who would rather walk two extra rows in the parking lot than have to fumble for her keys in the shadows at night.

She looked small. She looked afraid. And Katie knew that forty-four minutes later, probably half that, she would look like a bit of discarded meat. For the first time in years, Katie felt as helpless as the college girl staring back at the camera. She took a deep breath and closed the program.

3. Rookie

She spent the rest of the afternoon pushing paper. Unfortunately, the database reports she'd pulled didn't tell her anything new. When she found herself checking her watch more often than she was turning pages, she knew she'd reached her limit for the day. Her dad had taught her one of the old laws: "never leave work for the day before your boss does, especially when you're new." Rick seemed determined to work the sun down and back up again, though, and she still didn't really know what she was supposed to do.

Finally she saved off her desktop and cleared it out. She pushed away from the desk, one step back, and it looked just as it had before she'd even shown up. That thought resonated with her frustration. All she'd really done today was get to know a dead girl.

She stuck her head in Conference Room One and Rick cut off whatever he was saying to Reed mid-sentence. He blinked at her. "Good lord, Pratt!" He checked his watch. "Are you still here?"

"No, sir," she said. "On my way out." She stepped into the room so she could lower her voice. "Mind if I push the case file to my handheld? Or do you guys have some weird security rules I don't know about?"

He barked a laugh. "God, I wish everyone worked as hard as the rookies. Take a night off, Pratt."

She shrugged. "I just like to have it handy, in case inspiration strikes."

"Whatever you say. Sure. I mean, we have all kinds of crazy security rules, but Craig handles all that. If he'll push the case file to you, I don't have any objections. And if not, there's nothing I can do about it."

"Thank you, sir," she said, and stole out of the office.

Behind her, Rick barked, "Hey, knock that off!" but she ignored him. She asked Craig to push her case file to her handheld, and almost immediately she saw the screen light up from her front pocket. She also had Craig order a car for her. She'd meant to ask permission for that, too, but she could cover the price of a cab if Rick objected. She didn't think he would.

The building was surprisingly active for the late hour. As soon as she stepped onto the elevator, her remote personal assistant whispered the name of one of her colleagues in her ear, Bud Stanton, Finance, but she didn't need the favor this time. Bud introduced himself with a big warm smile as soon as he spotted her, and then he beat her personal assistant to the ID at every floor on the way down, as coworkers squeezed into the elevator car.

One floor below her, it was, "Mark! Mayer!" as the duo from Licensure joined them, and the three men immediately fell into an animated conversation that only broke for a moment when the doors opened on nine to admit Bill from Decency. He jumped right into the discussion, and Katie could have been a ghost herself for all the attention they paid her.

Bud bowed her direction when the doors opened on the lobby, but then she was forgotten again. She rushed out of the elevator, quickly separating from the rest of the crowd which came strolling along behind her in friendly conversation. As she crossed the cavernous lobby, an eerie double vision washed over her, bringing back her time in HaRRE that afternoon. The floor plan wasn't the same as the building in Little Rock, but it was close enough that she felt, for just a moment, like she was the disembodied HaRRE camera gliding across the marble floor toward the plate glass windows, a hostile, starless night waiting outside.

In her imagination, the killer was paused just outside the double doors, poised, invisible. Her heart thundered as she reached the door, and fear gripped her as she pushed them open, not knowing what monster she might find waiting in the night.

An explosive burst of laughter from Bud made her jump, and as the blush rose in her cheeks she found herself on the same busy sidewalk she'd used to come in this morning—packed with pedestrian traffic and glowing noonday bright from all the streetlights and storefronts. No one was waiting for her.

A black compact car at the curb immediately amended that thought by flashing its lights, and a recording of her voice called out, "Katie Pratt." She darted to it and dove in, slamming the door behind her. A monitor in the dash glowed in the dim interior, awaiting a destination.

First day in town, and she'd been late to work this morning, so she didn't have a place yet. She almost said, "Take me home," but that would be too much like running away. Even just for a night, it would be a sort of failure. She sank back in the seat and spoke into her headset. "Hathor, connect me to Hearth. I need a two-bedroom apartment. Tonight. Details to my handheld." As she said it, she pulled her handheld from her pocket and dismissed the "Transfer Complete" notification from Craig. A moment later a list of available apartments crawled onto the screen, each labeled by age, cost, distance from the office, and personal compatibility. She sorted the list by each of the criteria, and one apartment made top five on all of them. She tapped the "Lease" button, waited a heartbeat for a confirmation, then told the driver, "Take me home." Ten minutes ago that had been Brooklyn, but now it was Washington, D. C.

Then she settled back, eyes closed, while the car maneuvered itself into the dense flow of traffic. After a moment her stomach rumbled, and she said, "Hathor, order me some Chinese, to home. First match." She opened one eye to peek at the driver monitor. It was a twenty-minute drive, almost exactly, and that was fine by her. She had plenty of business to take care of anyway.

She opened the message center on her handheld and started scrolling through missed messages while she said, almost absently, "Hathor, connect me to Hearth. Apply my favorite color scheme to the apartment. Thanks. Hathor, connect me to Brooklyn MiniStore." She took care of the little chores that went along with setting up a new home. She checked in on a couple pending cases from her old job, then, just as the car was leaving the highway near her new apartments, she finished up with her mail and said, "Hathor, connect me...." She hesitated, just for a moment, but that was enough to mess up the voice command. She bit back a curse, and silently counted the seconds for the instruction to time out. Then she put away her handheld and said, "Hathor, connect me to Dad."

He didn't answer, but she had never imagined he would. She always tried anyway. It only took a few seconds for Hathor to give up on the connection, and ask if she wanted to leave a voice message. She said yes, and a moment later, "Hey, Dad. Just wanted to fill you in on my first day with the FBI." She made a story of it, interrupting herself mid-sentence when the car pulled up at her new apartment. The driver monitor lit up to show that payment had been approved on the Bureau's Midas account, and she saw Rick's signature right below it. She shook her head. Frustrating as her day had been, her boss was certainly trying to take care of her. She climbed out of the car and closed the door with a *thud*.

The apartment complex was a nice one, two-story white buildings with generous patios or balconies. She didn't need much in the way of luxury, but she had learned a long time ago that a separate room for a home office was a must. There was lots of covered parking near the street, with what looked like a stable of community cars. She'd have to check into that. It would be worth a few bucks a week to avoid the subway.

Hathor prompted her with a beep and played back the last few words of her message. Then in its simulated voice, Hathor asked, "Is this recording complete?"

"No," she said, her attention snapping back to the message. But as the cab pulled away from the curb, a car emblazoned "Chen's Chicken" replaced it immediately, so she said, "Just a sec, Hathor. Pause the recording. Thanks."

The window nearest her rolled down to reveal a small dispensary compartment, instead of a passenger interior. Her voice stamp announced her name, and the total for her dinner. She said, "Put it on my tab," and a payment light blinked from red to green a moment later. Her dinner dropped into view, a greasy bag almost too hot to touch, but the smell of her chow mein made her sigh contentedly. She grabbed it and turned back to the apartments as the delivery car disappeared into the night.

"Okay," she said as she turned. "Hathor, resume recording. Wait, no. Damn." The complex had a receptionist out front, no more than a couple years old. It was a pedestal waist-high, with a bright touch-screen that illuminated as soon as Katie approached it.

The screen said, "Welcome, Katie. Moving in?" She touched the yes button, and then skipped quickly past the confirmation screen listing all the complex's amenities. She trusted Hearth better than her own judgment, really. Two more button presses approved everything the apartment owner needed to know, and she chose "Map" instead of "Rendered Environment" to find her way to her door. Hers was the second building on the left of the courtyard, upstairs, third door past the stairs. Easy enough. She closed out the screen with a swipe of her hand, and headed across the courtyard. Her stomach rumbled again.

"Hathor, resume recording." She caught her breath, and shook her head. "Sorry, Dad. Anyway. My boss's name is Rick. Rick Goodall, and he's larger than life. Sweet enough to make you sick." And, because she knew her dad would worry, she added, "Too old for my taste, though."

As she approached her door, she heard the locks click open in response to her proximity. She made a mental note to activate the physical key requirement, out of paranoia more than anything else, and kicked the door closed behind her. "Anyway, Rick gave me the ten cent tour, showed me just enough of what they do to get me feeling really overwhelmed, then dropped a homicide on me."

She paused, imagining her dad's reaction to that. He would be grinning ear-to-ear, so proud of her. She could almost hear him say, "You're big time now, Katie."

"I won't forget the little people," she said. "Hey, I'm going to call you back. Ten minutes. I've got to get some food in me."

He wouldn't be able to take that call either, but she liked to pretend. She took a deep breath and let it out in a puff. "Later, Dad. Goodbye." Hathor killed the connection on the keyword, and Katie dropped her dinner sack on the little kitchen table before looking around the apartment.

Hearth did a good job. She'd only enrolled with them a couple years ago, but she'd liked the place they found her back in Brooklyn, and she liked this place, too. On her own, she would have picked something spartan, and this space wasn't luxurious, but it was a lot more comfortable than she would have chosen. Midas wouldn't have approved anything she couldn't afford, so that wasn't a concern. It was furnished, too, with a bed set in one of the rooms and an office set in the other. Perfect. The walls were a mute brown, almost gray, with just a touch of purple on the trim. Quiet, but appealing.

The living room was a small space that opened directly into the kitchen, with a three-place dining table tucked in a back corner. She had never done a lot of entertaining, so that was more than enough. She had eight small boxes of belongings in a storage unit in Brooklyn, and she could get those delivered while she was at work tomorrow, but she'd need a change of clothes and some toiletries. The complex would probably have a welcome service capable of setting her up, but she decided on a whim to run into town later and pick up some necessities. It would be fun.

First things first. She set upon her chow mein like a man starving, and finished her entire meal without stopping to take a drink. Hathor *had* ordered a Coke for her, so she took it over to the plush love seat in the living room and crashed in front of a dark television, taking occasional sips and enjoying a moment of deep silence.

After a while, her lips quirked into a smile, and she said, "Hathor, connect me to Dad."

She waited for the timeout, and started a new message. Then she discovered she had no words. She sat there in silence, staring at the wall as her smile faded. Once again, Hathor snapped her out of it with a buzzed warning.

She shook her head and said simply, "I'm scared." Her dad wouldn't like that, but it was the plain truth she'd been hiding from all day. "Dad, in Brooklyn I was the big dog. Out here, I don't even know where to start."

She took a calming breath and spread her hands before her. She thought about it for a moment and smiled. "But you know," she said, "after what I saw today, I don't think I could go back."

She told him all about it, forgetting her decision to go shopping. She told him about the Cincinnati kids and then went on to describe the doctored Hathor report from the Secret Service case. Even though she recognized the subtle buzz of Hathor censoring some of the more sensitive details, she laid it all out. In town for a day, and already she was caught up in plots she could barely imagine.

Again, she knew all too well how her dad would react if he were on the line. Even with thirty years on the force, he wouldn't have a clue how to investigate this stuff. In her imagination she could hear his low whistle, and the words that had been plaguing her all day long. "How do you even deal with somebody so far outside the law?"

And once again, she had absolutely nothing to say. After a long moment, she sighed. "I don't know. I know it's only my first day and all, but I've got my case and I've spent hours battering at it, and it just kills me because I don't have a clue what I'm supposed to be doing."

She frowned. "I know what you would say. 'Give it time.' That's what Rick says, and he's my boss, but...it's just...." Her breath caught, and she made sure it didn't come out a sob. She wanted to admit that she was only getting frustrated to hide from the fact that she was lonely. Or homesick. Whatever. She wanted to tell him she missed him. But, as she reminded herself for probably the tenth time that day, she knew how a cop behaved, and it wasn't like a scared little girl. Her dad didn't need to hear about all her little problems.

She glanced at her watch, just for something to do, and said, "Oh, holy cow. It's late, Dad, and I've got work to do tomorrow." She smiled. "Thanks for keeping me company." She wished for an answer, one real word of encouragement, but it was a voicemail after all. Her smile turned sad, but didn't go away. "Goodnight, Dad," she said. "Goodbye."

The click from Hathor let her know the line was dead. She glanced at her watch again, and thought about going shopping anyway. Someplace would be open. She didn't really want to anymore, though. She contacted the front desk to request a welcome basket, and the system told her one was waiting in her mailbox. She grabbed her handheld, pulled up her apartment details, and found a map to the mailboxes, right down on the other side of the courtyard.

The welcome basket was a cardboard box with a handful of necessities. She dumped it in a pile on the kitchen table, grabbed the soap and shampoo, and headed back to her room. She stripped down and threw her clothes in the wash, then settled in for a long, hot shower. Afterward, she had just time to whisper a word of thanks to Hearth for picking an apartment with a luxuriously soft bed before sleep wrapped her up and carried her away.

The next morning she learned that the complex's community cars weren't available for round trips over half an hour, inside business hours, but the nearest subway station was less than a quarter of a mile away. She caught a train downtown, and stepped through the doors into Ghost Targets ten minutes to eight. The other part of her dad's old law, "Always beat the boss to work," and she'd certainly managed it, but before the morning was over she found herself wondering why she'd bothered.

She spent two hours digging for dirt on the victim, anything to suggest a motive. She crawled backward through time, listening in on every conversation Ms. Linson had had on the day of her death (at least, she thought bitterly, every conversation that Hathor cared to remember). Rick stopped by her desk a little after noon to invite her to lunch, but she saw the rest of his team waiting for him—and Reed glaring at her—so she politely declined. As he was turning to go, though, she spoke up.

"Rick."

"Yeah?"

"I, uh...I have a case going before the bench tomorrow. Back home, I mean. Would it be too much to ask—"

"Not at all." He pulled out his handheld and glanced at it, probably checking the calendar. "No, that's perfect, actually. I know you've been chomping at the bit, but we're just swamped here."

"About that," she said, and he must have seen the frustration in her eyes. He threw a glance at Reed and the other three headed for the elevator. Rick finally turned his full attention to Katie.

"Look, kid," he said. "I'm sorry. I didn't mean to overwhelm you. Probably shouldn't have dropped a homicide on your first day on the force, but it would have been gathering dust otherwise."

"No," she said. "It's not that. It's just—"

"It wasn't fair of me," he said. "You should be watching over somebody's shoulder, not running blind. I can get you on—"

"Don't," she said. The word came down like a stomped boot, and stopped him dead. He raised an eyebrow in question, and she spoke a little more softly. "I haven't been pulled off a case since I was twenty-six. Don't do that to me. I can handle this."

He chuckled, but she saw a sparkle of pride in his eyes. "Dammit, girl, you've got gumption. Don't worry about it. It's the software that's the trouble, it's the tricks of the trade, and we're the only ones in the world who do what you need to learn. It's not a personal judgment."

"I know," she said, "but—"

"Reed told me you two talked yesterday. He told me how worried you are, and I should have known better than to ask it of you."

"No," she said, suddenly forceful again. "I want the case, Rick."

His eyes rested on hers for a moment, and then he smiled. "I told him you'd say that. Okay, girl. If you want it, the Little Rock case is still your baby." He raised a hand and pointed at her, mock serious. "But you do your civic responsibility. Take care of that New York case tomorrow. Maybe by the time you get back I'll have a minute to breathe." He started to turn away, then looked back at her. "You sure you don't want something for lunch?"

"No," she said. "I'm fine."

He shrugged. "Suit yourself." Half an hour later he brought her back a turkey sandwich. It sat cooling on her desk while she spent the afternoon eavesdropping on Linson's private life. She went back four days, peeking in on private calls, business conversations, Hathor requests. Nothing seemed out of place. The young woman was having money problems, but nothing exciting—just the sort of problems college girls always have. Her brother's wife was pregnant, and if it was a girl they were going to name it after her, and that tidbit had covered most of conversations for the time period. The company was doing well, but not quite well enough to keep a Junior Administrative Officer busy for eight hours a day. It was a quiet little life.

And then, all of a sudden, it was over. Nothing Katie could find made that any clearer. It all seemed surreal. Usually, once she had a murder victim, she could look in the database and find a big red arrow pointing at a suspect. Then, from there, she could follow the glowing lines between the murderer and the victim, seeing (usually from days out) the intersecting paths that would end in the victim's death. Tragic though it might be, there was an air of destiny about it all that made the crime almost mechanical.

A bug, certainly. A flaw in the system that had to be fixed. But not...random. Oh, sure, in the first moments after a murder, it always seemed random, but Hathor had cleared all that up. Almost always, the crime was set in motion long, long before it actually occurred.

She stopped the playback, freezing Ms. Linson in the middle of a call to her best friend from high school, who had just gotten a job at Disneyland and called to gloat about it. Katie shook her head. For no reason whatsoever, this girl was about to die.

Then she saw the clock on her desktop: after six already. Her day had burned up like a candle, listening to real-time audio streams. She put together a request to compile and transcribe the rest of the victim's voice audio for the previous week, then closed down her desktop and headed for the door. She could skim through that faster, anyway.

Katie stayed home Tuesday night and watched a movie, but she missed most of the details. Curled up on her loveseat, she spent the whole evening scrolling through chat transcripts on her handheld. At a quarter past ten, she glanced up and realized the TV screen was black, had been for an hour. She shook her head with a chuckle, put away her handheld, and headed to bed.

An hour passed, her mind buzzing here and there, and finally she grabbed the headset from her nightstand and hooked it over her ear. "Hathor, connect me to Dad," she said. She left him a forty-minute message, laying out her day for him, bit by bit, and as she talked it through the pieces fell into place. She had to fight a yawn when she finally said, "Goodbye," and she fell asleep with the headset still on.

Wednesday she woke up early, dressed in her most authoritative outfit, and had a bowl of dry cereal before she started her day. Then she checked her watch and checked her schedule again. "Hathor, get me travel details to the supreme court in Brooklyn, now."

The long-familiar voice of Hathor said in her ear, "From home to Supreme Court, Brooklyn, New York, now, by private car, will take two hours, twenty-one minutes. Conditions are optimal. Weather in Brooklyn, New York—"

Katie shook her head, confused, and interrupted. "Hathor, stop. Details to my handheld." The voice fell silent while Katie darted over to her loveseat and tossed aside throw pillows until she found her handheld. Her travel itinerary waited on the screen. She'd set it up last night, booking a seat on the train at eight o'clock. Now, the reservation showed as canceled, replaced by an order for a private car to pick her up at her apartment. She pulled up details on the reservation, and found it paid on the Bureau's account.

She rolled her eyes as her headset buzzed. Rick's voice boomed, "Pratt."

"Yeah," she said. "Connect him."

"Hey, kid," Rick said, and she could hear his grin. "Did you get my present?"

"You don't have to do that. The state of New York is happy to pay for my travel. The chief just wanted me to express his gratitude to you for giving me the day off—"

"Oh, forget that," Rick said. "Due diligence and all, I checked on your court date. You didn't tell me it was one of those piss-ant confidence appeals. I *hate* that stuff. The whole Jurisprudence Project was set up to avoid exactly that sort of wasteful motion."

"Well, yeah—"

"So I amended your credentials on the court docket. You're testifying as a Federal Specialist now. Tell your chief he can keep his gratitude. Just show the defense attorney for the clown he is, would you?"

"Umm...thank you, sir?"

"Stop that," he said, a touch of his irritation still in his voice. "Call me Rick. Besides," he said after a moment, "Craig would've blocked access to half our services from public transport. If I put you in a private car, I can keep you on the clock."

"Ah ha," she said, laying on the sarcasm thick, for his sake. "Well, thanks a lot, Rick." He chuckled, but she really was grateful for his forethought. Hours on a train with nothing to do would have killed her.

Rick said, "Gotta go. Luck in court. See you bright and early. Out." The line went dead before she could answer.

4. Brooklyn

Katie checked the itinerary again. She had another half hour before the car would arrive. She spent it all working on the Little Rock case, and she was still buried in her notes, standing curbside in a light drizzle and tapping on her touch-screen, when the car pulled up and called her name. She climbed right in and blacked the windows.

Half an hour down the road, she tore herself from her case and pulled up an old case file. Another homicide, but this one had been easy—seventy-seven percent out of Jurisprudence at the time of death, and eighty-nine percent before she'd slapped the cuffs on him the next morning. God bless him, he'd been a talker. Prints on the murder weapon had sealed the deal: ninety-two was enough, by law, to get a bench judgment against him, and the judge had handed down a sentence after twenty minutes of consideration, less than twenty-four hours after the crime.

She sat back in the seat and closed her eyes, recalling the details of the case. The appeals argument was a shallow one, a fallacious (and probably deliberately so) misstatement of the Jurisprudence numbers, and any judge with a functioning brain would understand that. Jurisprudence didn't make mistakes, after all. She grumbled, "Connecting the dots," and cleared the notes from her screen. A moment later, she pulled up the Little Rock file again. *That* was a mystery.

The car deposited her at the courthouse fifteen minutes before she was scheduled to take the stand. She stepped out of the car, and back into her real life.

It was like a punch to the stomach, the intense familiarity. Like any day of the week, climbing out of a cab to make a court date. She knew both of the lawyers presenting their cases upstairs. Hell, she knew most of the lawyers in the building, and half the judges. She waved to the security guard at the door as he nodded her through. This was her town.

She got a voice memo in the elevator from Eva, the prosecutor. "Glad you could make it. We're meeting with the judge in quarters, office three-oh-two down the hall on your left. Running a couple minutes fast, but you'll be fine." She could hear Taylor making her specious case in the background, and she shook her head. Taylor knew how to sell it, but the judge on the case was still in his forties so Katie wasn't much worried.

She pushed open the door in time to hear Eva announce, "Your honor, I'd like to introduce Special Agent Katie Pratt, Federal Bureau of Investigation, and formerly of the Brooklyn PD. She's the arresting officer on the case, and came up from Washington this morning to lend her expertise."

Katie took the introduction in stride, nodded to the judge, and said, "Sorry I'm late, Your Honor. I thought this was a court hearing."

The judge was a wiry man with an academic look to him. He leaned back in his desk chair, almost lounging, and measured Katie with sharp gray eyes. After a moment he shrugged. "Seemed like a fairly routine appeal, I figured we could handle it here and leave the courtroom free for more pressing business."

Katie didn't show her frown. That was a win, right there, but they hardly needed her for that. She nodded to him, then looked uncertainly to Eva. "What can I help you with?"

The prosecutor smiled reassuringly. "Defense has argued the unfairness of a bench judgment against a criminal with a ninety-two percent confidence. Specifically, she suggests that treating a ninety-percent confidence as a guilty verdict implies one in ten of our convicts are, statistically speaking, innocent." In spite of the informal setting, Eva was addressing Katie as though she were on the witness stand, and that eased Katie's nerves. She knew how to respond to that. "Can you comment on this?"

"Of course." Katie turned to the judge. She hadn't been there for defense's speech, but she knew how it had gone. This was, as the judge had said, a routine argument. "A Jurisprudence confidence score is *not* a raw assessment of guilt. Despite how it might sound, a ninety percent confidence against a suspect does not mean there's a ninety percent chance he's guilty."

She clasped her hands in front of her. It was easier to make the speech from the comfort of a chair. She felt like a professor lecturing, and that role had never suited her. "Rather, the Jurisprudence Project specifically compiles and analyzes available, definitive evidence against a suspect. The necessary and relevant criteria for individual crimes are...complex, but they are set in case- and trial-law. A one hundred percent confidence represents a theoretical, perfect preponderance of evidence against a victim—a case in which every possible incriminating record is available and positively identified, usually with an unbroken history of years. In fourteen years in law enforcement, I've never seen a perfect confidence. I am assured it's a technical impossibility."

The judge nodded. "Have you ever seen a ninety that was wrong."

Katie laughed. She shook her head. "I...can't say that I have. Honestly, I've never seen anything over a seventy that I believed was wrong, but I'm not a judge."

He smiled, tight-lipped, and nodded for her to go on.

Eva led her with, "Tell us about this case."

"First, I'd like to address the 'ten percent innocent' angle." Katie said. She'd only learned this figure a few months ago, and as far as she was concerned it put the nail in the coffin on the entire appeal. "For you to find a population large enough to trigger a false positive—and by that I mean anything over a confidence of *seventy*, not ninety, because seventy is the general standard for an indictment. Anyway, for you to find one false positive for the most lenient of felonies, you would need more than two hundred million innocent people. Jurisprudence compiles massive quantities of relevant data, positive and negative, and weighs probative value of every element, correlated to every other element."

Eva turned to the judge. "The chance of a false positive in this system is lower than the margin of error on DNA evidence—considered one of the most accurate methods of identification prior to the Jurisprudence Project." She turned back to Katie, "As to the particulars of this case...."

Katie nodded, and pulled out her handheld more for show than anything else. She knew the details by heart, but it looked more convincing if she seemed to be reading them. "Immediately prior to his death, as recorded by Hippocrates, the victim made an aggravated outburst that triggered authority and emergency responses through Hathor." She met the judge's eyes. "Specifically, he said...well, it's rife with obscenity, but the essence of his outburst was, 'Oh, no. Oh...lord, no. You can't do this to me. Help! Help!' a string of expletives, and then the clear sound of a gunshot. This recording coincides with a spike and then rapid crash of the victim's monitored vitals. Emergency services were automatically dispatched through Hippocrates, but the victim was dead on arrival. Based on several key parameters, Jurisprudence flagged the incident for review as a probable homicide."

The judge nodded. Katie went on.

"Concerning the ninety-two percent confidence on the accused. During a window beginning seven minutes prior to the shooting and ending two minutes afterward, the accused was alone in a closed room with the victim. They carried on a conversation concerning illicit activities that was picked up in fragments and reconstructed from audio sources outside the room. Hathor has an unbroken positive identification on the accused that precedes the event by one thousand, one hundred, twenty-four days, and continues unbroken since. The victim is likewise positively identified, up to time of death." Ugh. She remembered this one. She had watched it in HaRRE like a scene in a movie. The guy was guilty as hell.

"The presence of the accused in the same room as the victim at the time of death earned him a confidence of twenty-six percent. No one else was in the room—we have video proof of it. That alone would have earned him a guilty verdict at a jury trial."

The defense attorney complained at that. "Your Honor!" But he waved her quiet. Katie continued.

"Hathor has archived seven separate incidents prior to the event in which the accused discussed the victim, always in a hostile fashion, and two of those included direct threats of violence—in one case, he assured a compatriot that he intended to murder the victim. These accusations, individually, do not even factor in Jurisprudence, but taken collectively increase his score by four percent. Following the time of death, the accused confessed the crime on three separate occasions—twice in prayer, while on public transportation away from the scene of the crime, and once in conversation with his priest, whom he spoke with by Hathor audio connection. The combined confidence from these three confessions adds up to seventeen, weighted. Hathor provided seven lines of social connections between the accused and the victim, six of which represented illicit or illegal endeavors. Jurisprudence recognized a trajectory of conflict in these relationships, and that accounted for another seven percent confidence."

The judge sighed heavily, and Katie stopped in her report. She met his eyes in a question, and he shrugged. "I know how to read a Jurisprudence confidence report."

She bit back her first sarcastic response, but the second one escaped. "Does the defense?"

Taylor bristled at that, and barked, "Your Honor!" in objection, but Katie knew it was all playacting. Taylor was here on a simple crap-shoot, and really she had lost it as soon as she'd been assigned this judge. He still pointed a finger at Katie in rebuke, though.

"I'm sorry," she said. "That was out of line." She glanced back at the confidence report on her handheld and shrugged. "The murder weapon was positively identified with ninety-nine plus confidence, and linked to the accused before, during, and after the incident. Means, motive, and opportunity, as they said in the old days." As she said it, she realized the judge was the only other person in the room old enough to remember the phrase in common use, but the lawyers had heard it often enough in their history classes. "There's other incidentals, which account for the infinitesimally small likelihood of a false positive, but before Jurisprudence reaches a seventy percent confidence it has firmly established means, motive, and opportunity. We placed the accused and victim in the same location, we found a trajectory of violence based on a failed, illicit financial enterprise, and we associated the accused with the murder weapon."

She took a deep breath. "There's a reason congress authorized bench judgments above the ninety percent threshold, Your Honor. Jurisprudence has access to more information than eyewitnesses and search warrants could ever provide. The system is not wrong." She looked across at Taylor. "I understand that the system allows appeals of Confidence, for reasons of fairness. I also understand that process is under review, because confidence is *not* wrong. The report testifies to that, in this case."

She caught Eva's expression out of the corner of her eye, and realized she was stealing the prosecutor's lines. She'd been through it so often. She fell silent, and Eva delivered the punch line. "In this case, Your Honor, the accused is clearly guilty, and the bench judgment entirely warranted."

The judge looked at Taylor for a rebuttal, but before she could open her mouth, he shook his head. "I agree," he said Taylor sputtered, trying to voice an objection, but the judge shut her up with a look. "No, the prosecution has made its case. The court rejects this confidence appeal, with prejudice. I'll submit my remarks on the topic later today. Judge Grantham's judgment remains in force. Thank you."

Taylor didn't bother storming out or stomping off, but she didn't hang around to say hi to Katie, either. Under the circumstances, Katie supposed that was probably a good thing. Eva caught Katie's arm as they left the judge's office, though, and guided her to a quiet corner to talk. Katie watched the judge's door fall shut, then asked, "What the hell was that?"

Eva laughed. "I was going to ask you the same thing. Federal expert witness? When did that happen?"

Katie shrugged. "I made Special Agent on Monday. They didn't have any work for me to do, so my boss let me come testify here. I don't know he would have if he'd known it was just chambers—"

Eva laughed again. "That's *why* it was just chambers. I got a message from him at two this morning when your new credentials were posted. Apparently he was impressed."

Katie shook her head. "I guess that was the point. My boss did that, because he hates these appeals as much as you do." A shadow entered Eva's eye, and Katie said, "What?"

"Nothing," the lawyer said. "I mean, of course *he* hates them." Katie only looked confused, and Eva became defensive. "I mean, his cases are the reason we have these appeals at all."

"Ghosts?"

"Yeah," Eva said. "I wasn't sure you'd be able to sell your certainty, with your new position. Have you thought about what ghosts mean, to Jurisprudence confidence? What if someone else had been in the room with Tyler and Jay? We got twenty-six off the fact those two were alone in the room. Without that, for this particular case, you don't have a bench judgment. If you consider the possibility of a ghost, of someone else in the room that Hathor can't even guess at...you've got no confidence at all. We're back to jury trials for everything."

Katie just stared. After a moment, she snorted, then raised her hands in defense at the look of irritation in Eva's eyes. "No, no, you're right. You're absolutely right. But the system's not so fragile as you think. Maybe I couldn't have sold *this* argument before I became an agent, but I can tell you—Eva, there's thirteen agents in the FBI's *National* Ghost Targets division. Fourteen counting me, but I don't count yet. Thirteen, and five of them are working on one case right now. I checked, and Ghost Targets has eleven unresolved case files, and all but two of those go back far enough that there's just not enough database information to clear them up. Probably long since resolved, but we can't positively connect the ghosts with the new identities. Other than that, we're working five active cases, one of which is over but for the paperwork, and another is just two days old and sitting on the desk of an absolute rookie." She took a deep breath, and shook her head. "No, ghosts account for less than the one-in-two-hundred-million lottery of coincidence. Hathor was never made to fight crime, but in the process of making money, they built a hell of a justice engine."

Eva still looked doubtful, just for a moment, then she shrugged and let it go. "Whatever," she said. "Hey, you rushing back to DC, or do you have time for lunch? A couple of us are meeting up with some of your boys from the precinct." She made the barest of hesitations, then added, "Marshall will be there."

One of the detectives from her old precinct, Marshall was seven years younger than Katie. She felt a flush of excitement at the thought of seeing him, and then immediately regretted it when she saw the grin in Eva's eye. Still, there was nothing for it. "Yeah," she said. "I think I can make time."

Of course she knew the place. As soon as Eva had invited her, she'd known where it would be. A busy bistro, squeezed into a narrow block between a musty, cramped antique book store and a sprawling Duane Reade. As soon as she stepped through the door she sighed at the familiar smell of fresh bread. Everything about the place was familiar. Keith was saving a place for them, six tables shoved together on the far wall. Half a dozen spindly chairs stood rejected an arm's length away, just waiting for a hungry copper to scoop one closer with a boot, sandwich in one hand and large drink in the other. Richard was over there with Keith, leaning close, chuckling thickly and telling him some disgusting story. The blonde waitress she hated would be working their table today, unless she was out sick. Kenny was working the counter, and all she would have to say is, "Give me my regular."

And there was Marshall, just turning away from the cash register. So handsome in his uniform, with short blond hair and sharp blue eyes. He flashed her a smile, for all the world like he'd known she was coming, and headed over to the table. She watched him go, until Kenny called to her from his place behind the counter. "Hey, lady! You look familiar somehow."

She stepped around a crowded table so she wouldn't have to shout back, and rolled her eyes theatrically. "It's been a week."

"I thought you were gone."

"I am," she said, and just saying it hurt. "But I'm back for a day. Can I have my usual."

"Always, Katie. Good to see you." He winked at her as he passed her a cup, then yelled her order back to the cooks. "Thirteen-fifty."

"Put it on my tab," she said, and headed over to join the guys.

Conversation stopped as she approached the table. Then Keith raised his chin at her, challenging. "What you doing back? We already threw you a going-away party. Now this is just awkward."

"Oh," she said, playing hurt. She batted her eyes, mock fragile, and jerked a thumb over her shoulder. "I can just go. I didn't mean to—"

Several of them overwhelmed her with a groaned, "Whatever!" and friendly hands pulled her over to sit down at the center of the table, center of attention.

Marshall spoke through a mouthful of pastrami. "What's it like at the Bureau?"

She couldn't admit the truth to him, his eyes wide with interest, so she went on with the playacting. "Oh, you know, this and that," she said, all indifferent. "Their case files are a mess, and none of them know how to keep timesheets, but I'll get them whipped into shape." There were chuckles all around the table. She shrugged, and said earnestly, "I miss being here, though."

"Oh, go on," Keith said. "It hasn't been a week. You'll make it."

The sentiment was echoed, but Marshall cut through it. "Hey, seriously, what's it like chasing ghosts? I tried looking some up in HaRRE, but by the time the FBI case file hits the Register, all the ghosts are resolved."

She met Marshall's eyes, just for a moment, and her resolve failed her. He smiled as she leaned forward, elbows on the table, and launched into the story of the Cincinnati kids. She made the story as exciting as she could, then sat back afterward and just listened to the others talk. It was all mundane stuff, mostly concerning cases she was still familiar with. She reveled in it.

It turned into a long lunch, by virtue of her being there, but eventually everyone realized they had demands back at the office. They disappeared in ones and twos, and Marshall was one of the last stragglers, sitting across the table from Katie and joking about nothing. She finally, reluctantly, warned him that he was risking the chief's wrath if he stayed any longer, and his look of regret as he tore himself away was enough to make her day.

That left her with just Eva, who caught her watching Marshall's exit when she returned from the bathroom. "You are some kind of homesick, aren't you?" Katie tried to shrug it off, but something in her demeanor gave away the lie, and Eva's joking grin faded to concern. "Oh, gosh, Katie. *Are* you going to make it?"

Katie shrugged, suddenly miserable. "I'll be fine," she said. "It's just tough making a start in a new town, a new job. And I've got this awful case...."

Eva said, "Oh." She put her smile back on, and tugged Katie's hand to get her moving. "Well, we'll get it sorted out," she said. "Come on, let's walk and talk."

"Yeah," Katie said. "Good plan." She leaned across the table to grab her jacket, then followed Eva out the door.

They walked a couple blocks while Katie filled in the broad strokes for her, then she said, "You know what it's like? It's like the books I read when I was a kid. It's like...do you remember *Law and Order*? That old TV show? It's like that. I need to be hitting the beat. I need to be knocking on doors and asking the tough questions." She thought for a moment, and shook her head. "They always used to say, 'After three days, the trail's cold.' Maybe that doesn't matter when it's all in the database, but my new perps *aren't*. So all of a sudden it's like I'm an old-timey cop again, just like I used to dream about, and right now I'm looking at a trail that's gone cold. I'm spending day three hanging out with old friends and parroting back decade-old congressional talking points to a judge who already agrees with me. I need to be in hot pursuit, you know?"

Eva chuckled, and when Katie turned she caught the other woman just watching her. She'd always been a good listener. Katie said, "What?"

"Katie Pratt, Gumshoe," Eva said, and then laughed at Katie's frown. "Fine," she said. "Tell me about it. I bet you've already got more than you think you do."

So she laid it all out. She spent hours bringing Eva up to speed. Most of it they spent walking, strolling Katie's old beat, but after a while she summoned her car and they sat in its spacious interior while she pulled out her handheld to show Eva the HaRRE video.

She pulled off her headset and turned up the volume to use it as a speaker, then she opened her notes while the video was loading so she could skip to the really creepy part. It took a while for the video to render on her handheld, so she narrated while they waited. "Okay, so she's standing in the office, the elevator dings, and everything goes black." Even as she said it, the HaRRE screen resolved, already black. An unbroken roar came from the speaker. She stopped the video and checked the time in the environment, then double-checked her notes. "Weird."

"What?"

"She should be...." Katie skipped backward in time five minutes, and there was the girl, staring at a painting on the wall. Katie said, "Ooh, there she is."

"Pretty," Eva said in an analytical sort of way. "Shame."

Katie said, "Okay, well, here she's listening to some music. She looks nervous to me, but not exactly scared."

Eva nodded.

Katie went on, "Now she moves around behind the desk and—oh." The screen went black.

"Wow." Eva said. "That's spooky. It's not—"

"No," she said, and switched back to her notes. "It has shifted. We've lost...almost three minutes off the record, since Monday." She turned to Eva, eyes wide. "It's growing."

She shrugged. "So?"

"So I was already stumped. This...I don't know what the blackout represents, but it's totally blind. I looked, and it covers the whole downtown building and halfway down the block. I can't get details on anyone or anything within it. We're already pushing half an hour. That means unbroken positive IDs are about to start popping. Anyone inside that blackout—whether it's janitors cleaning up the building or an executive working late on a proposal across the street—if they stay inside the blackout past half an hour, the confidence level on their IDs plummets. It could take weeks for them to repair that. This has ramifications way beyond my homicide."

"How so? I mean, sure, maybe some bystanders can't get good credit for a couple weeks—"

"No. Eva, think about it." Their earlier argument was still fresh on her mind. "That blackout is manufacturing ghosts. The murderer was *already* erased, but this is ghosting everyone. Anything they do is lost to history. Any voice notes they record on Hathor, any last, precious conversation with a dying friend, any violent comment that could have shown motive in some crime of passion weeks from now. And any crimes. If someone was mugged out on the street, we would have no more evidence against them than against my ghost. This is a nightmare. And it's growing."

Eva opened her mouth, but she found herself at a loss for words. That was for the best. Katie said, "Hathor, connect me to Rick Goodall, high priority." He didn't answer, and instead of leaving a message Katie said, "Goodbye. Hathor, connect me to Craig, FBI. Craig, connect me to Rick, high priority."

This time Rick took the call, and Katie immediately said, breathlessly, "Rick, we've got a problem."

"What's wrong?" His concerned voice flooded the interior of the car.

"It's the Little Rock case," Katie said, turning down the volume a little. "There's something very bad there. It's not just a regular ghost. There's some sort of blackout—"

Rick cut her off, laughter in his voice. "Hey, slow down. Take a breath. I know how hard you're working on this case, so I took a look at your case file this morning and there's nothing to panic over. It's a little odd, but I can show you how to handle it as soon as I can get a minute free—"

"Rick, it's growing. It's a real problem—"

He chuckled. "We have ways of dealing with it, Katie. I appreciate your zeal, but this is nothing worth getting worked up over. How did your appeal go?"

"I trashed them," she said, trying not to sound petulant. Her voice just came out flat. "It went great."

"Great!" he said. "Take your time getting home. I'll see you in the morning. Goodbye."

They sat in silence for a while, Katie fuming. Eva finally spoke up. "Look, Katie, I know you don't want to hear this—"

"No," she said. "I know they're the experts. I know I'm just a rookie now. But there's no way this is routine. If it *is*—" She stopped, and took a deep breath. "If it is, the whole system is a lie. All our confidence...." She trailed off, furious and frustrated.

Eva waited a moment, then said. "I know a guy." Katie looked up and met her eyes. Eva shrugged. "Look, if they're as busy as you say they are...if it's the president, Katie, and they only have a handful of agents, your case isn't changing priority in their eyes. You just have to accept that." Katie's eyes flashed, and Eva hurried on. "However, if you want to get to the bottom of this on your own, there's a few things you can do. You can go to Little Rock and knock on doors—"

"I already have permission for that. I fly out Monday."

Eva smiled, a tightening of her lips, and went on. "That's a start. Interview everyone involved, and see if anything turns up." She glanced back at Katie's handheld on the seat between them, the HaRRE screen still solid black. "If you want to figure that out, though, you're going to need an expert."

"And you know a guy."

She shrugged. "I know *of* a guy. Runs a company called Database Archive Management, Inc. The *Times* ran a feature on him a couple months back, and I knew you were looking into Ghost Targets so I shared it with you." Katie looked away, and Eva said, "I know, you were busy. But this guy sells a...service. He 'manages' the database archives of the rich and powerful. The database in question being Hathor's." Katie's eyes grew wide, and Eva said, "Yeah. Right out in the open. They call him Ghoster."

She said, "Ghoster?"

A silky smooth, unfamiliar voice answered her, unnaturally loud from the headset speaker. "Ghoster," it said. "Pleased to meet you, Katie."

5. Ghoster

Eva started, then covered her surprise with anger. "Who is this? How did you connect to this line?"

"I thought we already covered that," the voice answered, sounding annoyed. "I'm Ghoster. Now, here's my question: why is a Federal Ghost Targets agent discussing me and my services with an officer of the court?"

Katie's eyes narrowed, but her voice was level. "Do you have any idea how much trouble you could get in for hacking the communications of a federal agent?"

He answered with a laugh in his voice. "I do. None. I'm walking away from this. Look, I know you're new to the department and all, and apparently you haven't gotten your orientation yet. So here's the most important bit of it. You forget about me. I don't exist, as far as you're concerned. In exchange, I'll throw you a bone now and then. That's the deal."

She caught Eva's eye, and hers were as wide as Katie's. She shrugged, just as confused as Katie. Katie said, "Look, umm...Ghoster. I don't—"

"That's all, Ms. Pratt. Leave me out of your plans. Goodbye."

Silence fell in the car once more. Then Katie shook her head. "What the hell?"

"Okay," Eva said. "I guess I don't know a guy. You're on your own."

Katie said, "No. Hathor, connect me to Ghoster." Her headset played a tone to indicate the name couldn't be resolved. She said, "Hathor, reconnect the previous call." The same tone played, and she growled. Then she barked, "Ghoster! Ghoster, Ghoster, Ghoster! Database Archive Management. I'm talking about you!"

He spoke from her headset once again. "Stop that. You trigger alarms when you do that."

"I know," she said. "You weren't taking my calls."

"I told you—"

"I need your help," she said. "Apparently you know a thing or two about Hathor. Someone has found a way to blind her, and I need you to explain what's going on."

"You couldn't afford me," Ghoster said. "Get your boss to show you how to track down ghosts. It's not as hard as you think."

"This is different," she said, and then her confidence wavered. "I think this is different. It's not just a blind spot. The whole scene is blacked out, in HaRRE. I've never seen anything like it. It's like the lights just go out."

"There are no lights in HaRRE."

He sounded patronizing, and she answered it with irritation. "I know," she said. "I'm trying to describe it. The murderer on my case is already a ghost, but somehow the entire office building goes black, just before the crime. Audio is just noise—a solid bar of noise."

She got no answer from Ghoster. After a moment, she said, "Hello?"

"I'm here," he said. "I'm thinking." Several seconds later he said, "Okay, that's weird. When do you get back from Brooklyn?"

Eva shot her a warning look, but she ignored it. "I'm heading back this afternoon."

"You'll be in the office tomorrow?"

She nodded, "Bright and early."

"Okay. I have a ten o'clock spot free. I'm going to meet you there."

Her eyes shot wide. "Really?"

"You've got me stumped," he said, then added quickly, "It's probably something stupid. No offense, but it usually is. But my Thursdays are usually slow, so I'll give it a look." Before she could thank him—before she really understood that he had volunteered to help—he cut off the conversation with a terse, "Goodbye."

She looked at Eva. After a moment, her face split in a grin. She said, "Thank you, Eva."

"I didn't really do anything," she said.

Katie laughed. "You've given me some hope, for the first time since I started this thing. It's probably something stupid, like he said." She waved away Eva's protest. "No, I've known that from the start. But this is my first opportunity to find out *what*. I just want to know how to do my job."

Eva smiled back at her. "You've got that, then. This guy sounded like a real jerk, though."

She laughed. She glanced at her watch, "Ah. I've used up your whole day."

"Don't worry about it," Eva said. "I took most of the afternoon off as soon as I learned you were coming to town." She glanced at her own watch, and groaned. "I do have an arraignment before long, though. I'm sorry—"

"Oh, no. Don't let me keep you any more than I have." Katie said. "I've got enough to keep me busy now, getting ready for Ghoster." She blanked the screen of her handheld and put it away, hung her headset back on her ear, and smiled at Eva. "Thank you again. Want a ride to the courthouse?"

Katie dropped her off, waved a sad goodbye, then sank back in the seat with eyes closed as her car sped toward DC. After a while she called up her dad, and left him a message all about her day. When she got home, her mind was abuzz with plans, details she needed to get sorted out to share with the database expert. She forgot about dinner, working in the comfort of her home office, and it was well past midnight before she finally shut off the lights and fell into her bed.

When the alarm went off the next morning, she cursed it roundly. The thought of her appointment with Ghoster got her out of bed, though, and she showed up at work smiling. Rick commented on it before he disappeared into the conference room. Even his disappearance didn't bother her, because she had found a mentor on her own. She went straight to her desk and pulled up the case file. Her first, highest priority was to learn more about the blackout.

It was indeed growing, in space as well as time. Two other buildings beside the Aggregator's were now fully engulfed, and she'd lost another forty seconds since she'd showed the video to Eva. She stopped the playback just before the blackout and left it rendered while she tried to do the math on her loss rate. She came up with a prediction just a moment before the video on her desktop dropped to black—easily an hour early. Aggravating, but she had no reason to expect the blackout's growth rate to be constant. She had an estimate, anyway.

It was alarming, too. If it took another ten days for the assassination case to resolve (one way or another), they would be looking at a dozen new ghosts in Hathor—people who were in the buildings or on the street earlier in the day. If it took a month, maybe a hundred other lives would lose some bit of information as their pasts wandered into the growing cloud. If it took much longer than that, the blackout could reach back into business hours, and then the damage would be catastrophic—locally, if not nationally. She found seven other people already caught in the blackout, all in one of the three buildings currently consumed. All of them had arrived at least an hour before the blackout started (most had been there since lunch), and the first to leave didn't do so until thirty-seven minutes after the end of it. All of them were less than a day away, real-time, from losing their positive IDs in Hathor, without ever leaving the office. At the very least, she thought, they needed to be warned.

Of course, one of those seven could be her killer. It was unlikely—Jurisprudence couldn't even find anything above single-digit confidence on motive for any of them. Besides, she'd already seen the ghost open the front door—seen nobody step out of the elevator, before that was lost to history—so there was no good reason to suspect any of the positive IDs. Unless the ghost had been a red herring all along. She sat back in her chair with a grunt. Maybe she'd been wrong. Maybe she preferred connecting the dots.

Then that same voice that had broken in on her yesterday spoke in her ear. "Katie Pratt, FBI," and she said, "Connect me." She waited a moment, and said, "I do appreciate you not breaking in this time."

He came right back, "I do appreciate you leaving me out of your conversations." He was silent for a moment, then said, "You're still having Hathor problems?"

"Yeah," she said. "I've got more details now, too."

"Always good," he said. "Come let me in."

She said, "Oh!" and turned in time to see the elevator doors slide open. He flashed her a smile and she said, "Craig, open the doors. I have a guest."

She got to the doors just as they slid open. Ghoster strode in, looking over the bullpen with all the scrutiny and pride of a general inspecting his troops. "So this is where the magic happens."

He was older than she had expected from his voice, easily in his fifties. His hair was black—naturally or artificially—and thick but cut close and slicked back. His eyes were sharp, clever, light blue. He shook her hand with a salesman's grip, and she went ahead and slapped that label on him. Silky smooth.

She jerked her head back toward her desk. "I won't waste your time," she said. "I want you to see this. Craig, pull up my case file on my desk."

Before she could turn, though, Rick stormed out of the conference room in a rage. Katie waited, curious, and blinked in surprise when Rick turned straight on her. "Ms. Pratt," his voice was a bellow in the bullpen. "A word please? My office." She blushed as all eyes turned on her, but held her head high and made her way across to Rick's office. He slammed the door as soon as she was in, barely missing her.

"What the hell are you trying to do to me?" He yelled, his face turning red with the force of his rage. "Are you trying to bring the whole damn department down? Hmm? Tell me, Pratt, why the *hell* would you bring that man into my offices?"

She shook her head, jaw hanging open. When he stopped for a breath she said, "I'm so sorry, sir. I just wanted some help on my case—"

"Do you know who he is? Do you have a *clue* who that man is? What he represents? If word of this gets out, that we brought in Archive Management—"

She spread her hands, and tried to explain. "He's not charging anything. He wanted to see the blackout on the Little Rock case. The one I told you about. He said he'd never heard of anything like it, and someone told me he would know if anybody, so—"

"So help me, Pratt." He raised his hand, like he meant to backhand her, then lowered it again. He shook his head, disappointed. "I don't know how I could hire someone so...reckless. This was stupid, Katie." She tried to stammer a defense, but he turned away. "No, it's my fault. You're new. God, I just.... Get him out of here. Now." He took a deep breath, and blew it out in an explosion. "Get him gone."

She said, "Yes, sir," and fled his office.

As she approached, Ghoster was standing behind her desk, fiddling with his handheld. She glanced at the screen, curious, and found him taking still captures of her desktop. Anger flared, white-hot in her chest. "What are you doing?"

He didn't even glance up. "Your secretary wouldn't give me copy access to your case file, but I was able to lock out your desk before he could clear it. I should be able to recreate most of this—"

"Are you insane?" She slapped his hand, sending his handheld bouncing off the wall before it smashed to the floor. He raised his eyes to hers, too astonished to be angry yet, and she said, "Do you have any idea where you are?"

He snorted. "So what? I'm in the lion's den," he said. He shook his head. "I'm not scared of any of you. All of this," he waved to indicate her desk, and then more generally the rest of the room, "all of this is public and corporate data. None of it belongs to you." He bent to scoop up his handheld and dropped it in his pocket. "You're eavesdroppers and gossips, Katie Pratt. You are not the law." He glanced to Rick's office, and she followed his gaze. Her boss stood framed in his doorway, huffing and angry, eyeballing the both of them.

Ghoster said, "Oh. I see." He tapped a couple rapid lines of code into the command line for her desktop, and the screen instantly blinked off. He met her eyes. "Sorry to trouble you." He brushed past her, out the door, and she fell into her chair. She could feel eyes on her, all across the bullpen, and from the conference room Reed's. His disappointed green gaze burned even blacker than Rick's. She couldn't bring herself to meet any of their eyes. She didn't even want to talk to Craig, to ask for her desk back. Instead, she pulled a notepad out of a drawer and started scratching some notes to herself with a pen. Details she'd figured out that morning, to share with Ghoster. Questions she'd meant to ask him. It only made her feel more miserable, but she couldn't bring herself to raise her head. She burned another hour staring at the little pad of paper, then slipped away early for lunch. She took a walk around the block, trying to find the nerve to go back and face her coworkers, but it wasn't there.

She knew what she'd done wrong. Ghoster's company represented everything they were fighting against. She had known that all along. She had invited the fox into the henhouse. Their whole *job* was to stop people doing exactly what he enabled people to do. But he had offered to help. He had told her over the phone, "Sometimes I throw Ghost Targets a bone." She had just assumed....

That was it. She had assumed she knew, and she didn't. She kept trying to drum up outrage at Rick for shouting at her, but hers had been a stupid rookie move. She knew that. Especially when she'd caught him trying to circumvent security measures right there in the office. How many of their secrets had she given away, hoping to get a bit of insight?

And on the heels of that thought, a far more terrible one. She had been used. He'd never meant to help her at all, he just wanted to see the inside of the FBI office. And she had given him the chance, complete with an opportunity to walk away unscathed. She hadn't just made a fool of herself, she'd put the whole department in jeopardy. How much harder would it become to track down Ghoster's clients, just because of what she'd done?

Without ever really thinking it through, lost in other thoughts, she looked up at some point and found herself at an entrance to the subway. She looked back over her shoulder, toward the FBI office, and heaved a sigh. She didn't have the nerve to go back. Not today. That's what had brought her here.

She didn't think she would be missed, either.

She took the train home, and walked the short distance to her apartment in a drizzle that fit her mood perfectly. The locks on the door popped open as she approached, and she made a mental note once more to get a key and start using the physical lock. She pushed the door open, irritated that she hadn't gotten around to that yet, and froze with one foot in the door.

Ghoster spoke from her couch. "Your fridge said you were low on margarita mix so I picked some up on the way here. I'll make it my treat if you'll mix some up for me."

She stepped all the way into the room and thought idly of drawing her weapon, trying to put a scare in him, but she was too well trained to follow through on it. Instead she settled for an angry growl. "What the hell are you doing in my apartment?"

He glanced over his shoulder at her, then back to the handheld in his lap. "Oh, it started raining." He changed some settings on the touch screen, then said absently. "After I listened to the conversation with your boss, I understood what was going on. The whole dog and pony show kicking me out. Still seemed like you would want to know what I found out, though, so I came here."

"You're a criminal," she said, without leaving her place by the door. "You're the bad guy. And I was a moron to bring you into the office—"

"Oh, knock that off," he said. "Rick's just upset about the president thing." He must have sensed her hackles rise, because he quickly added, "Which was none of my doing. Oh, hell, no. I wouldn't go near that kind of heat. No, I'm not your criminal. I do little cover-ups. I preserve marriages, Katie. I help family men keep their jobs. I'm like a saint."

She grunted, and he chuckled. "Regardless, I don't cross law. I'm too rich to go to jail. Prison life wouldn't suit me." He glanced around her apartment pointedly, as if to suggest it would be a relatively minor change for her. "Look. If someone comes to me looking to hide something really ugly, I have Hathor slip a little note under your boss's door. I guess he never figured out where those were coming from—too good at my own game—but I'm not breaking any laws."

"Except for a little harmless breaking and entering." She couldn't quite get the venom into her voice.

"Oh, psh," he said. "You invited me in. Besides." He rose and tossed her his handheld, still in good shape despite its tumble. "I have something you want." He moved to the kitchen area and started peeking in cabinets. "I'll make the margaritas, then, but I'm putting the mix on your tab."

She ignored him. The handheld showed her case file, complete with notes. It was running the same software they used, and she found a half-screen render of the HaRRE video stream, the familiar solid black box. An output window below it scrolled text, constantly adding fifteen-character codes that looked like personal IDs. She watched them roll for a moment, all different, and finally said, "What's this?"

"That's your blackout," he said, noisily mixing four ice cubes, three shots of mix, and two shots of tequila in her stainless-steel shaker. "Your math was wrong, by the way, but you would have figured that out pretty quickly. You got a fair average for three days, but it's decelerating. Sort of. It's actually growing at a one-dimensional rate in a three-dimensional environment. So it's not as catastrophic as you think."

"Oh," she said, trying to work out the full significance of what he'd said.

He went on. "Well, that is to say, this cloud isn't as catastrophic as you think. The fact that it exists, though... that it's even possible...."

She shook her head. "What is it?"

He uncapped the shaker and poured a margarita over ice. "People," he said. Then he stopped, and frowned at the countertop. "Noise is the right word for it. Just like the audio track."

"I don't understand that either—"

"It's all the same thing," he said. "Hathor is baffled. Ghosts are usually entries erased or moved around in the database. This is different. This is overload." He brought her the drink and pointed to the scrolling list of IDs. "Have you ever seen a ball made of rubber bands? It's just a huge mess. You keep making it bigger and bigger by wrapping little rubber bands around the outside. If you look at it from far away, though, it's just a ball. You don't see the individual...you know what? Never mind. That's not a great analogy. It's the idea, though."

He pointed to the black screen. "That's people. That's not an empty back office, that's what the office would look like in HaRRE if there were ten thousand people in it. A hundred thousand, whatever. I haven't done the math per square foot. The point is, it's overloaded. Instead of hiding one person from you—which, incidentally, is what *I* would do—your database manager has gone in and inserted millions of decoys until the software just isn't useful."

She stared at the screen for a moment, numbers ticking by at the bottom, and then she said softly, "Who are they?"

Ghoster shrugged. "I don't know. If it were my setup, they'd be phantoms. Fakes. You can cook up a reasonable-looking random ID with enough supporting background by running a quick script compile across a couple hundred real IDs. I've done that before," his eyes cut to her and he added too quickly, "as an exercise, you know. Just practice. Who knows with this guy, though? I never would have thought to throw this at Hathor, so who knows how he thinks?" He thought for a moment and said, "If these are real people, though, you have worse problems than a dead girl."

Katie had been thinking the same thing. She met his eyes. "What do we do about this?"

He laughed. "I don't know. You piqued my curiosity, so I'm going to poke around and see what I can find. I'll come up with a pretty good guess on the veracity of those blackout IDs in...say, half an hour. I can do that for you tonight, if you want. Anything beyond that...."

He shrugged, and finished his margarita in a gulp, then caught his breath. "Anything beyond that, I don't know what you're going to do. This is a mess. I guess pray for two things: that the cloud keeps growing, and that your boss has some miracle software to track down the source that's adding them. I don't know of anything that can do that, though." He shook his head, then took the glass back to the kitchen sink. "That's just my opinion, but there are only two people alive who know more about Hathor than I do, and neither of them works for Ghost Targets. I'd say you're better off canning the file and just hoping the cloud stops growing before it cripples Jurisprudence."

He held out a hand, and she passed him back his handheld. He grabbed one of the IDs from the stream at the bottom and pulled up personal details on it, his fingers flashing across the screen, and spoke absently while he worked. "Me, I'm just gonna spend my time praying whoever did this doesn't go into business. I can't compete with this." He moved to the couch, completely oblivious to the devastating effect his words had had on her. After a moment's silence, he spoke up again. "Hey, could you make me another one of those? That's good tequila."

She went to the kitchen, moving automatically. Everything he said hurt. She'd spent three days wrestling with an unsolvable case, constantly frustrated that she didn't know enough to solve it. Now she'd brought in an expert, and he promised her she never would know enough. *He* didn't know enough. If she weren't a cop, she thought, she would cry now. That's how bad it was. Instead, she mixed margaritas.

She brought Ghoster his, and when he reached for it, she caught his eye. "So, no justice?" she said. He frowned, one corner of his mouth turning down, and shook his head once. Katie said, "Then let's drink a toast to the poor girl's soul. Here's to Janeane Linson."

She let go of his drink, then, but he didn't catch it. It fell to the floor and soaked the pretty white carpet. He didn't even look down.

"What did you say?"

She shook her head. She was too upset about the case to care about the carpet. "That's the victim. Janeane Linson. May she rest in peace."

SURVEILLANCE

Ghoster licked his lips, nervously, then looked down at his handheld. "I never even looked," he said, quiet. Then his eyes darted back up to hers. "Umm...I may have a suspect for you."

She frowned. "What do you mean? You said—"

"I said there's two people in the world who know more about this system than I do." He tapped on the handheld for a moment and drew up personal details for someone new. "One of them used to be named Linson," he said. "And he grew up outside Little Rock."

6. Martin Door

Three hours later her boss's voice came through her headset, "Pratt," and she nearly jumped. She glanced at her watch, and remembered for the first time since she'd stepped in the door that she was supposed to be at work. She stammered the word "connect" just in time to catch the call. Then she shot a warning look at Ghoster to keep quiet. He was too drunk by then to pick up on it, though.

Her boss sounded surprised when he said, "Oh, uh, hey, Katie. I just—"

She interrupted him. "I'm sorry, sir. I know I should be at my desk—" Her heart pounded, remembering his fury at finding Ghoster in the office, and she prayed desperately that he didn't already know the man was in her living room, within arm's reach.

"No," he said, still hesitant. Then he took a deep breath. "Look, Pratt, I'm sorry about my outburst earlier. It was out of line. We've all been under a lot of stress lately—you included—and I know you're just trying to do your best. You just surprised me. That was an emotional reaction, not a good management decision." He heaved another big sigh, and said, "I'm sorry. That's what I'm getting at."

"No, sir," she said. "I shouldn't have brought him in to the office."

"You're right," he cut in, but his voice was kind. "But you couldn't have known how bad an idea it was, and I haven't been available for you to ask permission, so that's that. And stop calling me sir. I'm Rick, and I've told you *that* enough times I'll hold you accountable." He paused, and she could imagine him checking his watch. "Look, it's late. I can't say I'm surprised you didn't come back from lunch, but I don't want you walking out on me. Ghost Targets needs people like you."

"Thank you, sir." She said, then, "Rick," before he could correct her. "Thank you. And I'm not going anywhere. Although, I do wonder if I could move my trip to Little Rock up." She tried to sound hurt, but knew it was probably a little too late in the conversation to lay it on thick. "Just, it would be nice to have a couple days before I have to look any of the others in the face again."

He thought about it a moment, but finally said, "Yeah. No, I regret that most. I shouldn't have yelled at you in front of the others. I'll have a talk with all of them, set things straight, but yeah. Go do some old-timey police work. Interview witnesses, inspect the crime scene, all of that. Can you do that in two days?"

"Unless you want to pay me overtime to spend a weekend playing with my nieces."

He chuckled, and that turned into a rich laugh before he was done. "You're sharp, kid. I've got to give you that. But, no, your weekend is on your dime. Either way, I'll see you Monday. Maybe we'll have a break in the Service case before then. Luck to both of us. Goodbye."

She met Ghoster's eyes, and he nodded. "Seems like a smart opening move," he said.

"It gives us some time to look, anyway." She heaved a sigh. It had been an emotionally exhausting day. "Think we can find anything?"

He shook his head. "Man, if it were me...." He trailed off, and then barked a laugh. "Dude is not me, though. Martin Door is not me." He looked at her, and shrugged. "Who knows. But I think we'll have a better guess tomorrow morning." He glanced toward the kitchen, but they'd finished Katie's good tequila. He checked his watch. "Look, I'm going to find a place to stay tonight." He waved away her offer to stay there—one she'd had no intention of making—and said, "I'll be fine on my own. Make travel plans for both of us, would you? I'll see you in the morning." She expected him to stumble on his way to the door, but he didn't so much as sway. He did pull it closed behind him a little harder than necessary, and she heard him start singing about halfway across the courtyard. She laughed and threw the deadbolt.

Then she went back to her handheld, and continued making plans.

Her headset woke her early the next morning, and an hour later she headed out at a casual pace. She stopped for breakfast at a place on the corner, caught a train to the airport, and then pulled out her handheld to check on Ghoster. It showed him already waiting in the terminal. As she approached the identity gates, she thought again of the seven people caught in the Little Rock blackout, and hoped none of them had travel plans anytime soon. Without an unbroken positive ID, they'd have to go through screening. For the first time in years, she took a moment to be grateful for the system as she stepped up to one of the gates and it immediately fell open to let her through, snapping closed behind her. She was old enough to remember long lines at airport security, and extremely glad to be done with that.

Without looking up, Ghoster spoke as soon as she approached. "I can't believe you bought us business class."

"I can't believe there's anything else," Katie said, taking the seat next to him and glancing at his handheld. "What are you working on?"

"Your case," he said. "Still digging into the cloud. It helps me ignore the headache."

She laughed. "Figured anything out?"

"Nothing." He looked up, met her eyes, and said, "And that's scary."

She waited for more, but he remained quiet. After a few minutes she sat down next to him and pulled up the travel itinerary on her own handheld just as a voice announced over her headset, "Your flight is now boarding."

She said, "Details to my handheld," then jerked her head at Ghoster to follow. The display on her handheld guided her to the gate, and a simple "Hi" was enough to voice match her. Halfway down the narrow aisle, she took the seat by the window. As Ghoster settled in next to her, she said, "You know, I'm surprised they let you fly."

He rolled his eyes. "I keep telling you I'm not a criminal. The information I work with is all private property, and I am a licensed property manager. That's all. Every Aggregator out there sells the same services I do—I'm just better at it."

"So what's with the alias?"

He snorted. "Alias? It's a nickname. You've never had a nickname? My proper name is Jeremy. You could learn that from a Hathor search. My whole life story is available to the public. I'm no ghost. I grew up in Norman, Oklahoma. I have positive ID as far back as you'd care to check, and strong references from the highest levels of government."

"Really?" she said. "I'm surprised your customers would admit it openly." She said it offhand, her attention on her handheld, but his reaction caught her full focus.

He threw his hands up, deeply offended, and turned his back on her with a huff. She bit her lip, wishing she'd been more circumspect, but when she said, "I'm sorry," he just *hmph*ed again, and kept his back to her.

Giving up on him, she settled into her seat and pulled out her handheld as the plane began to taxi. She brought up personal details on her new suspect, Martin Door. She glanced over his financials first, and he fell squarely in the well-off-but-not-what-you'd-call-rich category. He seemed to be in the same line of work as Ghoster, contracting for huge sums with the major database services, though he apparently hadn't done any work for several years.

Then she checked out his identifying information. Five-eleven and graying—born in the previous millennium, he was pushing fifty. She had HaRRE generate a model of him, and considered it for some time while vocal samples played in her headset, familiarizing her with his voice. Her first impression was that he didn't wear his age as well as Ghoster did. Shown in jeans and a baggy shirt, he didn't strike the same cutting figure. He wasn't fat, but he was well padded. Soft. There was something inherently friendly about his face, though, clever eyes sparkling above rosy cheeks. He looked like the proud owner of an ancient secret, and it was quite inviting.

She hated when HaRRE made her suspects seem likable. She trusted the software—it drew on an amazing, unlimited source of data, and it could make remarkably accurate predictions—but sometimes she hated it. She knew as well as anyone how friendly criminals could be. Hathor gave her access to a person's whole life, not just the frantic, panicked moments that so often led to bad choices, but the quiet, happy hours at home with the kids, the deeply reverent contrition of a prayer of confession. She knew better than to let any of that interfere with an investigation.

Still, he looked so kind.

After half an hour of the silent treatment, Katie jumped when Ghoster suddenly spoke right next to her ear. "Same old Martin," he said with a chuckle. "He's looking good."

She glanced at the sleek salesman in the seat next to her, trying to guess if he was being sarcastic, but he seemed earnest. He reached past her and touched some controls on the screen, drawing up Martin's location details. He laughed. "Still kicking around in Argentina."

Her earlier train of thought rose up in her mind, and she asked, "How does the system generate a model?"

Ghoster didn't answer right away. He finished reading the information on the screen, then dropped back into HaRRE where Martin stood frozen against a white background.

"It's a weighted composite," he said. "Any time Hathor recognizes someone on a camera—whether it's a security camera, a Hathor Courtesy Recorder, or just a snapshot on someone's handheld—if Hathor can associate the image non-redundantly with an ID in the database, that image is stored forever. Over time, Hathor accumulates enough visual data to estimate a 3D model." His voice was lecturing, and she recognized a pride of ownership in it. "The magic number seems to be in the tens of thousands of images for a single model, and hundreds of thousands to get realistic animation. These days, that's generally a couple weeks out in public."

She nodded. "I understand most of that, but facial expressions, personalities—"

"All of that shows up in the photos," he said. "The weighting algorithms differentiate between short- and long-term characteristics, like the difference between height—which fluctuates rapidly in a person's early years—and general build, which really doesn't. Long-term characteristics are primary predictives, with more recent short-term characteristics applied for personalization. Basically...long-term characteristics have a constant weight, but short-term characteristics have a rapidly diminishing weight as they age. Between the two, you get a generally recognizable model that's always pretty up to date."

He zoomed in and pointed to Martin's friendly smile. "Ephemerals like facial expressions, clothing preferences or accessories, have extremely short lifespans, so this is probably what Martin most looked like in the last... say...week. Give or take twenty hours."

"I get all that," she said. "What I want to know is, could someone like you manipulate that?"

"The source data for the model? Yes, but it would be a lot of work—"

"I meant the expression, specifically. The personality. Can it be...hacked?"

He barked a laugh. "Well, yes," he said. "If you know what you're doing, you can go in and manipulate either the reference images themselves—all hundred-thousand-plus-per-week—or adjust the long-term weighting values and predictives associated with the individual identity. That's how I would do it, if I were doing it. But the old ways still work best. You want to look like an ogre in HaRRE, spend a week tromping around in public, making angry faces and flipping off little babies. It'll show up. You want to come off as happy and kind," he zoomed back out and waved at Martin's avatar, "casual and approachable and oh-so-innocent, all you have to do is spend some time making sure Hathor sees you looking like that. Ephemerals morph in so quickly, it wouldn't take much effort. Fake it 'til you make it, as they used to say."

Katie frowned. "Martin would know that? How to do that?"

Ghoster looked at her for a moment, clearly incredulous. Finally he said, "Yes...yes, I'd say so. You *do* know who Martin is, don't you?" When she just looked blank, he sighed. "Dear lord, little girl. It's time for a history lesson."

He took her handheld from her, ordered a couple Tom Collinses on her account, then blanked the screen. "Look, it was...jeez, thirty years ago now. Martin was a grad student at the University of Oklahoma. He and a friend had a little project on the side, just a hobby really. They invented a new database architecture. I think the big one back then was still SQL, and I'm pretty sure it was Martin who asked if they could maybe make something better. And these two kids, on their free time, did. It represented a massive efficiency increase for relational queries, and they took out a joint patent for it." He paused as the flight attendant delivered their drinks, and downed his in one gulp. Then he grinned.

"That was when I came on board. They thought they could make some money off their system, and I was a friend of a friend and the only business major they knew of. So they called me up and asked if I could work something out." He trailed off, thinking about it, and shook his head. "I put them in touch with AT&T, a big-time telecom back before Hathor destroyed all the telecoms, and they developed the first Voice Responsive Remote Personal Assistant."

Katie frowned, and he sighed. "Yeah," he said. "That was originally an AT&T thing. The first one was built on AT&T software, actually, but Martin figured out how to store voiceprints in their new Pantheon database, and locationally identify users by voiceprint and GPS signal. That was in the bad old days before we had location-aware microphones everywhere."

"Wait," Katie said. "I know this story."

Ghoster snorted. "You *should*," he said, and watched her eyes for a minute, but she couldn't place it. "Oh, my..." he said. "Okay, here's the pieces you're missing: just before I left college to start my own business, I helped Martin and his partner incorporate a business to sell database licenses and software support to AT&T and later, of course, everyone else." He chuckled. "Right. That business was called Total Awareness Monitoring Systems. It went public four years later under the name of Hathor."

Her jaw was hanging open long before he got to the end of that. "We're going after *that* Martin Door?"

Ghoster laughed. "How many do you think there are?"

"No, I just didn't... I mean, I haven't heard the name in so long. He's not much in the news." Ghoster grinned at that, too, but she didn't know why. She said, "So when you said there were only two people who knew more about the system than you, you meant the two people who built it." He nodded, clearly enjoying her sudden appreciation of the situation, but it felt like a lead weight in her stomach. She was in way over her head. "It was Martin Door and...the other guy. Something Mexican—"

Ghoster cut her off with a raucous laugh, and when she frowned at his outburst he laughed harder. Finally he took control of himself enough to explain. "Whitest kid you've ever seen."

"No," she said. "I mean—"

"I know, I know. Velez. Jesus Velez, plus four or five others tagged on there to make it sound more ethnic." He shook his head. "Lord, girl, you're supposed to be in Ghost Targets and you can't even spot an alias unless it's the name of a supernatural creature." She frowned harder and he went on. "Fine. Martin and Velez. They're both aliases. Like I said, Martin used to be David Linson, but no one has called him that since college. Velez had some privacy concerns when Martin went to add their voiceprints to the TAMS database—"

She nodded. "And that eventually became the Hathor identity database."

"And they never bothered to fix it," he said. "Precisely. And over the next decade, they had fewer and fewer reasons to, until everyone in the world, government included, preferred Hathor IDs over any others."

"That's crazy," she said. She sat back in her seat, thinking about it. "They're the original ghost targets, then."

"No..." he said, trailing off as he thought about it. "Not really. I mean, not for that." He shook his head. "Technically, there's no law against using a fake name in Hathor. It's awfully hard to do, especially today, but I can't see the FBI going after them for grandfathering themselves into their own system."

For the first time in the conversation, Katie realized she had some information Ghoster didn't. Her father *had* gone after them, and she knew exactly how it had turned out. She'd lost track of the names, but now that she knew who this Martin *was*, she had a lot more to hold against him.

She picked up her handheld and brought Martin's information back up, and switched to the location information Ghoster had been examining earlier. It showed him in Buenos Aires, Argentina. This morning he'd spent three hours in a corner coffee shop, and another two strolling through the neighborhood before he returned to his apartment where he spent the rest of the day. Looking back through the previous week, the guy had a pretty quiet lifestyle. Pizza, beer, and coffee defined most of his expenses. That explained his dumpy figure.

On a whim, she said, "Hathor, connect me to Martin Door." The connection buzzed twice, and then Hathor invited her to leave a message. She decided against it. She checked on his location at the time of Ms. Linson's murder, but it was just another day like today. He'd spent the morning at a coffee shop, and the rest of the day at home. She poked Ghoster, interrupting whatever he was listening to on his headset.

"How hard is it to fake an alibi?"

"Hmm?" He reached up to mute his headset, and then turned his attention to her. "What, like a location history?" He shrugged. "Aggregators are pretty shy about that, but there's dozens of independent operators who advertise the service. I don't know anyone but me I would trust to do it right, though." He grinned at her distrustful look and shrugged. "But, yeah, Martin could do it. Easy. Although... I have to say, I agree with your analysis. I couldn't reconstruct the elevator scene you described, but I was able to get a good look at the front doors when your ghost opened it. I poked around a little bit last night, and I can't find any glitches in the erasure, so...frankly, I don't see a reason for the cloud."

He took a deep breath. His brows came down. He shook his head. "I don't get it. That cloud—the blackout, as you've been calling it—that's basically a big red flag waving over Martin and Velez. Either one of them could do a clean ghost, spic and span, so I don't see any good reason for the cloud." He thought for a moment longer, then shrugged again. "But, yeah, *because* of that, you'd better bet he would be smart enough to paint himself a perfect alibi, knowing that cloud would look like his personal fingerprint." He waved at her handheld, which still showed a record of Martin's comings and goings. "That's almost certainly fiction, no matter how you slice it."

He watched her for a moment, to see if she'd have any follow-up questions, then turned the volume back up on his headset when she didn't speak up. For her part, she couldn't put words to the deep disquiet building in her chest. She'd built her career on the information Hathor provided. She had been good at tracking down suspects, predicting their movements and discerning motive out of the oily wash of information swirling in the system. She had been a damn fine cop. But now what was she? Without Hathor, with every word Hathor said to her a lie, she was pretty much nothing.

The thought nagged at her, no matter how she fought to push it away. She blacked the window, slouched down in her seat, and pretended to sleep for the rest of the flight. Her mind was buzzing, though, more accusation than ideas. When they landed in Little Rock, she had no idea what she needed to do.

7. Police Work

She stopped in the concourse, Ghoster almost bumping into her, and when he looked down she pinned him with her eyes. "I have an appointment at the Aggregator's office at two. I was too distracted to ask last night, but what do you intend to do here?"

He shrugged. "I don't know, watch over your shoulder. This is the regular police work, right? The part where you pretend Hathor doesn't exist anymore and do the hardcore sleuthing? I thought it might be fun to watch."

"It's not," she said. "Detective work is slow and tedious until inspiration strikes."

"Right," he said, a sarcastic smile tugging at his lips. "Nothing at all like programming."

"I guess what I'm asking," she said, still irritated and letting it show, "is what kind of help can I expect from you?"

"I'll find Martin for you," he said. "Hundred percent money-back guarantee." He watched her eyes to make sure she caught that. She wasn't paying him a dime. When he continued, his voice was less playful, dry. "I want to see how this thing shakes out. And, killer or not, Martin was my buddy once. I plan to make sure you make a clean bust."

It wasn't a friendly sentiment, but Katie could accept it. Either he didn't know her, and he was just generally suspicious of cops—or he knew more than she thought, about her father's involvement with TAMS, and he was worried she would make it personal. Rick's reaction to his presence at the office certainly gave him reason enough to worry either way. She was a clean cop, though, and she was prepared to prove it. Anyway, Ghoster had already proven useful enough to make up for his personality.

"Keep close, then," she said. "And keep your eyes open. And if you see something that I miss, feel free to speak up. I don't have your technical grasp." He nodded, once, and she turned toward the exit. "Hathor, I need a car to take Ghoster and me to the Helen building, now." By the time she got to the curb, the car was waiting.

It was a chill, sunny day, and as the car wove through traffic her stomach rumbled in complaint. Breakfast seemed a long way off, but a glance at her watch told her there was no time for lunch. The car deposited them out front of the Aggregator, and zipped off while Katie stood staring up at its facade.

She didn't need any time to consider it. She knew this building. She knew the whole block, from hours spent running up and down it, trying to gauge the exact size of the blackout. But now, seeing it in real life, there was an unsettling dichotomy of familiarity and strangeness. She'd never bothered to pull up source video, so she was used to seeing the blank white planes of the building's face, not the polished granite surface, sparkling in the early afternoon sunlight.

The people passing on the street were new, too. She hadn't spent much time in an active replay outside the young woman's office building, and all of that had been late at night, so the streets had been nearly empty. Now, in the light of day, the deathly alley she knew from all her research transformed into a bustling thoroughfare, and the people were all so cheerful, so friendly—something she definitely wasn't used to on the streets of Brooklyn or DC. For years, all her time in HaRRE had been in places on her home turf, so she'd long since forgotten what it was like to visit a familiar place for the first time, in real life.

So she stood staring until Ghoster looked up from his handheld, then looked up at the facade himself, then finally asked, "What?"

"Nothing," she said, then shook her head to try to lose the sensation. The thought of retracing her virtual steps through those doors, and riding up the elevator almost overwhelmed her, for just a moment, but she fought that down, too. "Nothing. Let's go."

She didn't stop for the receptionist, but said in passing, "Katie Pratt, FBI, I'm here to meet with Penelope Hein in Administrative." The second elevator on her left dinged open as soon as she approached, and Ghoster followed her in. She felt foolish for it, but she was glad he was there with her.

As the doors shut, he glanced at her over his shoulder, then fixed his eyes on the door once more. "It's weird," he said, "I wouldn't expect Martin to get involved with a place like this."

"What do you mean?" She felt awkwardly conscious of the courtesy recorder in the top corner of the elevator, saving everything they had to say, but Ghoster wasn't so shy.

"It's a skin market. Matchmakers, psh. I haven't seen one yet that stayed legit, once they saw the profit potentials on short-term matches." He shook his head. "Martin wasn't ever into that sort of thing. And, forget that. 'Helen,' for Helen of Troy? I'd think that would upset him even more." He trailed off, thinking. "I guess Cupid, Aphrodite, Venus—Adonis, even—they're already used up, but they could have done something better."

"What are you saying about Martin?"

"Hmm?" He glanced back over his shoulder again, and shook his head with a serious look. "Oh, Martin wasn't into the commerce side of his software. He was religious about it. This stuff was supposed to change the world." He sighed. "Maybe that's why he flipped. Finally—finally!—decided to take advantage of his wealth, picked up a trophy wife, and then she ends up working for a Hathor whorehouse." He nodded in a definite sort of way. "That's your motive right there. Guy would've gone ballistic."

Katie said nothing, but her eyes drifted back up to the recorder in the corner. She just hoped his imprudent words went unheard long enough for her to finish her interview. If Ms. Hein was listening in now, the entire appointment could be spoiled. The thought had barely formed in her mind when the doors fell open on a familiar foyer, and Penelope Hein stood waiting with a welcoming smile.

"Hey, y'all," she said, leaning on the accent for the sake of the Yankees, unless Katie missed her guess. "I'm so glad ya could make it down here. Terrible, terrible what happened to Janey, but we've got to get it behind us."

Katie returned the smile, and shook the offered hand. "As you know," she said, "I'm with Ghost Targets. We're involved because there are technical issues surrounding Ms. Linson's death that prevent Jurisprudence providing a reliable suspect, and your police department asked for our assistance to resolve it."

Penelope nodded vigorously, without her smile wavering. "Exactly, exactly," she said. "No, yeah, I'd heard there was something like that. It's just terrible. Terrible. She was such a pretty girl. So young."

"Well," Katie said, stepping past Penelope into the room. "All I need is a few minutes of your time. If I could speak with some of your other staff, too—anyone up here who really knew Ms. Linson, or might have known what she was working on recently."

Penelope frowned. "Isn't that...usually... I mean, we have courtesy recorders *everywhere* up here."

Ghoster pushed forward at that. "Actually," he said, "could you show me the controls for the recorders' access point? Sorry," he reached past Katie to extend his hand, and pasted on a salesman's grin to match the woman's. "I'm Jeremy Gustaud. I'm a technician supporting Katie's investigation."

"Of course," Penelope said. "We have...umm...."

"Maybe I could talk with your database admin?" His grin never slipped, but Katie could feel his opinion of Penelope change. "I mean, I wouldn't want to take up your valuable time with any of this."

"Of course," she said, and looked relieved. "Marco, send Diane up here to help out the technician." She turned to Katie, Ghoster forgotten. "We can talk in my office."

Ms. Hein's office was a vast space that felt more like a living room than a business office. On the far wall a monitor played some soap opera, and Penelope muted it with a spoken command as soon as they entered the room. There was no desk, but a pair of loveseats and a pair of plush armchairs gathered around a coffee table, next to a simulated fireplace. Penelope sank into the nearest armchair and waved Katie to the place next to her on one of the loveseats.

"Please, make yourself comfortable," Penelope said. "Can I get you something to drink? A snack? Anything?"

Katie feared her stomach would rumble as she said, "No, I'm fine, thank you." It stayed quiet. "Ms. Hein, unless my technician can learn something from your local access points, we're finding your Hathor archive unreliable. Can you think of anything going on with Ms. Linson in the days before her death that might be useful?"

Penelope bit her lower lip, staring downward in a pose clearly intended to show her deep consideration. Katie knew almost instantly she was going to get nothing informative from this one, but she waited politely. Finally the other woman shook her head. "No, dear. I'm sorry, but no. Janey has always been a good worker. She's quiet, and she keeps her nose clean. That's what was so terrible about it. No one could have wanted her dead."

"In what way, exactly, did she 'keep her nose clean'? Do you know of any financial or legal troubles?" She saw some hesitation in Penelope's eyes, and pressed on. "We're not looking to slander her name, Ms. Hein. If we're going to get her any kind of justice, I need you to tell me what you know."

"Well..." she rubbed her hands together nervously, and glanced toward a potted plant in the corner which almost certainly hid a courtesy recorder. Katie had spotted four others in the room, too.

"Please, Ms. Hein," she said. "We have no other angles on this."

"Fine." She took a deep breath and let it out. "It's just, Janey getting the job here *might* have been just a little...questionable. I mean," her voice lowered to a conspiratorial whisper, "she was *single*. And she wasn't even all that pretty."

Katie didn't answer at first. Her mind went back to Ghoster's comments in the elevator, but the girl had been working in a secretarial capacity. Katie didn't know how her appearance was supposed to affect things. Finally she shook her head. "I'm sorry, I don't understand—"

"Look," Penelope said, "far be it from me to speak ill of the dead, but that girl was the *worst* administrative officer I've ever met. She couldn't keep her mind on the job. Terribly slow learner. She was always asking *questions*. How hard is it to approve paperwork? God. Err...God rest her soul. Poor girl."

"Do you know if anyone else on the staff felt the same way?"

Penelope shrugged. "None of them had to work with her. It was just me and Dee—the Senior Administrative Officer at Headquarters. Janey was always bugging one of us, wanting us to hold her hand—"

"And how long had she been with the company?"

Penelope snorted. "Weeks. I've got girls on the sales floor who've been here years—who are getting on, if you know what I mean—and if I have any say one of them is getting the position. Ms. Linson walked in off the street...." She kept on, complaining, but all Katie really got out of it was that the suspicious hole in the victim's employment history seemed to be entirely accurate. Hathor didn't usually make placement errors, though.

She waited for the other woman to run out of steam, then said, "You said Ms. Linson was single? Is that right?" Penelope nodded, and that was another bit of Hathor data Katie had doubted. She frowned. She glanced toward the hidden recorder, and sighed. "Ms. Hein, I know you're trying to be polite, but I need your honesty here. What are your suspicions concerning the victim?"

"I think she's a *hussy*," Penelope said. She shook her head, "I don't know who she could have got to, but she must've got to someone, to land that job. I don't care if they hear it. She was awful, kept poking her nose where it didn't belong. We need someone with a level head to replace her, I don't care what Hathor says."

That last sent up red flags for Katie. She leaned forward. "What do you mean? What was she poking her nose in?"

Penelope huffed, still irritated at the deceased. Then when she realized Katie wanted a real answer, she looked flustered. "Oh, you know. *Details*. Things that didn't matter, I mean. It's not like she was ever going to be a system admin. Girl's a secretary, no matter what they call her. She didn't *get* that, though. She wanted to know how our program worked. She wanted to see the code. She kept asking us to give her access to all the tools our technicians use, when she should have been working on *her* job."

Katie sat back. After a moment she said, "Did she have any friends here?"

"Becca," Penelope said after a moment. "She was the only one, really. But they talked sometimes. Becca made it worse."

"Becca's a...."

"Sys admin," she said, and then nodded. "She probably put the idea in Janey's head. Of course Janey wanted to be like Becca. Becca's one of my best girls."

"Could I speak with her?"

Penelope spoke into her headset. "Marco, send Becca to my office." She smiled across at Katie. "You're lucky. If Janey had been any prettier, she could have made friends with one of the sales staff, and they're all out of the office this time of day."

Katie smiled, her lips tight. "Lucky break," she said. When Penelope remained in her seat, Katie said, "Maybe I could meet with Becca at her desk—"

"Nonsense," Penelope said, waving it away with a smile.

"Then perhaps you would be willing to leave us some privacy," Katie said, and dropped the smile.

Penelope blinked at her twice before she finally rose. "Oh," she said. "Well, yes, fine. I'll go see how your gentleman friend is getting along." She left the room, brushing past Becca in the doorway.

Becca came on in and threw a curious look at Katie. Katie rose and met her halfway, extending a hand. "Hi," she said. "I'm Katie Pratt, Special Agent with the FBI. I'm here about Ms. Linson's death."

"Oh," Becca said, and Katie could hear the numbness of grief in her voice. "Of course," she said. "What do you need?"

"Ms. Hein tells me you two were close." Becca shrugged, noncommittal, and Katie pressed on. "I'm sorry for your loss. I really am. I want to sort out just what happened, but we're having some trouble with the system."

"I know," Becca said. "I heard that guy talking to Diane. But I, uh..." she looked away, nervous. "I knew before. I've got a boyfriend in the PD. He asked me all kinds of questions."

Katie made a mental note to dig up that conversation, but didn't let it show in her eyes. "Ms. Hein gave me the impression Ms. Linson might have been snooping where she wasn't supposed to—"

Becca growled, cutting Katie off. "That..." she said, and then looked around, smart enough not to finish her sentence. "She hated Janeane. She always did. But, no, she's wrong. Janey wasn't involved in antyhing. That was just a hobby."

Katie frowned. "Your boss thought Ms. Linson might have had some thoughts of promotion."

"No," Becca said. "Nothing like that at all. Ugh." She sighed, then looked up to meet Katie's eyes, tears in her own. "Janeane never even wanted to work in Aggregators. But she grew up with it, so she was always a little curious."

"I understand," Katie said. She hesitated. "Ms. Hein told me Janeane was...single." Becca nodded, and Katie hesitated again. "I only ask because there has been some connection to a..." she pretended to check her handheld, trying to take the accusation out of the question, "Martin Door."

Becca laughed. "Martin Door? The system architect. You do know who that is, right?"

Katie fought down her irritation at the girl's tone. "I do," she said. "We suspect the name is an alias of a David Linson...."

"David?" Becca's mouth dropped open. "Martin Door is Uncle Dave?" She shook her head. "That's absurd."

"You know him?"

"Hmm?" She met Katie's eyes again, and frowned. "Oh, no. I knew Janeane in elementary school. I've known her forever. She...." Suddenly there were tears in her eyes again. "Her sixth birthday, her uncle Dave died." Her voice rose, dangerously close to breaking, at the recollection. "I remember everyone crying at the party, when they got the call. I remember her crying for a month. She wouldn't do anything. She loved him." She stopped and shook her head, tears flying from her eyes, then reached up daintily as she sniffled. "I'm sorry," she said, fighting to catch her breath. "I'm sorry. It's been—"

"I know," Katie said. She looked around and found a box of tissues on a bookshelf, and brought it to Becca. "I'm sorry, but I need to know what you know."

Becca dabbed at her eyes, then blew her nose noisily. When she looked back to Katie, her eyes were already swimming again. "I'm sorry. I don't know. That was fifteen years ago. I was five. I never met him, I just know how sad she was when he was gone." She took a deep breath, and a fierceness burned in her eyes. "He was a programmer." She chuckled, darkly, and shook her head. "No, I'm sorry, he wasn't Martin Door. You've got some bad information somewhere. But he *was* a programmer, and the way she talked about him was what made me want to become one in the first place. She never even considered it, though."

"Until she came here."

Becca teared up again, and Katie grabbed another tissue for her. Becca dabbed her eyes, then nodded. "She needed some money, and Hathor placed her here, and I kept telling her she could be sys admin if she just tried, but she wouldn't commit to it. She was... she was building up her courage to ask Penny for some training, I think, when...."

Katie nodded, and patted her reassuringly on the shoulder, but after that Becca was inconsolable. Katie finally left her to her grief, pulling the office door shut behind her as she stepped out onto the sales floor. Penelope Hein bustled up a moment later.

"Well?" she demanded. "What did you learn?"

"I can't say," Katie said. She looked past Penelope to Ghoster, just approaching, and asked him a question with her eyes. He shook his head, frustration clear on his face, and she nodded. "Ms. Hein, I think I have all I can get for now. Thank you for your cooperation, and keep a line open. We'll be in touch."

She turned toward the elevator, anxious to be out of there, but Penelope caught her elbow with a surprisingly strong grip. "Honey, sweetie, don't rush out of here." She smiled that sickly-sweet smile. "I looked you up, you know. I can find you someone perfect. It's not about confidences or numbers. It's about *love*. I can find you magic, dear."

Katie met her eyes for some time, incredulous, speechless. Finally she blinked, and her lips curled in something like a smile. "No," she said. "No, thank you. I can take care of myself."

Before Ms. Hein could renew her sales pitch, Katie turned her back and strode purposefully to the elevator doors. Ghoster followed a step behind, saving his smirk until the closing doors separated them from the office. "You could have had magic," he said.

"I don't want her kind," Katie said, stifling a shudder. "What did you find?"

"You wouldn't believe me if I told you."

Katie turned to him, finally really paying attention. "What do you mean?"

Ghoster frowned. "I mean I don't believe it. I found the cloud. I got into the local access point hoping it had a cache of real data. You never know how far back the logs go on these things, but this is a first-class operation. Brand new machines, local solid state storage, and honestly enough capacity to run every recorder in downtown Little Rock, even though they're just running this building."

"And?"

"And they're full." They left the elevator, and Katie had no time to be creeped out by the experience this time, because her attention was all on Ghoster. He shook his head, "I was worried the cache would be cleared out, or overwritten—and it's overwritten all right. Your blackout starts here. It starts in the recorders themselves. I never imagined that. I thought it had to be injected into the database after the fact." He stopped curbside, a moment before a cab pulled up to carry them to their next destination. When Katie reached for the door, he blocked her hand and caught her eyes.

"Katie," he said. "I'm out of my league here. Those were my two best ideas, dashed to pieces. I thought we could maybe get something incriminating out of the caches, but they give us what we've already got. And I thought maybe, somehow, with the right leverage and the right warrants, the FBI might be able to figure out where the database injection was coming from. But I just found it, right up there, and it's no help at all."

"Well, the recorders have to be getting the data from somewhere—"

"Nope." He shook his head, frustration clear in his eyes. "It's in the interpretation. The code in the cameras is interpreting...nothing...as hundreds of people. Hundreds of thousands. The cameras believe they're seeing it—"

"Then we should shut them down!"

He shook his head again. "No good. Hathor uses predictive algorithms to fill in blind spots in the database, so if we took away the recorders, it would go on assuming the same things were there, the same people, except for minute movements, until it received some information indicating otherwise. Our only shot would be to replace these recorders with new ones, but I fully verified the code base on these. It's all handed down from the server, completely homogenous, and any new recorders we got in here would do the same thing these are doing."

"We can wipe the slate clean," she said. "Clear out all identities making the blackout, and then put in new cameras—"

"Which are already reaching backward in time to create the cloud," he said. "You're right, actually. That's what we have to do, to slow down the problem. That, and get in touch with Hathor headquarters, but there's a bigger problem here." He drew a deep breath, and let it all out in a puff. "I don't know anyone who can fix it. All of Hathor's coders probably couldn't solve this. We can throw up some patches, but if the recorders are capable of doing this...." He shook his head. "Katie, *all* of the recorders are capable of doing this. I don't know what triggered this one, here, but I'm guessing it was some stupid mistake Martin made when he ghosted himself. It's just a byproduct of that, which triggered some bug in the recorder software."

"Okay...."

He shook his head. "Katie, if this can happen, it can happen anywhere. It could happen everywhere. There's a flaw in the source code for the recorders, and...what if it hadn't been this quiet office building late on a Thursday night in Little Rock? What if it had been the subway security cameras in DC, Monday afternoon at five? What if it had been *any* of the high res game cams at a professional football game, blanking a hundred-thousand identities in a flash. This is good equipment upstairs, or it would have died before the cloud filled the back office, but we have some real systems out there in the world that could cripple Hathor with a glitch like this."

"Well, then, we have to get it fixed."

"Dammit, Katie, that's what I'm saying." He suddenly looked tired, weak, for the first time since she'd met him. His veneer fell off, and he was a helpless old man who knew just enough to be truly scared. "I've been looking at this and looking at this, and I'm the best in the business, and I don't see a clue how to fix it." He met her eyes. "Without Martin—or Velez, if he's still around—there's just no way for you to get past this." He looked down at the car, waiting patiently behind him, and sighed. "I'm sorry, Katie, but I can't waste time chasing ghosts with this stuff going on. I have to get back to my office, and get in touch with Hathor about what's happening."

Katie said, "No, wait," but he ignored her. He climbed in the car and shut the door before she could take a step closer. She heard him ask the driver to take him to the airport, just before the door slammed shut.

She growled an obscenity at the departing car, but it didn't make her feel any better. Instead she reached up to her headset, and said, "Hathor, I need another car. Use my itinerary from earlier, but move the Linson house to the top of the list. Thanks."

She thought about what the girl had said upstairs, that David Linson was dead. Ghoster insisted David Linson was his old college buddy—the one he was hanging all his hopes on. Did he know Linson was dead? Or had Janeane been the one deceived? Katie needed to find out the truth: she needed Martin, but she'd been chasing him for two days now, and she was no closer. Every tool she knew of to track him down he had deprived her of by actions taken decades ago. She sighed, staring off down the street while she waited for her car, and wondered what her killer was up to.

8. In Little Rock

Katie had an appointment to meet with the Linsons, Janeane's parents, but she'd originally arranged it for Monday morning. When she pushed her travel plans up, all her appointments had been rescheduled automatically, but she hadn't actually confirmed with the Linsons since then. The thought hit her just as the car pulled up.

"Hathor, connect me to Paul Linson." She gave up on the call before the second buzz, ready to leave a message, but at the last moment it went through.

She heard a weary voice say, "Yes?"

"Mr. Linson," she said, "this is Katie Pratt, Special Agent with FBI Ghost Targets. I have an appointment to meet with you about Janeane's—"

"Yeah," he said, cutting her off. "Sorry, yes, I got the message. Can we possibly put it off? It's just, the funeral's in two hours."

Katie winced. "Of course," she said. "Of course, no problem. I'm so sorry for your loss." She started to disconnect the call, but he stopped her.

"No, wait." She heard him sigh, loud and long. "Just wait a moment." Another deep breath, and then he said, "How long would it take? Your questions?"

She frowned. "Shouldn't be more than ten, maybe twenty minutes."

"Let's get it done, then."

She waited, but he said nothing more. After a moment Katie said, "Really, it's no trouble—"

"No!" His breath was a hiss now. "I'm sorry, Ms. Pratt. I'm exhausted. I need to be done with this. Can you come over now?"

She glanced at the itinerary on her handheld and nodded. "I can be there in seven minutes."

"Then let's get it done."

It was a quick trip along the interstate, rolling down the wide bend around a forested mountain, and for the first time in a while Katie spent the drive looking at the scenery outside. There was still a surprising amount of green in the tumbling hills, and even in the heart of the city there were places the trees crowded in thick, right up next to the highway. Two hours before his daughter's funeral, and Katie had to question him about the murder. It wasn't her first time in that situation, but she'd never learned any tricks to make it any easier.

Paul opened the door as she approached up the stepping stone walk, her shoes brushing the browning leaves of wilted flowers that lined the narrow path. The front door was at the top of four short steps, and in spite of his grief, Paul Linson greeted her with a warm handshake and a convincing smile. "Welcome to my home, Ms. Pratt." He was tall and lean, with a thick shock of gray hair and a face as warm as his brother's. He waved her in ahead of him, and said, "Have a seat in the living room, just up there. Daisy's just out at the moment, but she should be home soon. Can I get you something to drink?"

"That's not necessary," Katie said. She sank down on the edge of a flower-print blue couch, and Paul took the armchair nearby. She glanced at her handheld, and then said, "I'm sure you're aware there are...complications with the record concerning your daughter's death?"

"We'd heard." Paul shrugged. "I'm not a super technical guy, Ms. Pratt, so I don't get the details. It's monstrous what happened to her, though."

"Do you have any idea why someone would want to hurt her?" That was often the question that started the tears, but Paul just looked down at his hands, and after a moment shook his head slowly. Katie said, "Did your daughter have any enemies? Was she involved in anything that could have gotten her in trouble?"

Paul looked up again, and met Katie's eyes. "I've got a son who can raise some real hell, Ms. Pratt. That boy's born for trouble." A sad smile stole across his lips. "But not Janey. Janey never did a bad deed." He held up a hand as though to stop Katie interrupting, and his smile quirked at the corners of his lips. "I'm not saying that to cover for her, it's the gospel truth. I never aimed to raise her a saint, but she went and did it on her own."

Katie tore her eyes from his, glancing down at her handheld. "Did she ever say anything about trouble at work? Her boss was concerned—"

He clapped his hands on his knees and pushed himself to his feet with a gusty breath. "I'm sorry, Ms. Pratt. I really am, but the cops here have done a good job chasing down the same trails you're starting on now." She rose with him, and saw tears standing in his eyes in spite of his defiantly warm smile. "I wish I could help. I want...I want the guy caught, whoever he was. But I've been over it and I don't know a thing that could help you. I'm sorry I brought you all the way out here."

"Mr. Linson—"

"No," he said, and his deep sigh was back. "I do have to get ready for a rough afternoon. I'm sure you understand."

"I'm sure there are some angles the local police haven't—"

"Ms. Pratt," he said, and his voice was suddenly stern. Something about it brought up a memory of her dad stopping her on the doorstep when she was a little girl, about to track mud into the house. "I know you flew all the way out here from Washington to try to lend some aid, but the local police are all over this, and they're probably better boys than you give them credit for, if you'll forgive me saying so. I just don't have time to go over things I've already—"

"Fine," she said. "Then tell me about your brother."

That stopped him short. He considered her for a moment, and then his eyebrows came down, and his expression darkened. "What could he possibly have to do with this?"

She said, "His name has come up in our investigation."

"He's dead fifteen years, Ms. Pratt. I doubt he has anything to do with it."

She took a deep breath, and held Paul's eyes for a moment. She waited, and after a moment, his shoulders slumped as he relaxed a little. She nodded. "I'm here to help you," she said. "And to do that, I need your answers. Does the name Martin Door mean anything to you?"

He frowned, thinking, and after a moment he shook his head. "Never heard of him."

"And you haven't heard from your brother at all—"

"He's dead," he said, with an absolute certainty. "It about killed our mom, and his was an accident. It's a blessing she wasn't here to see what happened to Janey."

"One of your daughter's coworkers said Janeane was starting to take an interest in programming, which she hadn't done since your brother's death."

He shook his head. "It was just a passing thing. I'm sorry, ma'am, but I don't see a connection there." He wiped a hand across his eyes, then shook his head. "Really, I don't think there's anything I can do to help you. David...he was a geek, Ms. Pratt. That's it. Too smart for his own good, but he never got into any trouble. That's something else he and Janey had in common. Nothing in his past is going to point you to Janey's killer. I'm sorry."

It was clear he was done with her. Katie said, "Thank you for your time, Mr. Linson. I'll let you know if we find anything."

"You do that," he said. He escorted her to the door, and stood framed in it, watching her leave down the sad front path. He waved to her as she climbed into her car, then withdrew back into the house and closed the door.

Nothing.

She checked her itinerary and scanned the notes on her handheld, then told the driver, "Take me to the North Little Rock police station. Thanks." As the car navigated the twisting roads back out of the neighborhood, she called ahead. "Hathor, connect me to Officer Larry Doan. Thanks." He answered right away, and she said, "Officer Doan, this is Special Agent—"

"I got it," he said, and he sounded like a kid. Hathor told her he was nineteen, and she shook her head at the thought of it. He said, "Becca told me you were at the office earlier, so I thought I might hear from you. Jake's actually leading up the investigation on this case...."

"I know," Katie said. "I'm on my way to the station. I was hoping I could speak with both of you."

"Sure. Yeah. I'll be here."

She checked the monitor, and said, "Thanks, Larry. I'll see you in ten."

She spent half an hour at the police station, and left there with nothing new. Everything they had to tell her was already in the case file. Katie fell into her car afterward, slamming the door shut behind her, and took a moment to control her frustration. She had two more appointments scheduled, but she didn't have much hope for those sources, if the local cops and the girl's family had given her *nothing*. She told the driver to find her some food, something quick and easy, and then went back to her notes one more time.

There had to be something. She reviewed what Ghoster had said about the cameras—it had been enough to upset him royally—but she just didn't know enough about the technology to understand the difference between what he was expecting and what he actually found. She looked over the Jurisprudence printout of Janeane's social web, but it was a small one and she'd already contacted the key players. One name stood out to her, though. She tapped the screen, the dim dot right next to

Janeane's father—Daisy Linson. She'd talked to Paul, but the mother had been out at the time. There could be something there, but Katie could hardly go back now. She checked her watch as the car pulled into a fast food parking lot, and sighed. The funeral was now. She could wait it out, but she didn't think Paul would be too happy to see her again.

The window lowered and she said, "Put it on my tab," without even looking, then reached out to grab the greasy bag. Burger and fries, and her stomach rumbled at the smell of it. She started an audio replay of her interviews at the victim's work while she got started on the burger.

She finished off her lunch before Becca started crying, crumpled up the wrapper and dropped it back in the bag with her empty fry container. A cursor on the driver monitor blinked at her, waiting for directions. She checked her watch one more time, then pulled up location information for the graveyard where Ms. Linson was to be buried. It was five minutes away. She said, "Hathor, show me location history for Daisy Linson on my handheld, starting now. Thanks." En route from the funeral home to the gravesite. How long would the burial take? She tried to guess, and gave up.

"Driver, take me to the graveyard. Thanks." She leaned back in her seat as the car merged into traffic, but she couldn't relax. Her left hand drifted up to her mouth, and she sat chewing on her thumbnail, anxious, until the car pulled to a stop on the curb next to the graveyard. Oak trees with thick trunks grew heavily in the grassy lot, just like the rest of the neighborhood, but she could see through the trees to the winding line of cars out in the graveyard. An open-sided tent stood over the gravesite, and Katie could barely see the mourners there through all the flowers gathered around the casket. There was a crowd. She could tell that much.

Daisy Linson was there, somewhere in the heart of it. When it came to daughters' secrets, mothers knew. That had certainly been true for Katie, anyway. Her dad never would have called her a saint, but her mother was the only one who really knew the full truth. Maybe Daisy would have the answers Katie needed. Maybe this whole day would be worth it.

She opened the door, the sound of it eerily loud in the afternoon stillness. She had no interest in being seen by the mourners, but she needed to be close enough to catch the mother before she left. Katie didn't want to go back to that house. It would be far better to catch her here and ask a few quick questions. That would be enough to find out if the mom knew anything, anyway.

She curved around to the left, keeping a line of trees between her and the gravesite mostly, and as she moved toward the line of waiting cars, she tried to pick out faces in the crowd. Gathered here was every one that mattered in Janeane's life. If Katie could interview all of them—but, then, that was what the local police were for. Presumably, they were already chasing those leads. Katie was looking for something else, something different. A ghost.

And then she saw him, not in the crowd at the gravesite, but hiding back among the trees, maybe twenty yards ahead of Katie. He had on a baseball cap pulled low, and big sunglasses that were ten years out of style, and he was leaning against a tree trunk, peeking around it, spying on the ceremony off to the south. He turned at some noise, Katie's footfall, and she barely ducked behind a tree before he spotted her. But in that moment she saw enough of his face to be certain. The bastard was here. Dead fifteen years, and standing twenty yards away. She needed him.

She waited four seconds, five, listening intently for some sound of movement and hoping he hadn't seen her. She heard nothing but the beating of her heart. Then she moved, throwing herself around the trunk of the tree and into a low, stealthy run. She was sure he would be gone, a hallucination born of her desperation, as ephemeral as his ghost in the machine, but she came around the tree in a full run and there he was, dead ahead.

She saw his eyes widen through the tint of his sunglasses, and he reached desperately toward a pocket inside his jacket, but she was on him too quickly. She crushed him between her body and the tree, one of his arms trapped behind him and the other pinned beneath her weight. She threw a hand up to clap over his mouth, silencing him. The motion slammed his head back against the tree, hard enough to daze him for a moment.

She risked a glance around the tree's trunk, but no one at the gravesite was looking their way. She batted the older man's hand down, away from his jacket, and reached into the inside pocket with her left hand as she drew her pistol with the right. She fished out a handheld, old and battered, and withdrew two paces with it, her gun trained square on her prisoner. She watched his movements, but his eyes were fixed on her gun, and he looked genuinely terrified.

"I'm sorry," he wailed, but she stomped a foot to get his attention, and silenced him with a glare.

"You're Martin Door?" she said quietly, and after a moment he nodded. He looked like a hurt puppy, pitiful.

She woke up his handheld, but it only showed location details for the graveyard, and a minimized window tracking Paul's movements. She gestured with it. "You're also David Linson."

His eyes crinkled, like he was about to cry, and he nodded. "Yes." The word escaped him like steam from a boiling kettle.

She considered him for a moment. He was nothing like Ghoster. Ghoster was cool, collected, and way too sure of himself. And yet he'd talked of this man like an idol—his superior in every way.

The Martin Door standing before her was a wreck. His clothes were dirty and disheveled, and he seemed emotionally frayed, ready to break. Katie had intended to cuff him, but instead she holstered her gun. "Come on," she said, jerking her head toward her car. "We need to talk."

He didn't move. He said, "Who are you?"

"I'm Katie Pratt," she said. "Special Agent with FBI Ghost Targets." She looked him up and down, then tossed him his handheld. "And I'm trying to figure out who killed your niece."

He hesitated a moment longer, then acquiesced with a bob of his head. She turned away, showing him some trust, and he rewarded the gesture by pushing off from the tree and stepping up to walk alongside her. As they headed toward her car she said, "Your brother believes you're dead."

She glanced up in time to see a tear escape his eye. Martin nodded. "They all do," he said. "Everyone thinks David Linson is dead."

"How much do you know about the circumstances of Ms. Linson's murder?"

Once again she glanced up to measure his reaction. His eyes squeezed again, webbing his face with wrinkles, and he took a slow, deliberate breath through his nose. "Almost nothing," he said. "I just found out. Last night."

His voice cracked on that, and she couldn't believe he was *that* good of an actor. The man was broken. She said, "You two were close?'

He snorted. "I haven't been able to talk to her for fifteen years, Ms. Pratt, but I can still remember her smile. I can still remember her laughing in the backyard swing and shouting, 'higher, higher.'" He took a deep breath, trying to fight his tears, and said, "Hathor didn't tell me when she died. I just found out last night. I try to stay away, but I...I had to be at the funeral." He took a deep breath. "I can't even call Paul to tell him I'm sorry for his loss."

Katie walked three paces before she found an answer. "He's handling it well. He seems like a strong man."

"He is," Martin said, nodding sadly. "He is." He pulled up his handheld and started typing on it, fingers flashing like a secretary hard at work, and Katie fought down a wave of irritation, but it was his coping mechanism. He was a geek, like Paul had said. Hell, if she understood right, he'd practically invented the things.

So she tore her curious eyes away from his screen and focused on his face. "There's something strange going on with Hathor, Mr. Door, and it has to do with your niece's murder. It's why I'm here." She paused. "I need your help."

He finally glanced up from whatever he was doing to meet her eyes, just for a moment, and there was an absent curiosity there. "What do you think I can do?"

"It's apparently a bug in the recorder software. I brought in Ghoster, and he said you were an old friend. He said you're my only shot at figuring out what's wrong—"

Martin shrugged, without looking up this time. "Ghoster always gave up quickly," he said. "You're with Ghost Targets? Rick can figure it out." The corner of his mouth turned down at that, his distaste for Katie's boss unconcealed.

They were at the car by then, and Martin looked up in surprise when Katie stopped walking. He blinked at her car, then went back to work on his handheld. "Am I under arrest, Ms. Pratt?"

She sighed, her irritation getting the better of her. "You are certainly a person of interest. I was hoping you would come along with me and answer a few questions."

He nodded, tight-lipped. "Yeah," he said. He looked back over his shoulder toward the gravesite, where the ceremony was still wrapping up, and then met her eyes again. "Could I...could I have just a moment?"

"Of course." She walked around to the other car door and climbed in, leaving him a moment's privacy. He could run, but he didn't seem in much shape to escape her, and he'd already had a chance to try it. She could risk giving him a moment with his grief.

Even as she was thinking it, the driver monitor flashed at her, and a route to the airport appeared on the screen. She reacted immediately, but the car door was already locked, and a heartbeat later the car darted into the flow of traffic, leaving the graveyard behind.

"Driver, stop!" she shouted. She pushed up and twisted, searching frantically out the rear window, and just caught sight of Martin jumping into another car at the curb, which promptly sped off in the opposite direction. "Driver, stop here! Stop now! Dammit! Dammit!" She lost track of Martin in the traffic, and turned back to the driver monitor. A red emergency button no larger than the head of a pin stood on the bottom lip of the monitor, right next to the microphone. Every auto-drive car on the roads had one, but she'd never had a reason to press it before.

She did now, and it overrode whatever commands Martin had managed to push to the car. It immediately started slowing, and quickly pulled out of traffic to stop by the road. The doorlocks disengaged once it fell below five miles per hour, too, but by the time she was out and on the sidewalk, Martin was long gone.

She buried her face in her hands, trying to comprehend everything that had happened in the last few seconds. She had been ready to catch him in a footrace, and he'd hijacked her car. The man was a ghost, invisible to Hathor, impossible to find, and she'd had him in her custody.

She dove back into the car and pulled up an All Points Bulletin form on her handheld. She filled it out hastily, and sent the command over her headset. "I need all local law enforcement on the lookout for David Linson, alias Martin Door, last seen at the corner of..." she took a moment to look up the street names, but before she'd found them a voice spoke through her headset.

"Please don't do that, Ms. Pratt."

The rage that bubbled up within her nearly overwhelmed her. She fought it down, snarling, and finally said in a deceptively cool voice, "Mr. Door, you've made a huge mistake."

"I'm sorry," he said, and he sounded genuine. "I know that must have been quite a shock for you, but I wasn't ready to let you march me into a police station. There's too much I don't know."

"You can save your apologies," she said. "You just lost all credibility with me."

"Let me make it up to you," he said, and then he fell silent for long enough that she thought she'd lost him. She glanced around, to see if maybe he'd come to turn himself in after all, but he dashed that hope when he spoke again. "I'm going to lay low for a bit, and do some reading. But my first blush says you're somebody worth talking to." He fell silent again, and she realized he was checking up on her, reading through her Hathor profile. She ground her teeth, but while she waited for him to continue she finished up the APB on her handheld and sent it out.

"Yeah," he said at last. "I want to talk to you, Ms. Pratt. Wait." He sighed, and her handheld flashed an error message at her. "I'm not letting that APB through, okay? I'm sorry, I hate to do this to anybody, but I'm going to have to lock out your handheld and headset until I know I can trust you." The car engine revved to life again, and the driver monitor rebooted. Once again, she saw it receive directions to the airport, but this time the doors remained unlocked.

"Here's the thing," Martin said. "I am unwilling to act out of ignorance. Surely you understand that. At the same time, I'm not terribly excited about making an enemy of the FBI." His voice trembled there at the end, as though he were earnestly afraid. With the power he'd already displayed today, she couldn't quite understand it. "So here's the deal. Go to the airport, and wait for me. In the..umm...food court there. Please. Don't try to chase me, don't try to get the police after me, just wait. I won't take long, I promise. I just...if we're going to have this conversation, Ms. Pratt, I need to come to it with a little bit of dignity." When she didn't answer right away, he pleaded, "Can you understand that?"

"I understand that you're asking me to give you an even larger head start than you've already got." It wasn't the smartest thing to say, but she wasn't feeling terribly clever at the moment.

Instead of retorting, though, Martin seemed to crack. His voice broke in a wail, and Katie pulled off her headset, staring down at it incredulously. Eventually Martin took control of himself enough to huff into the microphone, "You have my offer, Ms. Pratt." He caught a ragged breath, and went on. "Give me an hour, okay? One hour. I'll be there, and we can sort this out."

Before she could answer him, her headset beeped and shut itself off. A moment later, her handheld did the same. She crossed her arms with a little huff, wishing for some more effective way of expressing her frustration, but nothing presented itself. Finally she rolled her eyes and slammed the door shut. "Fine," she said. "Driver, take me to the airport."

Five in the afternoon on a Thursday, the Little Rock airport wasn't extraordinarily busy. She entered through the identity gates and headed straight toward the food court.

There were recorders everywhere here. Martin had locked her out of her headset, but she could do almost as much by talking into a public recorder as she could talking into a headset, and there was no way Martin would shut down all the courtesy recorders in an airport. She knew that, but she kept quiet anyway. She had let him go, and now her only chance of seeing him again was playing by his rules, and hoping against reason that he actually showed up.

It was a miserable hour, though. She spent it sitting and waiting, knowing he was probably running as far away from her as he could possibly get. She couldn't wake her handheld, either, and she felt powerless without it. Her instinct at a time like this was to research, learn everything she could while she waited for her moment to act. And, of course, that's exactly the favor Martin had asked of her. She could understand that, but it didn't make her plight any more comfortable.

Unable to access Hathor, she turned to her memories instead, dredging up whatever she could about her quarry. Even with Ghoster's brief history to go off, she knew almost nothing about the man she was trying to contact. Thanks to HaRRE, she'd known his voice, known him by sight, but apart from that all she had to go on was a reputation for genius, and the personal, corrupt power necessary to hide himself from the eyes of the law.

Her father had faced him in a Senate subcommittee. He'd never really used names, just called him "that man" with enough bitterness to twist the words into a curse. But now she had a name to put on "that man," it told her something about him. From everything her father had said, she knew him to be dangerous. Not violent, necessarily. Not even necessarily evil. But powerful in a way no one man should be, and entirely unaccountable. That had been damning, in her father's eyes. He answered to no one—not even Hathor—but through Hathor he held everyone else's secrets.

Back then there had *been* secrets, and politicians terrified of them, and Martin Door had walked onto the Senate floor in jeans and a t-shirt and, without a word spoken, reminded everyone by his presence that he had cameras in all their closets. He had high-definition footage of all the skeletons. After that day, her father had been "retired." After that day, Hathor's databases weren't subject to any external audits. After that day, the government had paid for access to Martin Door's information just like all the marketers and other businessmen. Hell, they had hired Martin Door to write Jurisprudence for them, at great expense to the taxpayers. After that day, "that man" had become more powerful than ever, and perpetually unaccountable.

To her father, that had been his greatest sin. Now, she thought, she might have a new one to lay at his feet: a dead girl. She'd been ready to acquit him, back at the graveyard, with the performance he gave, and even after his hi-jinks with the car she had trouble believing the man so broken up back there had been the killer. In the end, it didn't matter. Maybe he was a monster, mad with power. Maybe he was a devastated man, an absent-minded professor grieving over the death of a loved one. Either way, he was the only person left in the world who could, maybe, pierce through the shadows and tell her what had happened to the girl, and it was Katie's job to figure that out.

So she sat, and she waited, and the minutes felt like hours.

And then, out of nowhere, the voice spoke in her ear again. "Hello, Ms. Pratt," and it took her a moment to sense his presence, right behind her. She started to rise, to turn on him in a fury, but he cut the motion short with a firm, warm hand on her shoulder, and she thumped back down into her hard chair. He said, "I would appreciate it if you would keep your cool. I showed up, after all. I didn't have to."

She nodded, a terse gesture, and he seemed satisfied by it. He moved around the table, squeezing past abandoned chairs from the next table over, and sank down opposite her. He had taken some time to clean up, and lost the hat and sunglasses. Now he looked just as HaRRE had drawn him, except for the expression. He wasn't smiling, and there was no sparkle in his eyes. He was somber, grave, and when he met her eyes, his gaze was like a hammer. His voice was kind, though. "I'm not unlocking your handheld yet," he said. He spread his hands apologetically. "I'm sure you'll understand the precaution." He reached into the wide pocket of his jacket and pulled out a paper notepad and flipped it across the table to her. From his other pocket he pulled out a cheap ball-point pen, and set it on the table.

"You'll want to take notes," he said. "Because nothing we say here will end up in the archive. Do you understand?" He gave her just time to nod, and then continued. "Ms. Pratt, I've had a few minutes to look into what's going on, and it seems to me like I'm your only suspect."

She arched an eyebrow at him. "You know," she said, "I was just about ready to rule you out, before you pulled that stunt at the cemetery."

He spread his hands again. "I don't know you, Katie Pratt. I've been checking you out, as much as I could, but I don't know you." He looked away. "I do know Rick Goodall, though, and I'm not ready to put myself in his hands."

"You might not have a choice, Mr. Door."

He considered her for a moment. "I do." He blushed at the simple arrogance of the statement, and shrugged. "I do, Ms. Pratt, and I came here because I want to help you find Janeane's killer. You can go ahead and rule me out."

The cop in her answered him. "You'll forgive me for wanting more than your word on that."

He looked down at his hands, on the table. "I never had kids. I remember when Janeane was born. She was...." He shook his head. "She always laughed. I don't remember her ever crying, and all babies cry, right? She just laughed and laughed. Happiest little kid I've ever known." He clasped his hands together, squeezing until his knuckles turned white, and then suddenly relaxed. He looked at Katie. "Have you seen her?" Katie nodded, and he nodded. "She was so pretty, before. Why would someone do this?"

Katie knew offhand half a dozen reasons people killed pretty young women. People were violent animals, no matter if God or Hathor were watching over their shoulders. But she didn't say anything. For a long time he just stared at the tabletop, and when he spoke again his voice was almost inaudible.

"I heard you and Jeremy talking about me, back in your apartment. That's how I found out." He took a moment to catch his breath. "Velez wrote that code, fifteen years ago, then Jeremy perfected it, and we all use it." He sighed. "I knew you were looking for me, so I looked you up, and when I saw you were Ghost Targets, my first thought was to break in and yell at you."

He smiled again, tight-lipped this time. "Just like Jeremy did. Then I remembered your name." He looked away, and Katie fought down a sudden surge of anger. He said, "So I kept quiet, and I peeked into your case file."

Katie said, "Oh."

He nodded. "That was, oh, six o'clock last night." He took a deep breath. "I haven't slept. I can barely think. I came straight here, but they all think I'm dead." He shook his head. "I've been hiding in the airport all day. I saw you get off the plane this morning. Jeremy looks good." He said it offhand, automatically. His eyes were on something far away.

"Mr. Door," Katie said, "I don't know how much you know, how much you've listened in on, but there is something extremely weird about the Hathor record of the crime."

"I assumed as much, if Ghost Targets was involved."

"Not just that," she said. "Actually...the reason we suspected you, before we knew you were her uncle...there's something going on in the camera code. Ghoster calls it a 'cloud'—"

"And you call it a blackout." He nodded. "I haven't had the nerve to look at the footage, but it sounds confusing."

"It's worse than that. Ghoster is genuinely scared of it. It's packing false identities in so densely that it's threatening to overload Hathor. Or something like that, I don't get all the technical details."

Martin frowned, his eyebrows meeting over his nose as he tried to picture what she had described. "I don't think I understand. Can't you just go in and pick out the legitimate identity to find your man?"

"No, he's been ghosted." She pulled out her handheld, but remembered that he had disabled it. She dropped it on the table and said, "Look, I got in HaRRE on the day the crime was discovered, I saw the moment before the killer stepped off the elevator into the office, and there was no one there. The database had *already* been scrubbed. But then, on top of that, the lights just went out, total blackout within HaRRE, and it's growing in time and space. Ghoster thought maybe you—" she cut herself off as he winced, and started over, "maybe whoever cleaned the database triggered some sort of bug in the recorder software."

Martin shook his head. "That software has been running for ages. It's on billions of machines around the world and has been for years." He frowned, bitterness in his voice. "And they've been tampering with the archive from day one. I can't imagine something that would do what you're describing just happening *now*. There's a lot of money resting on the fidelity of those recordings."

"The way Ghoster tells it, our whole society is built on it."

"Well, yes." Martin shrugged. "The board doesn't care about our society nearly as much as the sales numbers, though."

"I can show you," she said. She took a deep breath, and let it out. "Mr. Door—" She cut herself off, and met his eyes. "May I call you Martin?"

"Please."

"Okay. Martin." She saw an opportunity. "I tried to tell Ghoster that our only shot at solving this—at bringing justice to your niece's killer—is to get back to Ghost Targets, and get the rest of the team helping. I'm sorry to say it, but I just don't have the know-how yet. But my boss does. If you'll just come with me—" His look was enough to tell her he had no intention of doing that, but she leaned forward and kept him from tearing his eyes away. "Martin, if nothing else, we have authority. You have the technical skills. Ghoster has already said he can't tackle this. If you will come to DC with me, we *will* get to the bottom of it. All of us working together."

He bit his lower lip. "Show me," he said. When she looked blank, he said, "Hathor, unlock Katie's headset and handheld." Then he met her eyes. "I'm trusting you."

"I understand," she said. When she tried to load the case file, though, she got an access error. She held up a finger, "Hathor, connect me to Craig. Craig, share my case file to my handheld."

The simulated voice answered her, "That action is prohibited. You're in an unsecurable public place. Apologies."

She frowned, and said, "Hathor, connect me to Rick—"

Martin cut her off. "Hathor, no. Lock Katie." When her eyes flashed at him, he shrugged. "I'm sorry. I don't trust you that much, yet."

"I'm trying to help you."

He considered her for a moment, then said, "I believe you. I do." He sighed, and once again looked exhausted. "Hathor, I need travel arrangements for Katie and me to DC within the hour. Have a car waiting for us at the airport. We're going to FBI headquarters. Return." He didn't meet Katie's eyes.

After a moment she said, "So that's it then."

He nodded, still looking away. "I guess it is."

9. FBI Headquarters

Their plane touched down in DC at nine-fifteen, but Martin seemed anxious to get to work. Katie had no objection. Chances were good Rick would still be there, and if he wasn't, she could at least show Martin the HaRRE footage. As tender as his emotions were proving, it might help to get that out of the way before he had to meet the boss. Either way, she was ready to move, so a few minutes before ten o'clock they stepped off the elevator onto her level. And Martin would get his time for grief, she saw, because the lights for the floor came on as they approached the frosted glass doors.

Martin whistled. "Rick has done well for himself," he said. "You've got a class operation here."

"Just wait until you see our conference table," she said. "Craig, let us in and show my case file on my desk." The doors flew open, and the two walked into the empty office. She turned back to Martin. "I'd still like an answer, if you're willing to give it. Why does Hathor insist you're in Buenos Aires?"

He shrugged. "Another of Velez's ideas. He was obsessed with privacy, so he made us doppelgangers to roam the streets of Buenos Aires. It's a pretty clever program, random enough that it looks realistic." He paused, and looked around the room. "How smart is your boss?"

"What do you mean?"

He didn't answer right away. Then he said, "Hathor, what's going on?" He looked at Katie, and his eyes narrowed. She saw a flash of emotions—anger, betrayal, and panic clearest among them—and he moved with surprising speed as he darted back toward the office doors, but they didn't budge when he pressed against them.

She frowned, uncomprehending, but he didn't seem in a mood for reasoning. She said, "Craig, open the doors for my guest."

Craig answered immediately. "That action is prohibited. Explanation unavailable."

Martin wheeled on her, fire in his eyes. "What are you trying to do to me? I've done nothing!"

"*I've* done nothing," she said. "I don't know what's going on."

"Shut up. Shush." He waved her to silence, and tilted his head listening to his headset. After a moment he said, "Details to my handheld," and dug out that ancient, battered handheld she had taken from him earlier. It looked like one her dad might have used. He scanned it quickly, shaking his head, and said, "Oh, this is not good."

Katie said, "What?" She was starting to feel panicky herself. Martin didn't answer her. "Craig, open the doors." But she only got the same error message. She realized for the first time that the layout of the floor was one big trap. There was only one way in or out, and that was through three-inch thick, beautifully-frosted and probably bullet-proof glass doors. She decided if she didn't get an answer soon, she was going to test that last theory. "Hathor, connect me to Rick—"

Once again Martin cut her off, this time rolling his eyes. "That's not going to do you any good," he said. Two tones later, he was proven right. Rick wouldn't take her call. She left a message, and tried for building security, but she got no answer there, either.

"Hathor, connect me to the building receptionist," she said, trying everything she could think of, but Martin finally looked up with exasperation in his eyes.

"Could you be quiet, please?" He tapped several controls on his handheld and shook his head. "You don't have access to anything right now. Within this scenario, they were smart enough to realize that they probably can't trust you."

"Me? What did I ever do?"

"Just—wait. Okay?" He stepped away from the front doors and looked around, his eyes lingering on the big glass windows overlooking the sparkling city. He went into the conference room, and ducked out of sight. When she followed him in, he had his eyes closed and he was talking into his headset like a man deep in prayer.

It sounded like gibberish to Katie. "Rick is get ID Rick Goodall, Department Head, FBI Ghost Targets. Display ID details to my handheld. Stream is get audio stream using Rick. Do duplicate stream to my headset using background is true, no input is true. Done." He waited for a moment, listening and nodding. Then he frowned, thinking, and finally shook his head. "Hathor, reroute all vehicles heading here to, umm, the airport." He listened for a moment longer, then said, "Say something." He waited, then opened his eyes and looked at Katie, impatient. "Say something."

"Oh!" she said. "What?"

His eyes narrowed, and he said, "Hathor, lock out Katie's headset." Then he asked her point-blank. "Have you led me into a trap?" When she didn't answer, he growled. "Did you do this on purpose?"

"Do what?" she shouted. "No."

He nodded and closed his eyes. "Good news for me, bad for you," he said. "They're listening to you—"

"Who?"

He took a deep breath, clearly impatient. "Your office is a ghost trap. It makes sense. If I'd thought of it before—and I should have—I probably could have detected it remotely. I trusted you, though." He sighed. "Anybody without a solid ID walks in here, the whole floor goes into lockdown and an alarm sounds on your boss's headset. There's six agents on their way here, right now."

"So—"

"They were listening to your headset, too. That's the only reason I trust you at all. You're new, but you could have known about this. But I checked, and they were listening and they weren't talking, so you're not getting coached. Sounds like they don't trust you." He stopped and held up a finger, listening. Then he glanced down at his handheld and cursed. "Your boss is a smart man."

He watched his handheld for a moment, then continued. "He's not coming directly here. Probably routed to one of the buildings next door, but I don't know for sure. Hathor...never mind. Crap! I don't know how to get to his car. Hathor, coding. Get driver using Rick." He shook his head, probably at an error message, and spoke over it. "Get driver ID using Rick. Get driver by passenger using Rick. Get vehicle—no. Done. Argh!" He jumped to his feet, looking around in a panic. "He's getting closer. Katie, he's mad."

Katie said, "Calm down. I'll talk to him when he gets here—"

"No," he said, listening to an audio stream she couldn't hear. "He's not going to listen. You brought Jeremy here, and now you brought me here, and he thinks you're trying to bring down the department." He shuddered. "You wouldn't believe the language he's using."

"But why? All I've done—"

He caught her by the shoulders, his nose an inch from hers, and screamed, "I don't know, Katie. But he's coming in hot. He just learned that I rerouted the other agents, and he responded with a shoot-to-kill order. Got it? He thinks we're dangerous."

"No...."

"Hathor, coding. Do duplicate stream to Katie's headset using background is true, no input is true. Done."

She heard Rick, then, his familiar bluff voice. He didn't sound cheerful, but he didn't really sound angry, either, as he had when she brought Ghoster in. He sounded...determined. "Reroute to checkpoint delta. Jesus, guys, you should've done that in the first place. Elevators are locked until I get there. If any of you get there first, don't try moving without me."

"What about Katie?" Reed said, and Katie held her breath.

Rick answered right away. "She killed her audio feed, Reed. That was the last straw. She's rogue, and whoever she's with is in trouble. You have your orders."

"No!" she shouted. "No, I'm here! Craig, connect me to Rick. Hathor, connect me to Rick!"

It didn't work, Martin's handiwork cutting her off, but she heard Reed speak up. "Dammit, Rick, you need to think this through."

Katie stopped, astonished. Reed? *Reed* was standing up for her.

Rick's answer was a low growl. "Careful, Reed."

"No, Rick. You're the one who needs to be careful. I don't know what's gotten into you, but you're running way too hot on this. There's no way Katie—"

"She's a mole, Reed."

"She's not a mole! She's not a rogue. She's just a dumbass rookie who didn't know any better, and you're out of line."

"That's it," Rick said, that same calm in his voice. "You're relieved, Reed. Go home. Everyone else, I'm ninety seconds from checkpoint delta. Guns hot."

Katie's eyes snapped toward the elevators, as though he were already there, and she shouted, "No! Martin!"

Martin wasn't paying attention to the audio, or Katie's shouts. As soon as he'd shared the audio with her he had turned away, looking around again with his head swinging wildly. Now he was reading over location details for the building on his handheld. He tapped the screen and said, "Got it." When he looked up, he saw the fear and the fury in Katie's eyes. "What?"

"What? They think I'm rogue!" Katie said. "Just unlock my headset. I can sort this out."

"Can't." Martin shook his head. "He's coming here to kill me. You heard him, Katie. If I gave you voice, he'd maybe tell them not to shoot you, but there's no way in hell you could talk him out of putting a bullet in me."

"I can take you down," she said, and she didn't know if she was floating an idea or threatening, but it didn't matter. "If I have you under control when they come through those doors, if I can report that I've restrained you—"

"Then I go to prison, Katie. For the rest of my life. There's no Hathor record to clear my name. Your word wouldn't matter once a judge saw my doppelgangers roaming the world. I'd be in prison for the rest of my life, and," he stopped and caught her eye to make sure she picked up on his point, "I wouldn't have access to the tools I would need to find Janeane's killer." Before she could argue, he shook his head. "Not for the stuff they'd pin on me. No way in the world they'd give me command access to Hathor."

"So—"

"So we have to get out of here." He pushed himself to his feet. "If we can just get out of this building, I'm gone. I'll reconnect you to Rick, you can arrange a surrender and once they hear your story, you're in the clear. I'll make sure Hathor has the information you would need to clear you. But first we have to get out, and I have an idea." He tapped his handheld again. "If we can trigger a fire alarm, it should let us out."

Rick spoke into their ears, "I'm here," he said, loud and clear, and they both jumped. "Where are you guys?"

"Minutes out."

"Arriving now."

"Driver says six."

Katie and Martin stood frozen for three heartbeats, listening, and then Reed's voice came through, chillingly quiet. "Don't do this, Rick."

Rick grunted in response. "Screw it," he said. "I'm going in. You guys catch up."

Martin's eyes shot wide, then he ran out into the bullpen, rapidly scanning the walls, spinning in circles like a little kid. "Nothing," he said. To Katie, frantic, "Do you have a lighter? No, why would you? That's how they used to do it, though. Lighter under the sprinklers." He stopped, and for a moment she thought he had calmed down, then he started hopping up and down, bouncing on his toes and screaming, "Fire! Fire! Help, fire!" as loud as he could.

She followed him out of the conference room and walked past him. Then she scanned the windows, drew her weapon, and fired three shots through the window directly above her desk. The gunfire thundered in the room and Martin dove to the ground, hands covering his neck and head. The glass shattered, exploding down in a rain of shards, and Katie rushed to the window. She leaned out, and saw the telltale markings of an emergency escape, pinhole-sized jets perforating the building's facade in a horizontal line just below the window. She said, "Craig, deploy emergency escape," but nothing happened. "Building receptionist, deploy emergency escape." Still nothing. She turned to Martin. "Do you think the sensor will work during a lockdown?"

He nodded. "Has to," he said. "This place is not registered as a holding facility, so they'd be breaking so many laws if they deactivated emergency mechanisms for a private—"

"Then we have to jump." He said something, probably in objection, but all she heard was Rick announcing he was in the elevator. For a moment she thought about trying to fight him at the door, to take him down, but she knew she wasn't prepared to fire on him, and from the sound of it he wouldn't even hesitate.

She climbed up onto her desk, took a deep breath, and then stepped out through the window.

She fell. The sensors outside her window didn't trigger, or the emergency escape really *was* locked out, but she plummeted down through the chill, dark night, too terrified to scream. It lasted for just a heartbeat, until she saw the windows of the floor below flash past, and then she landed in a bag that ripped upward to close over her head.

She'd never used an emergency escape before, so the sensation was unexpected and awful. Intense claustrophobia welled up inside her, and she scrabbled against the fine, almost invisible net that held her. It wasn't necessary, though, because the net broke an instant later, dropping her lightly past the windows another floor lower down, where another nanofiber net shot out of the wall to wrap around her. This time she had time to see it deploy, spiderweb threads blasting out of thousands of tiny jets in the wall, out and up and twisting around her as she drew level with the jets, clinging for just long enough to slow her fall before the web tore free of the wall. After that first free fall, the rest of the way wouldn't be nearly as frightening. The nets would pass her along, from one to the next, gently down to the ground.

She had almost calmed herself with the thought, just as the second net released her, when she heard a terrified scream above. She twisted her neck and just had time to recognize Martin plummeting past the floor above before the net below fired. As it twisted up to catch her, some of the fibers spun around Martin, too, but not all of them. She grabbed his wrist with her right arm but her left was already pinned under her in the cocoon, and he was falling too fast. He fell against her hard, slamming her back against the building, and then tore free of her grip just before the net broke underneath her. At the next floor he was the one caught in the net, and she landed with a thud on top of him. This time the net caught them both, and the next was enough to slow them to a safe descent together. The pain and fear in Martin's eyes took a moment to subside, but as the next net broke, he wrapped his arms around her and they fell together the rest of the way to the ground.

As soon as they hit the ground she was on her feet. The net fell away easily, and she hauled Martin to his feet and dragged him down the street, away from the corner that should already be swarming with the rest of Rick's agents. She could hear Rick shouting down at them from above, but couldn't make out the words, and for that she was grateful.

Martin limped along, and she dragged on his arm urging him forward. "Come on," she said. "They're going to know exactly where we are."

"No," he panted, his breath coming ragged. "No, I locked out his headset before I jumped." He pulled free of her grasp and stopped, doubled over with his hands on his knees, gasping for air. "We should have a minute or two."

"That's not a lot of time—"

"I know." He looked up to meet her eyes, and she saw his pain. "I know, Katie, but I'm—"

Her eyes grew wide. "Are you shot? Martin, did he get to you?"

He chuckled, wheezing. "No, Katie. I'm just an old man."

"And you need your freedom for Janeane's justice," she said, taking a step back toward him. "You can do it, Martin. We have to get out of here, or all of that was for nothing."

He nodded, still panting, and then forced himself upright. They ran to the end of the block at a full sprint, then Katie squeezed his hand tight and dragged him out into the street, darting through the traffic. They went another block down, cut across the street again, and then down into the subway, Martin stumbling along behind her all the way.

She pulled him toward the first train at the platform, wanting to put more distance behind them, but he dug in his heels and stopped her. When she turned, ready to urge him on again, she found him looking determined. Before she could say anything, he put a finger to his lips, then looked around and led her toward a back corner. It stank of urine and spoiled trash, but it was darker than the rest of the platform.

"We can't just hide here," she said. "That's the FBI chasing us."

"I know, I know," he said, his voice a whisper barely audible above the noise of the station. "Keep your voice down. There's only so much I can do."

She answered him with a whisper. "What do you mean?"

"I didn't expect any of this. If I'd been prepared...." He shook his head. "None of this had to happen. I'm sorry, Katie."

"He's nuts," she said. "Rick, I mean. He seemed perfectly normal, but when I brought Ghoster in, when he found out you were there—"

"He's very good at what he does." Martin sighed, then shook his head as though to wake himself up. "Katie, this is important. You don't want to meet Rick like this. You've got to shake him, wait for him to cool off. Do you think you can stay off the grid for a couple hours?"

She shook her head, looking blank. She could maybe figure it out, but she'd never even thought about it. Most people worked their whole lives at making sure Hathor had a good solid read on them.

Martin sank back against the wall until it was supporting him. "All you have to do is make him give up running. We may have already done enough. If you can just force him back to his office, he'll think to check his recordings, and he'll know enough to clear you." He took a deep breath, and nodded as if to comfort himself. "Man like that, I guarantee you he has his own recorders running. Wouldn't trust Hathor as his only source."

"That helps," Katie said. "I wouldn't have a clue how to get away if he had all his tools available. I don't even know what they are."

"No, you shouldn't have to do that. I'm assuming he'll check the recording first, because he'll want to know exactly what happened. They're short enough, he should have the patience for that. He might even be doing it right now."

"Good," she said, straightening up. "Then we can go back. Unlock my headset and I'll talk to him. We'll—" She stopped, because Martin was shaking his head. "What?"

"I'm not going near that man." He closed his eyes, and let his head fall back against the wall. "I don't trust him. He's smart, but he can be wild. To turn on you so quickly...." He sighed again. "I'll go home. I don't need FBI software to figure this out. I'll go home and I'll figure out who did this. I'll...I can get in touch with you. Okay? I can be anonymous, and provide you the information you need." He laughed bitterly. "Or Rick, if they pull you off the case. Whatever. That Reed sounded like a good guy." He looked her in the eyes. "I can't go back there, but I'm not going to let this go."

She nodded. "I understand."

"I'm sorry, Katie. This...this is going to be really bad for you. There's no getting around that. We can keep you out of prison, but—"

"I know," she said. "It's okay, I guess. Whatever. We did what we had to do."

"I can take care of you." He hesitated, clearly uncertain. "I can... I have a lot of power inside Hathor. I can—"

"Don't worry about it," she said, faking a bravado she didn't really feel. "I'll figure this out. This isn't the first time I've pissed off my boss." He smiled, relieved, and she clapped him on the shoulder. "Now get out of here."

He nodded, stepped away from the wall, and then his eyes grew wide and he shoved her, hard, both hands to the chest. He caught her so off guard that she fell, and he tumbled down next to her. At the same moment a voice barked from twenty feet away, "Freeze!" and she thought she recognized Phillips from their brief conversation Monday morning. At the same moment, two shots rang out from somewhere behind Phillips, to the left, and ricocheted off the wall Martin had been leaning against a moment earlier.

She heard Phillips curse, and rolled to her feet in time to see him drawing his gun. Behind him, Rick was charging forward from the stairway, looking for a clean shot past Phillips' shoulder.

Martin was on his knees, and she caught his shoulder and hauled him up onto his feet, wrenching her shoulder with the effort. A departure message played over the public address system as a train prepared to leave the platform, and Katie shouted over it, "Come on!" Dragging Martin behind her, she darted headfirst into the crowd. She heard another shot and hated Rick for it.

She fought through a sudden press of panicked people, elbowing and outright shoving others out of the way, with Martin in her wake. She forced her way on to the train seconds before its doors slammed closed. The train jerked into motion, and she breathed a sigh of relief.

Suddenly the butt of Rick's gun slammed against the glass window, inches from her head, and spiderwebbed it with bright white cracks. She could see him running along beside, and when she met his eyes, he raised his gun to fire, at full sprint. She ducked out of sight and shouted, "Down!" for the rest of the train as much as for Martin. Rick was wild now. It had been mad for him to take that last shot on the platform.

He didn't fire this time, though. The train rapidly outpaced him, and as they left the station behind, Katie finally caught her breath. She rose and turned to Martin, who stood pale and terrified, just inside the door. "Are you okay?"

He nodded, mute, and she breathed another sigh. They were moving away. For now, they were safe. "It's a good thing you locked out Rick's headset," she said. "He has the authority to stop this train." Her eyes widened in sudden concern. "Lock out Phillips's headset." Martin nodded and stammered the instructions. She shook her head. "I'm disabling FBI agents," she said, and sank into an empty seat, directly below the broken window. "I'm going down for this."

Martin stepped around in front of her, and lifted her chin up until she met his eyes. "It will be okay," he said. "We can fix this." He sighed, then sank down to crouch on his heels in front of her. "It will take some work, but we can fix this."

"Thanks." Her voice was flat, and he looked offended.

"Katie, I'm...I'm a powerful man. You are in this predicament because you, alone in all the world, wanted to find justice for my little Janeane. I'm not going to forget that." He growled, his upper lip curling in his anger. "That Rick is an animal. I put plenty of blame on him. But you had your chances to throw me to the wolves and you didn't." He patted her hand reassuringly. "I'm going to fix this."

She forced a smile, and said with more sincerity this time, "Thank you, Martin."

"First," he said, looking around. "We're going to have to make you a ghost."

10. Ghosting Katie Pratt

They switched trains at the next station, but as soon as they were in motion again, Martin explained that it wasn't really that useful. "Katie, Hathor is tracking you everywhere you go. That's how the train system knows how much to charge to your Midas account. As soon as Rick gets back to the office, he'll be able to follow every switch we make."

"So what do we do?"

"First," he said, digging in the big pockets of his jacket, "you stop talking. Voiceprint is still the cornerstone of Hathor tracking. Until we've got things sorted out with the FBI, you don't say a word." He dragged out the same pad of paper he had tossed her at the airport in Little Rock, earlier that day, and the same cheap Bic. "If you need to communicate with me, write me notes. How's your cursive? Write something." She scribbled "something" on the pad, and he glanced at it, then nodded. "Very funny. But that'll do."

He sank down on the bench next to her. "Courtesy recorders only use video to supplement established IDs, but some of the more expensive private security cameras are running all sorts of visual identification software, and all of them end up reporting back to Hathor eventually, so we need to change your appearance quickly. Changing ephemerals won't throw them off long, but we're not trying to make you disappear forever. This is a temporary thing."

He leaned his head back against the broken window, and closed his eyes. "What else?" After a moment he shook his head. "You just *have* to keep quiet. That is the most essential. Not a word. Not yes or no. Don't sob or sigh. If you can help it, don't sneeze. We did a damn good job with voiceprinting." He saw the doubt in her eyes, and shook his head. "Okay, no, not literally *that* good, but the guys hunting us now are also the world's experts at working with low-confidence triggers. They don't need positive IDs, just partials. Ugh, this isn't going to be easy."

The next stop was Union Station, and as the doors slammed open and he got a look at the busy platform outside, the crowded shopping concourse just visible at the top of the staircase, his face split in a grin. "Perfect," he said. He hauled her to her feet and dragged her out into the packed train station. His earlier breathlessness was gone. He'd apparently been overwhelmed when it came to running, but hiding was his business. He led her up the stairs, then dragged out his handheld and pulled up a directory for the train station. Even at nearly midnight, the station was active and bustling. "Okay, you're getting a haircut and dye, makeup, I'll find you some new clothes." He glanced down the list, all high-end shops, and sighed. "Okay, never mind, you can find you some new clothes. I'm going to get us tickets out of here." He glanced around, then stepped closer to her and lowered his voice.

"Give me your headset, your handheld, and your watch. That's a Hippocrates, right? Yeah. And your gun. Oh, dear. Have to have the gun." She shook her head, but the look he gave her brooked no argument. She raised the pad to scribble an answer, but he pushed it back down. "Every one of those things reports your exact location to Hathor every time you use them. Your watch reports in ten times a second. Keeping quiet does you nothing if you're wearing that." He gestured at the gun under her jacket. "Or carrying that."

She still wasn't sure she was ready to hand over any of those things. Among them, they determined who she was, and made up most of the tools she had for dealing with the world. Of course, that was the point. She was supposed to be taking herself out of the world.

She saw that Martin was getting antsy. He started twitching again, looking in all directions, glancing back down the stairs to the subway platform. She grabbed his elbow to get him moving, and then he led the way. "Look, I'm not asking you to give up your stuff forever. There's a baggage claim with concierge service right up here. I'll ship your stuff to your apartment, okay? It'll be waiting for you as soon as you're safe to use it." He caught her eyes and said, "I don't *want* your gun, if that's what you're worried about."

She frowned, started to write something on her notepad, then changed her mind. She pulled the headset off her ear and tucked the pen in its place. She stuck the notepad under her arm and dug out her handset, then unclipped her gun in its holster, and passed him the whole bundle.

"The watch," he said, and she flinched at his insistence. "I'm sorry, Katie. I really am. But the watch is the worst of them all." She glared at him, wishing she could at least say something mean, even if she knew he was right. She unbuckled the watch, though, and added it to the stuff in his hands. He held it all awkwardly, but he smiled.

"Good. Now, let's get you into a salon." He checked his own handheld once more, and started walking up the concourse.

"I know how you feel," he said, glancing at the watch on his own wrist. "That was the worst thing about Velez's plan, really. The whole doppelgangers bit. I mean, yeah, it's nice to be able to go where I want, say what I want, and know that Hathor is only interpreting it the way I want, and then forgetting about me, but there was no good way to tie that in with Hippocrates. I *wrote* half of Hippocrates, back when I believed in the services, and I could never find a way to hack the two together. It's a beautiful system. I hated being left out. I mean, if I got shot where I stand, or if, say, I had a heart attack...." He chuckled and glanced meaningfully toward his belly. "I'm not the healthiest guy you've ever met. Sure, if I broke my ankle I could voicecode something, but if I had a heart attack, or severe head trauma or something, Hathor would send ambulances screaming to some imaginary address in southern Buenos Aires."

He glanced over at her. With her forcibly mute, he was proving quite chatty. "I came up with a solution, though. I have a miniature, private Hippocrates server running at my house. I custom-built this watch, so everything it records gets bounced through local network connections, straight to *my* house, instead of the Hippocrates main server. I'm still hidden, but if anything critical ever happened—anything that would normally trigger a medical emergency with Hippocrates—my home server will relay the real data from my watch to Hippocrates, and backdate their records with anything relative to the event." He let out a long breath, puffing out his cheeks. "Pretty cool, actually."

He glanced over again, and he could see from her eyes that she wasn't impressed. "I just...I understand what you're going through," he said. "That was my point."

She imagined he did, at that. She nodded, and tried to say a sorry with her eyes. She felt alone. Surrounded by all these people, she felt like she was alone in the wilderness. Naked, helpless. The man next to her had her entire life in his hands, and he was about to drop it in a mailbox.

She had been on Hippocrates since her fourteenth birthday, and it had saved her life twice. The first time had been a car accident, back during the switch over, when some idiot in a manual-drive had overridden his system's security to change lanes, and clipped the rear wheel of her mom's new autodrive. They'd spun across the median and a motorist going the other direction had smashed into the passenger side, and Hippocrates had gotten an emergency crew to her side in just under four minutes from the time of impact. The second time had been in college, when she'd learned she was allergic to shellfish. She knew half a dozen cops in Brooklyn who were alive today because of Hippocrates watches, and she'd worked a solid score of homicides that would have been batteries if the victims had been subscribers.

She loved her Hippocrates watch. She loved her headset and her handheld. She felt like she could barely walk on her own without them.

And then he stopped in front of the salon, bright lights and big mirrors and rows of barber chairs, and the next reality of it struck her. He wanted her to change her hair. For a moment she had an overwhelming urge to just state, loud and clear, "I'm Katie Pratt, at Union Station, and I just want to go home." She knew better than that, though. It wouldn't be home. She tried to fight her emotion with reason. They wouldn't let her have her headset or handheld in jail. If Rick showed up without calming down, she might not even make it to jail. Martin was right, this was her best chance, but she hated it. She *liked* being Katie Pratt.

She didn't argue, though. She didn't speak, let Martin speak for her, and he told the stylist, "Cut it short and make it yellow."

Yellow? She'd never even *tried* blonde, but in her condition she wouldn't have a chance to improve his instructions. The stylist must have caught a hint of her despair, because she arched a questioning eyebrow, but Katie could only shrug and nod. When that didn't work, she forced a tight smile, and the stylist finally turned away, ready to do what Martin had asked. Katie wouldn't have any input at all. She sighed, a tear threatening the corner of her eye, and followed the stylist to the first empty chair.

He knew what he was doing, after all. She remembered their meeting, on the outskirts of the graveyard where his family had gathered to mourn. He had done this, too, she thought, as the scissors went *snip, snip*. Sure, he could talk without fear. He could order Hathor around, and he even had his precious private Hippocrates server, but he had given up far more than she was. Her hair would grow back, and her stuff would be waiting for her at home. He'd walked away from his family fifteen years ago, let them believe he was dead, just so he could go unseen by Hathor's greedy eyes. She remembered his tear-stained handkerchief. He'd missed his niece's funeral. Fifteen years in, and still unable to break his disguise. That was his burden forever.

She could live with this. If he could put up with that, she could go a couple days with yellow hair.

Martin showed up while her bleach was still processing, and stood impatiently just behind her left shoulder. "What's this?" he said. "How long is this going to take?"

The stylist glanced at her watch, and shrugged one shoulder. "'Nother ten minutes, maybe."

Martin checked his handheld, and asked uncertainly, "Ten minutes?" He tapped something on the touchscreen, then sighed. "Okay. Can I sit down?" He sank down onto the couch just inside the salon's door and spent several minutes tapping on his handheld, muttering into his headset rapidly all the while. Katie had a hard time keeping quiet, anxious to know what was on Martin's mind, but he wasn't about to talk openly in front of the stylist. He just kept glancing up, catching her eyes in the mirror so she could see his concern, then looking back down and working some more.

Finally the stylist let her go, rattling care instructions at Katie even as she walked out the door, still pushing whatever hair care product was paying her the most. Katie ignored the girl, all her attention on Martin. He hurried to catch her up to speed, his eyes darting again, checking every face for Rick.

"He's got another headset," he said. "He was in the office, but he's on the move now. It's hard to track him, sometimes. He does weird stuff with his driver." He shook his head. "I didn't get to it in time to hide our stop at Union Station, but I put you on another train heading out at twelve-oh-seven, express toward Shady Grove, and with any luck he's chasing after that. As long as you keep quiet, it *should* show you riding that train until he gets on the train and flags that as a false ID."

He pulled up some notes and glanced over them. "Reed is with Rick now, so we've either got no problem or two problems. Phillips was coming here, but he didn't learn his lesson earlier. I sent his driver toward the Washington Monument, and I don't think he's even realized it yet."

He glanced up from his handheld as they mounted the stairs up to the next level, moving with the flow of the crowd. "I have blocked out a private cabin in a train leaving town at seven-fifty-five tomorrow morning. I think I figured out how to jack one of the identity gates, but we'll see. I want to test it out real fast, so be ready to run if it doesn't work. Now that you're clean, we should be able to ride the subway. I *know* I can outsmart their sensors." He glanced at his watch, and said offhand, "Oh, your stuff is in the mail. Look, we still need you to pick up some clothes." He pointed to one of the boutiques at random. "Go pick out whatever you want. I mean, whatever you don't want. Pick stuff you would never wear. I'll wait at checkout."

He was true to his word, clearly disinterested in accompanying her as she wandered among the racks. He stood at the counter at the front of the store, leaning against it and ignoring the dirty looks from the cashier there while he worked on his handheld. She left him behind, glad for a moment's quiet. It was weird, spending so much time in a conversation she couldn't participate in. She had always thought of herself as a kind of authority—even before she enrolled at the Academy—so being completely in someone else's control made her skin itch.

He was in charge, though, and for the moment her liberty depended on her obedience. His last instruction had been to pick out clothes she normally wouldn't wear. Nearly everything in the store was much nicer than anything she owned, so she felt like she was meeting his main criteria just by being here. She tried to take his advice to heart, though. She chose a pink top, frilly and thin, almost slinky fabric. She always wore pants—always—so she chose a knee-length skirt to go with the top, purple leather, and gold bangles for her wrists. When she brought it all to the front of the store, Martin glanced up for a fraction of a second, then back to his handheld. "Shoes," he said off-hand, as she dropped her pile on counter. To the cashier, "Put it on my tab."

She went back into the store, then, and picked out a pair of stiletto heels, to complete her Halloween whore costume, and then shook her head and dropped them back on the rack. She was on the run. These were only ephemerals, after all. She needed to be able to move more than she needed to make some magazine's Worst Dressed list. She chose a pair of pink open-heel sneakers, and on her way to the front of the store picked out some hip-hugger white cotton pants. She got to the counter and swapped out the skirt for the pants, daring Martin with her eyes to object. He didn't even look up. "Put it on my tab," he said again, and then pushed himself away from the counter. He looked up to meet Katie's eyes. "We ready?"

She nodded, and he turned away. "Train terminal first, then you change, then we're going to get out of sight for a bit, okay?" He didn't look back for her nod, but led her straight to the terminal. Pass-through identity gates, like a more secure version of the turnstiles of old, formed a long flat wall at the top of the stairs. The gates flew open and closed, green lights flashing above them, as passengers climbed the stairs to board one of the late-night trains, or headed into the station to do some shopping. Martin stopped halfway up the stairs, a yard short of the sensors that would have opened for him, and waited for a lag in the foot traffic.

Then he said, "Okay, let's see how this goes. Hathor, coding. Gate is get nearest security gate using style is Union Station. Do open gate using gate." The green light flashed on, and the gate flew open. He jumped up and turned, landing facing Katie with a huge grin. "Pow!" He said. "How do you like that? Oh!" He frowned. "Do close gate using gate. Done." He blushed. "Hathor did *not* like that." He shook his head, his smile still there. "Awesome," he said. "Awesome. Let's go."

She raised an eyebrow, to ask him, "Where?" and he pushed past her, pulling her down the stairs as he answered.

"You've got to change. Then...our train doesn't leave for another six and a half hours. I thought we might be able to grab some sleep, but we can't do it here. One way or another, eventually, they'll be here."

She nodded. They found a public restroom just off the food court and she ducked into it to change. When she came back out, her old clothes now bunched up in the bottom of her shopping bag, Martin was standing right in the doorway. She bumped into him, and he gave her a little shove. "Back, back, back," he whispered. "I'll tell you when." She retreated, wishing she knew why, and waited in the quiet bathroom, straining to pick some meaningful sound out of the subdued roar of the crowded concourse outside.

Minutes ticked past, painfully slow, and Katie reached for the door handle more than once, imagining all sorts of horrible things that could have happened to Martin. Rick could be standing right outside the door, just waiting for her. He could be waiting for backup, to come in in force. Martin could be dead, or hauled away in cuffs. She had no headset, no handheld to find any of that out. She was alone, standing in a poorly-lit bathroom in the middle of a crowded shopping mall, and dreaming up nightmares to pass the time. She glanced up into the mirror, and barely recognized the woman staring back at her.

It was disconcerting, and the shock of it derailed her fear. She looked younger, in spite of the fear that wrinkled her face. Hip, stylish. That wasn't really something she went in for. Ghoster could call them "ephemerals," but the insignificant little details added up. The reflection in the mirror wasn't Katie Pratt. She stepped up to the sink, and put on her meanest cop face, so silly under that mop of blonde hair. Still, she tried to look tough, the way she pictured herself, and pointed an imaginary gun at the girl in the mirror. She barked, "Freeze!"

A sound caught her attention and she whirled. At her right elbow, Martin stood looking in through the cracked door, his eyebrows threatening to climb into his hairline. "*Shh!* Are you crazy?" He tilted his head. "What are you doing?"

She still had her arm extended, a pretend gun now trained on Martin, and she put it away with a blush. He shook his head. "Rick and Reed were here. Rick still doesn't recognize me. I know because he was within arm's length before I spotted him, and he didn't react at all." He grabbed her hand and pulled her out the door, then set off at a quick pace toward the subway station. "I think they came straight here earlier, assuming my spoof was a spoof, and they finally decided they regretted that, because they tore out of here like bats out of hell, aiming toward Shady Grove station." He glanced back over his shoulder at her, his severe tone spoiled by a quirk at the corner of his mouth. "I have no idea if 'freeze' would be enough to voiceprint you, but single syllables usually aren't." He frowned. "Usually. I don't want you feeling comfortable with them, though."

She shook her head emphatically, and he nodded. "So here's what I'm thinking. It's two stops over to the green line. We get on a train there, and just ride it up and down until morning. You sleep three hours, I sleep three hours. Something like that. Come morning, we'll check on your buddies back at the FBI. I'll listen in and see if they're down to common sense yet. If not, you hop on a south-bound train with me, and give them all the time they need to cool off." He stopped, and turned to her. "Katie, I know this isn't how you wanted to spend your night—"

She laid a hand on his mouth, worried she might start laughing. Spend her night? She'd never been in as bad a spot as this. Even that accident, when she was sixteen, bleeding out in the crumpled shell of her mom's new car, help had been on its way. This time....

Martin was her help. He might be the one who had gotten her into the mess, but he was her help out of it, too. She leaned forward, tilted her forehead against his, and tried to tell him with her eyes, "I'm with you. Whatever you say."

He got the message. He smiled and blushed and turned away. "This way, then," he said.

He insisted on the first shift standing guard, and she reluctantly accepted, stretching out on her side on an empty bench seat in a mostly empty subway car. He sat in the seat across from her, working on his handheld, muttering into his headset. He was always busy with something. She watched him for a while and tried to sleep, but her mind raced. She thought about everything they'd done since they left the office, and tried to imagine the whole scenario from Rick's perspective. He had to be pissed.

His pride was in it. She knew that much. He'd shown it when she brought Ghoster into his office. She didn't know the man, but she knew enough about men to make that guess with a high confidence. He'd gotten where he was by taking pride in his work. He was single, Hathor had told her that much. He had two grown kids, and a wife who had died the year before he started climbing ranks with the bureau. As far as she could tell, he had been married to the job ever since.

He had built Ghost Targets up from a case file to a file folder, then a full-time position, then a task force, and now he had his own department. He cared about what he did, and he was good at it. And then she'd brought Ghoster into his environment. Top dog in a rival pack, or something like that, and, yeah, he'd gone feral. He'd chewed on her, that was for sure, and then the very next day she had brought a true ghost right into his office. She'd shot out a window to help the ghost escape, and then made him look like a loose cannon on a packed subway platform.

Hathor was watching. Every time an agent's gun was fired, it reported back to Hathor, same as a police officer's. The system had already generated a case file for the incident, and on Friday morning, somewhere down on floor three, someone would be looking over footage of the scene. Katie would sure look bad, but Rick would look worse. He'd fired blind in the direction of a crowd of bystanders. That was a permanent scar on his record. His pride had driven him to a stupid, stupid move, and now his pride was in for an even bigger hit.

She shook her head, and realized she still hadn't fallen asleep. She glanced up and saw Martin sound asleep sitting up, his head titled back at an awful angle, his handheld forgotten in his lap. She glanced around, but the car was still empty. She went across and pulled on his shoulder until he lay over on his side, snorted once, and then fell into a deep sleep.

She took his handheld, and discovered he'd been tracking location information on all the active Ghost Targets agents. He must have done a good job, because they were all chasing red herrings, running all over town. A blessing and a curse: they were safe, for now, but that was another slap in the face for Rick. He would come down on her like a hammer. She had no doubts about that.

That was a problem for another day, though. For now, it was enough just to survive and get out of this alive. The train rolled on, thundering along beneath sleeping streets, and she watched as one-by-one, Rick's agents called it quits and went back to their homes. Rick kept prowling the town, all night long, and she stayed awake to watch him.

At seven o'clock the train pulled into Gallery Place, and she roused Martin with the toe of her shoe, prodding him in the ribs. He snorted waking up, then looked over at her. "Was I asleep?"

She nodded and jerked her head toward the doors as they opened. He shook his head, and then climbed clumsily to his feet in time for her to lead him out the door just before the train left. She pointed across to the red line platform that would take them back to Union Station, then checked to make sure he was paying attention. He wasn't. His eyes were wide as he patted his pockets, then turned as if to chase after the train that had already left.

She caught his elbow so that his motion whirled him around to face her, and she almost fell off-balance in the process. She pressed his handheld into his hands, though, and as soon as he saw it he relaxed. "Oh, thank goodness," he said. "Oh, you scared me." She shrugged. Worry clawed into his eyes again. "Wait, what's going on with—"

She raised a finger to stop him, then tapped the screen that still showed location details on Rick. He was at her apartment, waiting across the courtyard with a good view of her door and the approach path. He might still be there when the courier dropped off her stuff, for all she knew. Midas showed he had already picked up six large coffees, over the course of the night, and Hippocrates had him into the yellow on stimulants, which meant he'd probably been doing something else besides the caffeine. He was a man driven, and he was in the wrong place.

She wasn't sure how much of that Martin picked up from a glance at the handheld, but he could at least see that Rick wasn't waiting for them in Union Station. Martin grinned. "Come on, then," he said. He stumbled into a trot, toward the platform they needed. "We have a train to catch."

11. That Man

Katie walked a step behind Martin as they entered the train station, both of them frantically searching the flood of faces for some alert security guard or one of Rick's agents. They saw none, though, and Martin was still able to open the identity gates with a word. Together they made their way up the long line of trains to the one they needed, a luxury passenger train with an antique toy-train motif.

The doors stood open and the two slipped aboard, unseen by Hathor and ignored by the scurrying porters who were busily prepping the train for departure. Martin led her to the cabin he'd reserved and unlocked it with a couple taps on his handheld. "In here," he said. The cabin was spacious, two three-person benches facing each other, with bunk beds up above, and a picture window looking out on the city as the train began to move. He closed the door behind him while Katie watched the town roll by. Behind her, Martin said, "Oh, wow. You made a real impression on Jeremy."

She turned, arching an eyebrow at him in question, and and Martin frowned. "Ghoster. Sorry. I checked on your message log, and Ghoster hasn't stopped trying to get in touch with you since we jumped out of the FBI building. He sounds genuinely concerned."

Katie shrugged. It was hard to reply, since she hadn't heard the actual messages and didn't *really* know Ghoster at all, but then she thought back on their last conversations before he'd left Little Rock. He'd thought for sure Martin was the killer, and now all he knew was that she was on the run, in his company. Chances were good he imagined her a hostage.

Martin watched Katie's train of thought play through her eyes, but he couldn't possibly have guessed what she was thinking. She reached for her notepad...and realized there was way too much to capture on a little scrap of paper. She shrugged and put it away again.

Martin frowned. After a moment he shook his head and finished relaying his report. "Anyway, he's in touch with Reed now. I'm sure they'll fill him in on the details."

Katie smirked, imagining the kind of details Ghoster might get from Rick Goodall, but Martin was already on to something else. He frowned again, eyes on something far away, and said, "Hathor, coding. Reference is my voice. List is get all input sources by reference using reference. Print list to my handheld. Done."

He fell silent, and she turned to see what he was up to. His eyes were locked on his handheld, scanning rapidly, and he was nodding all the while. At last he looked up with a grin. "Perfect," he said. "My headset and..." he trailed off, looking around, then pointed up above him to a pinhole camera above the door, "that recorder are the only listening devices that get a good read in here. I've got my headset exempting your voiceprint now, and I'm just going to lock out this recorder...." He did it with a flourish and grinned again. "And there you go. You've got your voice back."

She raised an eyebrow by way of asking, "Really?" and he nodded enthusiastically. "Go ahead. It's safe."

She cleared her throat, and after a moment said, "Is *that* what you've been working on?"

He nodded, clearly pleased with himself. "I had never actually looked at the privacy scripts Velez made for us, but they weren't as complicated as I'd always assumed. Especially for private headsets. The reporting functionality on overheard identities is explicit, not passive like I would have thought. Maybe that's just mine." He pulled his headset off his ear and considered it critically. "Hmm...."

Katie cleared her throat again, this time to get his attention. "What I *meant*," she said, a hint of acid in her voice, "is, 'You were working on that, instead of the blackout?'"

"Oh!" He looked suddenly sheepish, and wouldn't meet her eyes. "Well, it was such an inconvenience, you know? I felt bad for you, so I thought I should fix it. It didn't take long."

She shook her head. "That was nice of you, Martin. Really. But we have much bigger fish to fry."

"Of course," he said, taking a seat by the window and patting the bench next to him. "Let's see what we can see."

Katie sank down with a frown. "I don't think it's smart to try to get at my case file."

He shook his head, "Wouldn't dream of it. Don't need to. I've got my own HaRRE here—"

"On that thing?" She couldn't keep the surprise out of her voice.

He chuckled. "You'd be surprised what this old thing can do. But yeah. All we need is time and location. Hathor, load HaRRE on my handheld using the real-time stream from the Helen office building in Little Rock, Arkansas at record time...." He trailed off, counting backward in his head, and she saw pain crinkle his eyes just before he turned to her. "When did it—"

"Thursday night, the twelfth. Blackout starts around nine twenty-one."

He nodded, gratitude in his eyes, and repeated the information to Hathor. Seconds later, the HaRRE display filled his handheld screen, and there was Janeane Linson, considering a painting on the wall. Martin's breath left him in a *whuff*, and Katie looked away.

"No," he said, drawing a ragged breath. "It's okay. We have to—" He stopped talking and paused the simulation, going automatically through the same motions she and Ghoster had.

He scoured the building, found the telltale scenes that indicated a ghost—the doors opening on their own, the elevator button lighting up with no one there to call it—and drew up some additional database reports almost instinctively, looking for some clue to the ghost. Nothing caught his attention, though. He took a deep breath, visibly steeled himself, and then returned the camera to Janeane's office. He resumed the playback, and almost immediately the screen went black.

He said, "Hmm."

"Ghoster said it's just a ton of identities, packed in until HaRRE can't render them."

"Sounds right," Martin said, switching to a text log of the playback data. "Oh, goodness. Look at this mess. And you said it was in the camera code?"

"Ghoster said that, yeah. He went with me to interview Janeane's coworkers, and checked the local access point—"

Martin frowned. "Odd," he said. "He shouldn't have access. I do, though." He hid the log and pulled up a remote connection utility. "Probably. I used to." He tried to log in, two different ways, then gave up and said, "Hathor, load the control scripts for courtesy recorders and display them on my handheld." The browser he was using immediately filled with the files he was looking for, and he mumbled a quick, "Thanks," as he scrolled through and opened one.

"There we go," he said. "I still have access." He closed the first file he'd opened, and picked another one, skimming through it rapidly. "I think I remember this stuff," he said. "I haven't looked at it in forever." He closed that one, and opened three more in quick succession. Katie had no idea what he was looking for, and she had so little programming experience she didn't even bother trying to read it.

Finally he exited back out to the file list, and sorted it by date. "Aha!" he said, then he frowned. "Oh."

The first file in the list, the most recent, showed a modification date less than a week before the murder. Katie spotted that as quickly as Martin did. "That's odd," she said.

"Indeed." He tried to open the file, but an error message denied him access. He frowned and pulled up the details. "This is a new module. Most of this code hasn't changed in..." he looked at the next script in the file list, and nodded, "years. Six years since we've made a change to the courtesy recorder code, and here's a major module." He switched back to the file details, and whistled softly. "Look at the file size on this. It's huge, and he just added it in July. Hathor, show me my message center."

Katie said, "He who?"

He considered her for a moment before answering, and still didn't give a name. "Do you have that notepad?"

"Yes, why?"

He gestured impatiently and she dug it out of the bag with her old clothes while he explained. "We need to be...careful." He frowned, thoughtfully at first, but with more and more anger in his eyes. "Katie, why did you suspect me?" Before she could object, he shook his head. "I don't mean that. I'm not upset anymore. But what got you looking for me in the first place?"

"The blackout," Katie said. "Ghoster—Jeremy—he was helping me out, and when he saw it he said he only knew two people with the know-how to make something like that: you and—"

Martin put a hand over her mouth to shut her up, and nodded. "And him," he said. He took the pad from her and wrote out the name. "Jesus Velez Vasquez Carlo Guzman." He tapped it with the pen, a fire burning in his eyes, and said aloud, "He has been trying to contact me." He shook his head, like an angry bull. "Katie, he's been trying to contact me since July. He said he was working on a project for Hathor." He looked over the list of messages in his message center, and filtered out just the ones labeled "Velez."

"He left a dozen messages. He called, he wrote, he hacked into my handheld, and I just never responded. I don't work for Hathor anymore. He knows that."

"Then why—"

"There are parts of the system he never understood." He sighed, and all the fire went out of him. He looked over at Katie, and she saw self-loathing in his eyes. "He's a far better programmer than I am, but he couldn't dream. He never saw past the code, and Hathor was more than just a program. He made it work, but he never understood the whole of it. The purpose."

Martin wrung his hands. "I walked away from it all, because all any of them wanted to do was make money." He sighed. "Money is dangerous stuff, Katie. They destroyed everything that made Hathor special, so I stopped working for them. I guess...." He stabbed a finger at the name on the white square of paper. "I guess *that man* was so angry that he did this to get to me. No, it's not punishment. He doesn't believe in punishment. It's coercion. It's a threat." A tear leaked from his eye. "It's a message, Katie, and he'll do it again. He knows about all the people that matter to me."

She just listened, eyes wide. After a moment's silence, she said, "Do you really think—"

"Yeah." Martin nodded once, definitely. "Everything that pointed to me, points to him. He's as much a ghost as I am, and the code that triggered your blackout is here." He switched back to the file properties on the script he couldn't read. The very first line read, "Access rights: V." He pointed at that. "It's always 'DV.' Always. Most things are 'General' or 'Dev One,' 'Support' or 'Technician,' but every file in the system is 'DV," for 'Door' and...well, him." He took another shuddering breath, and let it out slowly. "He wanted me in on this, and when I wouldn't agree, he did it on his own. I don't know what else this code does, but your blackout is coming from there."

He let his head fall back, eyes closed. "He killed my Janeane." For a long time he said nothing, then, "I bet he didn't even care. He just did it, because it made sense to him." Another silence, then. "I wonder how much money is involved."

"Martin, we can get to him. I found Ghoster, I found you, I can find...that man." The phrase swam up out of her memory, her father's nickname for the man behind the curtain at Hathor. She wondered, now, if he had meant Martin or Velez. She tried to put some fight in him. "We'll turn Rick loose on him."

Martin smiled at that, without much heart. "I did it," he said. "I knew he was some kind of crazy. Always has been. And he has never come to me for help, in all these...what, fifteen years since we parted ways. We've been in touch, but even that was usually my doing." He met Katie's eyes again, tortured. "I should have known something was up. I should have done the job."

Katie didn't want to upset him further, but her curiosity got the better of her. "Why didn't you?"

He turned and looked out the window, and for a while she didn't think she was going to get an answer. Finally he said, "Do you have time for a story?"

She laughed in answer. He glanced back at her, then threw his handheld across the cabin. It bounced off the padded back of the seat across from them and landed on the bench. He ripped off his headset and tossed it to land beside his handheld, then turned his back to her, his eyes locked on the landscape outside.

"Here's your story, then." He sighed. "I don't know how much of this you already know, but I'll start at the beginning."

He took a moment to collect his thoughts, then nodded once. "We made the database in grad school. *That man* and me. Jeremy helped out, some. We brought him in late, and he left just before we applied for the patent, to pursue some project of his own. As far as I know, there were never any hard feelings, but I didn't ever really have the nerve to ask him. He missed out on a lot of money."

He sighed and shook his head. "There was money in it, from day one. I had this side project, working on voice recognition stuff, and once we got the database working, Vel...that man realized we could tie my Spoken-Language Syntax into a database that tracked people's movements, and provide location-aware services better than anyone else on the market."

Katie nodded. "That's when you signed on with AT&T."

"Basically, *he* sold them my personal assistant software to push adoption of the database architecture, which he knew was the real money-maker. AT&T created Butler—you probably don't remember Butler, because I renamed him to Hathor when we bought out AT&T three years later—but at the time, AT&T started pushing Butler while we set up Total Awareness Monitoring Systems and licensed out the data storage."

He shook his head. "It was amazing how quickly things moved after that. Privacy was a big deal back then, but we could offer people services they couldn't get anywhere else. Mostly...it was nothing. Nonsense. We'd give them movie showtimes and driving directions and all the sorts of things you could already get on your phone. At first, we were just serving the information *to* their phone, but we gave it away for free. AT&T was already paying us for the storage, so we wrote up little programs that would make location-specific recommendations and gave those out for free, and people ate them up. They would give us access to every last dirty secret they had, in exchange for easy access to voicenotes and remote downloads of popular music."

He fell quiet for some time, remembering. "It was supposed to be something bigger," he said, wistful. "My goal was to archive all human behavior, and we had the technology to do it. For the first time, we could efficiently record every thing people did, and that man was frantically working out deals that let us record personal preferences when it came to stupid videos or pictures of cats in funny hats. I wanted politics. I wanted religion. I wanted the things that mattered, and he gave me gaudy, colorful 'personal profiles' and truckloads of money."

He sighed. "He always said it would end up where I wanted it to. He used to say, 'peddlers today, gods tomorrow.' It was like a mantra for him. He always said the first goal was market saturation, and once the system was in place, once everyone was comfortable feeding it their data, *then* we could change the world."

Katie said softly, "I think it worked."

Martin shook his head. "No. Not yet, anyway. We have some amazing technology, but we haven't made any gods yet." He glanced up at the camera above the door, blind and deaf. "There's too many loopholes." He sighed. "I got impatient. I convinced a couple state senators to push through a bill that switched state IDs over to TAMS. It wasn't easy, but there was a certain state pride in this explosively-popular new technology coming out of Norman, Oklahoma, and they got the bill through the senate and we got our first government contract. They gave us social security numbers, addresses, census history, criminal history, everything they had on everyone in the state, with the understanding that we could provide them more accurate identity verification for cheaper than anyone else. And," he said with a sarcastic smile, "the next day, Oklahomans started getting *much* better service out of TAMS programs."

He sighed in disgust, "The database was never compartmentalized. On a fundamental level, it was massively relational. That had been my goal all along. When we put in all the extra personal information, it fed directly into our commercial recommendation algorithms. The reverse was true, too. Some of our customer information immediately began flagging against some false or missing identity stuff the government had given us. Within a week of accepting the contract from Oklahoma, we handed over information that led to the arrests of *dozens* of wanted criminals. That was before

Jurisprudence. That was before the legal system even really knew we existed. But suddenly, nothing was secret. We knew who lived where, what names they went by, where they had their video game consoles shipped when they bought them online. We knew everything about everyone, and no one really expected that yet."

He turned, tired of staring out the window, and slumped in his seat. "It went national after that. Privacy groups threw fits, we had our asses handed to us in half a dozen lawsuits, but AT&T made them all go away. Meanwhile, other state senates started wondering if we could find all their outstanding warrants for them, like we'd done in Oklahoma, and customers in other jurisdictions wanted us to recommend quality housing and provide free tax advice—the extra services Oklahoma residents were getting. We signed contracts with thirty-two states in less than three months. We hired hundreds of college kids to do our data entry, and dozens of programmers to fill in all the gaps we kept coming across, but we always kept the core of it to ourselves."

Katie said, "Then—" but Martin didn't want to be interrupted.

"Then some ambitious district attorney in Brooklyn got mad because some kid used our database to buy drugs laced with something vile, and he came after us. We were in negotiations with New York State at the time, and I think maybe he wanted to interrupt that, and he sure did." He tapped the pad of paper, Velez's name. "*He* got pissed off, and walked out of negotiations, and the state government came down hard on this DA, and I think the DA walked away, but his star witness wouldn't. Stubborn as a mule, this old cop just kept filing complaints and scheduling meetings and bullying his way through the state and federal government."

"Dad," Katie said, and Martin nodded.

"Your father hated it almost as much as I did. But we had Virginia and Maryland by then, and we were already doing surveillance work up there, and...ahem...*he* waited until your father took things all the way to the United States Senate *just* so that he could take care of the lawsuits once and for all. He dug up all the dirt we needed, hacked into systems and left private, anonymous emails letting key senators know that we knew."

He sighed. "I didn't know. I didn't know about any of it. He convinced me that our entire future depended on that hearing, that he didn't have the nerve or the passion necessary to win the case, so he sent me in to make the desperate appeal based on my *belief* in the system. I showed up and heard your father give his speech, and he was right. He was complaining about all the stupid, pointless services we offered, about the reckless way we used and shared out private information. About the vast amounts of money we made off of every transaction facilitated by our software, legal or not. He made good points, and I agreed with them all."

He looked over at Katie and said earnestly, "I'm not telling you this because of what happened to your father. I'm not trying to whitewash my role in the company. But this is the answer to your question, and one your father never got the chance to learn. I was ready to cede the case to him, to open up all of our resources to federal oversight and start steering the company toward policies dedicated to the public good." He sighed and shook his head. "I didn't get to say a word. The senators already had their answers ready. That man had them by the balls, before the hearing ever started. It was a sham."

"I got out of TAMS, then, right when they changed the name to Hathor. I cashed out my stock and started working on a service that could use the TAMS database for good. That was Jurisprudence, and it's probably the best thing I ever did. I worked with Midas until they started pushing high-interest loans, and then seven years later I bought them out, and now it is *just* a money-management service. In all, I helped start sixteen different services, and I walked away from nine of those because they sold their souls for profits, and I couldn't steer them back. Two more went under, but the other five contribute more to society today than everything else running. I'm confident of that." He was genuinely proud.

Katie smiled, "You sound like a saint, Mr. Door."

He rose and crossed the cabin, scooping up his handheld in one hand and his headset in the other. Calmly, deliberately, he hooked the headset back around his ear. When he turned back to her, his eyes were dead.

"I'm a fool," he said, defeated. "Because I have known for fifteen years what kind of a man Velez is, what he's willing to do to get his way, and I ignored his threats until he decided to kill someone I loved."

Her eyes shot wide when Martin said the name, but he didn't seem to care. "Hathor, connect me to Velez," he said. Katie tried to object—at the very least to learn his plan—but Martin lay a heavy hand over her mouth to shut her up, and then he nodded. "Velez!" he said, his voice thick with insincere excitement. "Hey, I'm sorry I didn't contact you earlier. I've been busy with things. But I got your message." His breath escaped him then, but he forced the fake smile back. "I would love to work with you."

His smile fell a moment later. "Oh," he said, sounding genuinely disappointed. "Well, let me know if that changes, okay? Thanks." He reached up and shut off his headset.

Katie said, "What?"

"He's not interested," Martin said. "He sounded surprised to hear from me. Not...repentant or anything. Just surprised. He was perfectly polite...."

Katie grabbed his hands, and tilted her head forward until she caught his eyes. "Martin, you don't have to work for him. We can protect you and your family. With your help, we could catch him."

He barked a sarcastic laugh. "I don't plan to work for him," he said. "I plan to hunt him down and kill him."

She said, "You don't mean that."

"I do. I'm not setting Rick on him. I'm taking him down myself."

"How?" She moved around to his elbow to watch him work as he brought up location details on Velez on his handheld, but they were exactly what Katie would have expected. He was in an open-air market in Buenos Aires, after grabbing a coffee at a little cafe on the corner near his apartment. All lies.

"I go to the queries," he said. He opened some software Katie had never seen before, and nodded when she narrowed her eyes at the program's name. "I can check every read or write to the database. That was what your father wanted the Senate to be able to do. Your boss has been making noise about it for years, too, but Hathor won't release access and the government just doesn't have the power to make them. Not anymore." He entered some search terms and started scrolling through the results.

Katie said, "How does this help us?"

"It gives me direct access. When you—or your boss, or even Jeremy—when somebody asks Hathor where somebody else is, the answer you get back is a prediction based on all of the data stored in the database. In my case, or *his*, those entries are all automatically modified on insertion so that they provide a false prediction. *Here*, though, I should be able to get the raw input. In fact..." he stopped for a moment, changing his search terms. "I can probably get a list of just insertions that don't match the database entries they created." He scrolled down. "See, here's where I shut down the courtesy recorder in our cabin." He scrolled up higher in the list. "Here's my call to Velez." He frowned, eyes scanning up and down the list rapidly. He bit his lip.

Katie thought he might be close to drawing blood. "What's wrong?"

"He's not in here." He tried another search, and apparently didn't like those results any better. "I don't understand! If I'm here, he should be here!"

"Calm down," Katie said. "Don't worry, we'll figure something out." She pointed at the screen. "Do you know the code that does this? Can you get at it?"

He shook his head. "It's all in the kernel. I could access it, but I don't have a clue how it works. That was all his doing." He dropped the handheld on the bench next to him and hung his head. "If he's doing something different now, if he's running his own privacy stuff, I wouldn't begin to know how to track him down."

He fell down on the bench, looking dazedly out the window. Katie picked up his handheld and started looking back through the lists he'd accessed. After some time she poked him in the shoulder. "Give me your headset." He looked up, with sad eyes, but didn't respond. She took the headset and put it on her ear. "Can I use this?" she said. "Will it work?" Her eyes widened, "Will he be able to hear me?"

Martin shrugged, both hands palms up. "I don't even know, now. He's doing something totally new." He shook his head. "Might as well try, though. If you have an idea, go for it."

She didn't have an idea, but she had a starting spot. She played back the earlier conversation between Martin and Velez, heard Velez turn down Martin's offer. He had been right—there was no trace of a guilty conscience in the other man's voice. But there was something else she thought she could use.

She didn't know all his tools so she tossed the headset back to him, and the handheld, too. "Play back that audio. That's your call. There's other voices in the background."

"So?"

"So get a positive ID on one of them. Hathor can do that, right?" After a moment, he nodded reluctantly. "There you go. Get a positive ID on a bystander, someone who *doesn't* have your special privacy code running, and find out where that guy is."

His brows came together for a moment as he thought through her plan. "That's not a bad idea." He spent some time talking into his headset then, reading results on the screen and passing new instructions. Katie couldn't help but grin, proud of herself for figuring out something the expert couldn't, but he shattered her pride when he put down the handheld again, shaking his head.

"It's no use," he said. "He's too smart for me. For either of us." When Katie looked up in surprise, Martin shook his head. "Don't get me wrong, that was a very clever plan. He's still one step ahead of us, though."

"How so?"

Martin tossed her the handheld, and it showed a list of six identities, all of whom were apparently in an open-air market in Buenos Aires at the time of the call. Martin said, "I don't think my privacy measures go that far, but I've never really tested it. It wouldn't be too hard to do. It's unfair to them—messing with other peoples' records like that, but it would keep him hidden." He sighed. "Face it, Katie. We're out-classed."

"I'm...I'm not so sure of that. Play the audio again." He reached up to hand her his headset, but she used the handheld to switch it to speaker mode so they could both hear. She played back the conversation, but the conversations in the background were just noise to her. "How do I..." before she finished the question, she figured it out. She pulled up the list of other identities, and found a control that offered audio playback at the time she wanted. She heard a different voice, loud and clear with the background rumble of an open-air market. The voice was clearly speaking Spanish.

"Better and better," Martin said, still sounding defeated. "He didn't move the people around him, he just added background noise from Buenos Aires to his own—" He cut off at the sound of Velez's voice, clear in the stranger's microphone, shouting, "Martin!" over the noise. His opening, "What's happening?" the only English in a babble of Spanish.

Martin blinked. "That's complicated." Katie left the audio playing, picking up snippets of Martin's call within the crowd noise, but Martin spoke up again. "Still, he could have merged the two together—"

Katie held up a finger to cut Martin short, just as Velez said clearly in the audio, "Goodbye."

The stranger they were eavesdropping on said, in halting English, "You're ready now, sir?"

Velez answered him distinctly, "Yeah, sorry. Lo siento. Whatever, two mangoes."

"Dos mangos? Bueno." Katie's grin crept back as she turned down the audio on the headset again. She looked up to meet Martin's wide eyes.

"I think that man is hiding in plain sight," she said, and Martin nodded, flabbergasted. Katie laughed. "I think we need to start looking in Buenos Aires."

12. Buenos Aires

Martin got to work on his handheld, mumbling instructions into his headset from time to time, and quickly became so absorbed that Katie left him to it. She tried thinking about the case, but her mind kept drifting, and she couldn't concentrate without her handheld. She wanted to ask Martin if she could use his again, just for a few minutes, but he looked busy and she didn't have the nerve to make the request. She finally gave up and stretched out on the cabin's empty bench. It was soft enough, and she hadn't slept in almost thirty hours. She drifted off quickly.

She woke sometime later to find Martin regarding her with his head tilted to the side, a thoughtful look in his eyes. She pushed herself upright and said, "What?"

"Close enough," he said. "Hathor, save and commit changes on that identity, and activate the process. Thanks." He smiled at Katie. "I have good news."

Her eyes narrowed. "What's that?"

"I figured out how to spoof an identity." He glowed with pride. "I don't have the tools to spoof a voiceprint in real-time—that's over my head—so you're back to being seen and not heard as soon as we leave the train."

She nodded. "I can handle it. What does the other part mean?"

"Oh! I've got a...there's a new fake you. Or, well, not really. There's a fake identity with positive ID and full federal clearance trailing along three feet behind me, wherever I go. That should take care of identity gates, even the gate attendants when we get to the airport."

She interrupted him. "The airport?"

"Yeah," he frowned, surprised by her confusion. "It's like you said, we need to start looking in Buenos Aires."

"I wasn't planning on *going* there," she said. "What did you have in mind?"

He blinked. "Umm.... Well, this train stops in Atlanta in about half an hour. I have a car waiting for us at the station, and two first-class seats to Argentina. Should be a pleasant flight. We can both get some more sleep while we're in the air."

"No. No. I'm not ready to go jetting off to South America. Besides, isn't that a little risky for *you*? I'd think booking a flight would take a lot more safeguards. The airline will have records—"

"Not a problem," he said, shaking his head. "The airline we're using licenses a Pantheon database running the Hathor architecture, so my regular security scripts should kick in automatically. Real-time responses will trigger off my actual presence, but all stored data entry is either falsified or forgotten between the recorder and the file write. The reservations are held under a single-use, randomly generated nickname, the seats will be paid for automatically and anonymously through Midas, thanks to my work in the last few hours we'll walk through the identity gates and past the boarding gate with pretty green lights, and then for all of history the records will show that the two seats we used were empty on this particular flight. Velez was quite thorough in his design, and between the two of us..." he frowned, obviously irritated, "We've had our hands in almost every major implementation of the core architecture. And even if they *weren't* running Hathor, it wouldn't matter. Interconnects take so long to correlate that I'd be free and clear before Ghost Targets or anyone else could find out what city I'd flown out of, let alone what flight I'd taken."

"You're telling me an awful lot of your secrets, Martin." She tried to sound off-hand, but she watched him as she said it, hoping to gauge his reaction. For a long time he didn't react at all, and she was beginning to worry he hadn't heard her when he finally answered. He didn't meet her eyes.

"Katie," he said, "I don't like ghosts. I don't like being one. I'm... it's just...." He met her eyes then, begging her to understand. "Hathor could have been something new in human history. Think about it. For the very first time, we have the ability to see everything people do, to hear everything they say. For the very first time, we can demand immediate accountability. We're not talking about morality dependent on belief in some un-provable, horrifying afterlife. We're talking about human behavior, here and now, completely exposed and permanently recorded by the all-seeing eye."

He let out a long breath. "That potential is still there, but right now the system is corrupt. It's not *Hathor* that's broken, it's the people who present Hathor to the world. While the system is trying to genuinely, honestly watch over the lives of men, someone at the heart of the system is selling indulgences to those rich or powerful enough to buy blindness. And those corrupt administrators—whether we're talking Jeremy or the system administrators at Hathor Corp.—they are making money hand-over-fist off of the sins of those people so small-minded that they don't *want* a new age of man." His hands clenched in fists. "Today the database services are just soulless corporations, but they really could be gods tomorrow. All that stands in the way are the ghosts."

She shook her head. "If you believe that," and it certainly sounded like he did, "why—"

"Why have I been a ghost all this time?" He sighed. "Because I had the opportunity. Because I was a young man, offered extraordinary power, and it was fun. More than that, it's because I know there are other guys out there, guys like Jeremy, yes, who are short-circuiting the system for personal gain. And as long as that's going on, I thought, maybe the system needs someone else on the inside, someone equally powerful, to try to hold things together."

"I understand that," she said. "What you said about working with Jurisprudence earlier...Martin, I've been using that service all my life, to do real good. You have changed the world for the better. You can take some pride in that."

He looked out the window. "No, Katie. I was wrong. From the very first, I was wrong. I tried to play the game. I walked away from my family so that I could keep the power. I indulged in a life of privacy and authority most people will never know, and I have known for *years* that it was wrong, and I've just gone along. At first it was loyalty to an old friend," his mouth twisted into a sneer, "then for a while it was complacence, and eventually, it was fear." His eyes met hers with a deep self-loathing. "I didn't *want* to be on the outside, just a normal man. I wasn't sure I could live without the power. Instead, it was Janeane who died, for my pride and foolishness."

He blinked away tears. "It helps to have you," he said, and drew a shuddering breath. "I never trusted Rick, Katie. He's too driven, too ambitious. And he hates the system. He hates Hathor, not just the ghosts. I can't trust a man like that."

For a while after that, neither said anything. Martin stared out the window. Katie lost herself in her own thoughts, trying to grasp the depth of the old man's heartache. Ghoster had nailed it—Hathor had been a religion to Martin. He had built a life inside the system, protected, powerful, and now he risked everything in search of reform. What must it have been like to carry that burden through so many years?

And what about the man who had built the system with him? The man who broke Martin's god, corrupted Martin's religion? Jesus Velez, an ironic choice for an alias, and she wondered if it had been deliberate, almost two decades ago.

As if in answer to her thoughts, Martin said, "I'm going to kill him." There was no emotion in his voice, and he never turned from the window. "Jurisprudence can't touch him, so I will kill him. Then you can arrest me, Katie. You can take me back to your boss all tied up with string, like a present on Christmas, and I'll tell you everything you need to know, to fix Hathor once and for all. You'll be the FBI's little darling, and my Hathor will be whole. But first...." He turned away from the window at last, and Katie caught a glimpse of Velez's personal details on the handheld as Martin got back to work on it. "First I'm going to kill him."

She couldn't draw him back into conversation after that, to talk him out of it or even learn more of his plans. And she couldn't let him go alone, either. Katie didn't know if it was her responsibility to prevent Martin committing murder, or to protect this broken, defeated man from a monster who had already killed before, but either way, she couldn't let him go alone. When the train pulled into the station, Martin immediately jumped to his feet and headed out into the corridor. She followed along, three feet behind him, walking in the footsteps of her ghostly avatar.

The plane ride was eerily silent, too. Without a private cabin to seal off, every headset in the plane threatened to announce her location directly to the FBI if she so much as asked for a Coke. So she shook her head politely whenever a flight attendant spoke to her, and looked around the cabin at all the other passengers, busily working on their handhelds or watching movies, listening to music or recording voicenotes through their headsets. She had nothing. Her only connection to the world was Martin, so she sat close to him and watched over his shoulder as he researched Velez.

He wasn't watching the man's movements anymore. He'd probably long since learned all he could from immediate data. Instead he was digging back through time, looking up anything of significance Velez had done. There wasn't much to find, and Martin was apparently a rapid reader, because he often opened articles, scanned them, and then closed them out before Katie had finished reading the leads. He read up on Argentina, particularly its tech policy, over the course of the last five to ten years. At one point he glanced over and saw her reading over his shoulder. He looked down, then back to her again.

"We haven't been in touch for a while. I'm starting to think he left the states a long time ago. It's weird, though...." He trailed off, and didn't respond when she raised an eyebrow for an answer. He hadn't given her the pad of paper back, either, so she was left without a voice, while his thoughts carried him away, back into his research.

She couldn't keep up, so she finally fell back into her chair and tried to sleep. She dozed for hours at a time, but never really slept. Finally, after what seemed like days, the plane touched down in Buenos Aires, and they disembarked into a crowded airport. Martin leaned close as they bustled through the concourse, and shouted so she could hear over the noise of the crowd. "I've found where he's staying. It was tricky, but there's a shop in town with a ridiculous energy bill, and the bulk of it is getting paid on the sly by an anonymous account. I'd bet my last dollar it's Velez's hideout." He didn't smile, but there was a bounce in his step, and a dreadful determination in his face.

Then it hit her, with a dreadful force. He had her gun. He had to, to talk of killing Velez with such certainty. She'd given it over to him back in DC and just trusted him to drop it in the mail, with the rest of her stuff. She watched him stride toward the exit, full of purpose, from her place three feet back.

They left the airport and immediately a car called from the nearby curb, shouting out the alias Martin had used to board the plane. He reached for the door, and while his attention was diverted Katie hit him with both hands, knocking him back against the side of the car. He gasped in surprise, but she ignored him, intent on what she was doing.

She started at his shoulders, slapping the outside of his jacket, then reached inside to check under his arms and the inside pockets. She patted him down, top to bottom, but didn't find what she was looking for. He didn't have the gun on him. She did find the battered notepad, though, and pulled it out of his pocket with the pen, while he watched her in sheer astonishment.

Then she nodded toward the car door. He cautiously slid past her and ducked into its interior. She followed him a second later, and fell into the seat behind him, already scribbling on the pad.

"What was that about?" He reached around to prod at his side, where she'd hit him, and winced.

She shook her head, unwilling to voice her suspicions. Instead she showed him the questions she'd written. "Is it safe to talk? Can you secure the car's interior?"

He squinted at her penmanship, then shrugged. "I can, maybe. Probably. But it would take too long. It's not worth it. We could be at his place in ten minutes—" She held up a finger, a stern look in her eyes, and he stopped short. "What?"

She held the glare for a moment, then went back to the notepad. "If we're going to do this," she wrote, "we're going to do it smart. He seems like a dangerous man. We're not rushing straight to his house."

Martin frowned, considering. "Well, what would you suggest?"

She wrote, "market," and when he looked uncomprehending, she underlined it with some force. It seemed like the best way to catch him out of his element. He went to the same market every day, like clockwork. For all they knew, his house was fortified against intruders, but if they could catch him out in the open air, they could take him where they wanted. Maybe the local police station, maybe some dark alley. They would have time to figure that out later.

She didn't have time to explain any of that, though. Just as she put pen to paper, a delighted voice spoke from the driver's monitor. "Ah, Martin. I'm so glad you've finally come to visit me."

Martin stammered, "Ve—Velez."

Martin's eyes widened in surprise, then whipped to the monitor even as the same route from Martin's handheld appeared on it. Velez's lair. "It works out well," Velez said, "because I've reconsidered. I will accept your help, after all."

Martin met Katie's eyes and shrugged. "Umm...excellent. Good." Sweat beaded on his forehead.

Velez laughed. "I'm glad you brought the girl, too. I think I would have had to get her delivered, if you hadn't. You know what they say about loose lips, Martin."

Martin's face fell, and she could see the guilt and concern in his eyes as he said, "Velez, she'll be helpful. She's...she's trustworthy. I'd swear to it." He pulled himself up, tall in his seat, and said, "And besides, she's under my protection."

"Of course." She could still hear the laughter in Velez's voice. The driver said they had eleven minutes until arrival. She couldn't imagine what to expect. Velez said, "Enjoy your trip. I'll just get a place ready for you."

The monitor's audio switched off, but there was no way to know if he was still listening. Katie raised an eyebrow at Martin, asking permission to speak, but he took it for a different question.

"I don't know," he said. "Technically, he...he wrote everything. The actual code, it's all his. He could easily be listening in now. He knew you were here, when even your boss at the FBI couldn't know that. I don't *think* he could listen in on my headset, because it all routes through my home server, but I don't even know that. He might have heard everything...." He looked down at his hands. "Maybe you should run, Katie. When we arrive, as soon as the doors unlock, just run for it. I don't feel safe bringing you to Velez like this. Not after what he said."

She shook her head, then touched his arm to get his attention and shook her head more forcefully. She touched her chest with one hand, then touched his. "I'm with you."

He caught the meaning of that, and smiled sadly. "I'm sorry for dragging you into this. I...that's what I did to Janeane, too. But without your help, I never could have...." He took a deep breath, and let it go. "I'm glad you're here, Katie. I'm sorry for everything, but I'm glad we're here together."

She couldn't have answered him, even if he'd allowed her to speak.

The car stopped shortly after that, and Katie took a breath to calm her beating heart. She wished for the reassuring weight of her gun in its holster, or the lifesaving cinch of her watch on her wrist, but she was alone here. She opened the door and climbed out into the breezy night. The car zipped back into the traffic, leaving them standing on a sidewalk before a run-down electronics store. Most of the wares in the window were worthless, relics of a past when new gadgets dominated the market quarterly. For a moment she considered plunging into the store, purchasing a handheld that would look as old and battered as Martin's, just to have something to record some notes on. Just to have something to hold, really, but it was a fleeting thought.

It was driven from her mind at the sight of the man standing outside, waiting for them. Ghoster's description sprang immediately to mind: "the whitest kid you've ever seen." He was in his fifties now, but the description still seemed to apply. He was a couple inches past six feet tall, skinny and pale. Clean-shaven, balding, and wearing clothes that had been unfashionable when they'd been for sale decades ago. When he caught her considering him, he grinned.

"Katie Pratt. Charmed, I'm sure. Martin, you always picked the pretty ones."

Martin growled, "Stop it."

She expected Velez to carry on his patter, to throw some rejoinder back at Martin, but he actually seemed cowed. He flinched away and shrugged, looking hurt. "Fine," he said. "I'm just trying to be friendly. Come on." He waved over his shoulder, and led them to some stairs that descended below the sidewalk. "I've got a basement apartment."

The apartment was below the electronics store, dimly lit with a handful of dying light bulbs in a shabby living room decorated with the sort of relic electronics sold upstairs. Velez didn't stop in the living room, though, and didn't bother giving a tour. He headed straight toward the back of the house, down a narrow hallway, and Martin and Katie followed behind. Katie's fear rapidly gave way to curiosity.

The bedroom had barely room for the unmade single bed and the cheap chest of drawers beside it. Velez slipped around the foot of the bed and opened the folding closet door, then shoved aside a rack full of clothes much like the ones he was wearing, revealing a door in the back of the closet. He glanced back over his shoulder at them, a sparkle in his eyes, then said, "Okay, we're coming down."

The door swung inward, revealing another narrow staircase. Katie looked back at Martin, concern in her eyes, but he only shrugged. She turned back and saw Velez watching their silent exchange. His smile widened. "Ladies first."

The stairway twisted down in a spiral, the same cramped quarters and poor lighting she'd seen in the rest of the house, but at the bottom of the stairwell she stepped through an open doorway and into a vast workshop. The rathole apartment above was clearly nothing more than camouflage for the extravagant underground lair. The floor plan was wide open, with a kitchenette off to the left boasting a well-stocked wet bar, and an entertaining area farther ahead with suede couches and a rich leather armchair circled around an expensive wall-mount monitor. The back wall of the wide space had three doors set within a shallow alcove, and she was prepared to guess they opened onto two bedrooms and a bathroom. It would have been a luxurious apartment in a tower in New York City, but it felt fake somehow. She could tell, whether from Velez's personality or some subtle clues in the room itself, that he had no use for the creature comforts it boasted. His time was all spent in the right half of the room, the workshop.

Two full computer desks, each one easily the size of hers back at the office, stood end-to-end, and a programming monitor taller than the TV was wide stood mounted on the wall above them, currently displaying some computer code she probably couldn't have deciphered with years of training. Half a dozen handhelds lay forgotten, here and there—some of them resting on the desktops, one in a desk chair, and two apparently dropped casually on the floor. Another lay against the wall across the room, smashed to pieces, and a tear in the wallpaper showed how it had been damaged. They were all of them cutting-edge technology, nothing like the battered and much-loved device Martin carried with him.

She noticed one other thing out of the ordinary as Martin followed her out into the room and began his own inspection. She pointed, subtly as she could, to draw his attention, but she wasn't sure he noticed.

There were security cameras throughout the room—half a dozen here in this one open space, and now that she was aware of them she could recall another one looking down on her as she'd descended the stairwell. They weren't the discreet, miniaturized courtesy recorders Hathor had installed in every public space, every office building in the developed world. These were the big roving cameras with powerful microphones she knew from the police station, the courthouse, the federal building. There was something odd about them, though: a barrel mounted on the left side of the camera, opposite the microphone, nine inches long and about the diameter of a man's wedding ring. Despite her attempt at discretion, Velez caught her looking as he stepped into the room.

"You've noticed my security system," he said, and clapped Martin on the back to get his attention. He pointed at one that was scanning aggressively back and forth above the two computer desks, surveying the whole of Velez's domain. "Do you recognize these, Martin? I designed them for that DARPA job. I always thought it was stupid Hathor wouldn't spring for the target locators."

Martin shook his head. "Hathor didn't need them. The point was always to match passive observation with active self-reporting from individuals' possessions. I told you it would be enough. I told you something would come along, and the Hippocrates watches proved me right."

Velez pouted. "It was a risk. That way makes you dependent on an outside source. What if there had been no Hippocrates?"

"It would have been something else."

Velez shook his head. "It costs pennies, Martin." He chuckled. "Well, not these. But a laser range finder and some pretty simple triangulation technology could have gone into every courtesy cam out there—"

"But that's millions, Velez. Hundreds of millions. You don't understand the scale. You never did. My goal wasn't to make perfect hardware, it was to see everything. Everywhere. To do that, you have to sacrifice some of the cool factor."

"Whatever." He held up a hand and walked away. Katie looked back and forth between them, fascinated. Their argument had the feel of old familiarity. Velez caught his desk chair with one hand and dragged it behind him to the computer desk, then climbed up in it to tap the camera on the side.

"These are special," he said. "Remember that magnetic projection system Dewey needed math help on?"

Martin frowned for a moment, thinking, then his eyes shot wide. "For the Navy? Back in college?"

Velez nodded, grinning. "He never did anything with it. Lost the contract to Lockheed Martin, and they just took the money and delivered excuses until the Navy gave up. Ten years later, technology being what it was, I put this sucker together from scrap and worked it through DARPA for millions. I don't think they ever really deployed them, though."

Martin just stared, fascination and horror battling in his eyes. Velez nodded, grinning.

Katie said, "I'm sorry, I don't get it."

"It's a gun," Velez said shortly, and for just an instant his eyes bored into hers, then he put his grin back on. "A very advanced one."

"It's a rail gun," Martin clarified, moving closer to examine it. "That's what we used to call them. It accelerates dumb payloads to extraordinarily high velocities and how on earth did you get one this small?"

Velez shrugged. "NASA tech. I mean, that one's not going to sink a battle cruiser through seawater drag, but it's enough to protect me from intruders. Ooh, watch this. Lock target on Martin."

The roving camera jerked back from its slow pass to train directly on Martin. Katie caught tiny movements from the corner of her eye and turned to find half the other cameras in the room now stationary, too, all of them pointing directly at Martin.

"Oh, that's eerie," Martin said. He took a step back, away from the computer desk, and three cameras moved smoothly to follow his motion.

"Stop it," she said.

Velez considered her for a moment, and again Katie saw that threatening glint in his eyes. He had taken his opportunity to threaten them. She knew that, and she was pretty sure Martin was smart enough to pick up on it, too. This whole place was a deathtrap. They needed to get out of there.

"Martin," she said. He waved her to silence. She wasn't interested in hiding anymore. She'd seen enough from Velez to know he was their man. The man wore social courtesy like a cheap suit, something sinister and snakelike slithering behind his eyes. So what if she brought Rick straight to them, now? "Martin, I think—"

"Just a minute, Katie. We haven't seen each other in ages. Speaking of which..." he said. The last was directed at Velez and she could tell he was trying to fake casual. "What's this project you've been working on? You've clearly done well for yourself—"

"It's Hathor," Velez said, cutting him off. He stepped in front of Martin, square to him, and when Martin's eye still drifted back to the camera, he said with a hint of irritation, "Reset cameras. Martin!" He snapped his fingers, and Martin's eyes snapped to his. "It's Hathor, Martin. We have to do something about it. I had thought that the easiest way would be to go through you, but when you wouldn't answer me, I took matters into my own hands."

"Wait," Martin said, his brows drawn. "Why would it be easiest to go through me?"

It was Velez's turn to look confused. After a moment, almost as though he thought Martin was tricking him, he said, "You run Hathor."

"No." Martin barked a laugh and looked at Velez like he was insane. "You do."

Velez shook his head, then looked pointedly at Katie. "Is this an act for her? Jesus, Martin, the stuff you've already told her, I didn't think you'd be trying to pull something like that over her eyes—"

Katie held up her hands, annoyed. "Stop it! Both of you." All eyes turned to her, and she said, "Who runs Hathor?"

Martin and Velez glanced at each other. Velez shrugged, and Martin sighed. "After the senate hearing, AT&T severed all ties to Total Awareness Management because of the embarrassment.

The demand for the tech was still there, though, so TAMS just rebranded as Hathor Corp. and struck out on its own. But I was disgusted with what Hathor had become. That's when I left, like I told you—"

"Wait, what?" Velez's laugh was almost shrill. "Are you kidding me? You were disgusted, so *you* left? No." He turned to Katie, like a witness to a judge. "I walked away from Hathor. It was dangerous. I said that all along. It was a fun project, it was cool to make it, but I said from the start that it would go bad—"

Martin cut him off with a shout. "You also thought it was going to be AI. It was never AI—"

"Tell me how AI is distinguishable from 'predictive recommendation algorithms' apart from built-in error. That's a semantic point—"

"Boys!" she shouted, and the two older men turned to her, Velez panting and Martin a little flushed from the argument. "Who runs Hathor?"

They each pointed to the other. Velez narrowed his eyes. "The senate expressed some concern about two men wielding so much power, so we built a board of directors out of whole cloth."

"Fake IDs," Martin clarified. "For *those* we built AI."

"And then I walked away, and left Martin running the behemoth he was always so in love with."

"No," Martin shook his head. "No, if you didn't want to run Hathor, why did you send me in to convince the senate to protect it?"

Velez laughed. "After all these years? You still really.... I sent you there to go off on your little romantic sermon about human perfection and make us look so irrational they would have to shut us down." His shoulders sagged. "It didn't work. You never got a chance to talk."

Martin shook his head. He looked crushed. "How...why would you do that? Who's been running everything, then? The AI?"

"No," Velez shook his head definitively. "No, there's a hand on the tiller, I can see that clearly. I just thought it was yours."

Katie had a guess, but she didn't have a chance to voice it, because Martin drove to the point that she'd lost track of.

"It doesn't matter who is running Hathor," he said, his breath coming fast now. "You needed a favor from me, or you thought you did, and you attacked where it hurt me most." There was no recognition in Velez's eyes, no realization that the tenor of the conversation had just changed. For a moment, Katie thought they had been wrong again, misled by another hasty assumption based on who could or couldn't do what to the cameras. Martin stepped forward, close to Velez, and grabbed his shirt in both hands. His eyes begged Velez to confirm what Katie was already starting to suspect, that he was wrong, but his words formed the accusation. "You killed Janeane."

For a moment Velez said nothing. He understood, now, enough that he was paying attention. He tilted his head to the side, like a curious bird, and looked into Martin's eyes for a moment. Then he laughed lightly. "Little Janey?" he said. "That little blonde girl was Janey? I didn't even think to check." Martin fell against Velez's thin chest, collapsing into tears, but no emotion touched Velez's voice. "Huh," he said. "What a coincidence."

"You bastard!" Martin said it before Katie could. He rose up and launched himself at Velez, grappling for his throat, but Velez moved like a snake, darting to the side and whipping an arm up into a lock around Martin's extended shoulder. He turned and pushed, and Martin flipped over onto his back, breathing hard.

All of that happened in the time it took Katie to close the distance to Velez. She approached him from behind, aware now of the threat he posed, and waited for him to straighten, then moved fast. She shot an arm forward past his shoulder and bent it back, locked around his throat in a sleeper hold. "That's enough,

Velez," she said. "You're under arrest. I'm taking you back to DC. We'll get this sorted out."

She looked down at Martin, struggling to catch his breath, and said, "You okay?"

She didn't hear his answer. She remembered too late that the real threat Velez posed had nothing to do with jujitsu. He said the words offhand, unconcerned, even with her grip tight on his throat. "Wound the girl."

There was no gunshot, no sound at all, but she felt an excruciating explosion of pain as a high-velocity chunk of metal destroyed her left calf and glanced off the side of her shin bone, sending splinters, muscle, and blood exploding out the front of her leg. She saw the splash of red, and heard Velez's gulp of air as she fell, then the blackness took her.

13. Bloodthirsty

Katie woke sometime later in what was apparently the guest bedroom of Velez's underground lair. Her first thought was to wonder if Velez had killed Martin. She didn't get much past that because of the pain. Her left leg throbbed, fiery white heat, and she was afraid to look down at it. Her teeth ground together in the effort not to scream, and tears burned in her eyes. She blinked them away and tried looking around the room, but nothing really registered. There was furniture, bookshelves, and another computer desk, a couch against the wall, but she couldn't concentrate on details.

She was lying on the floor, on her side. She tried to push herself up, to get a better view of the room. As she rose she heard a voice, probably Martin's, but her vision swam, accompanied by a wash of pain and nausea, and she passed out again.

The next time she came to, she was lying face-down on the floor, and her left cheek and nose felt raw from being pressed into the carpet. She worked her jaw, forced her head around to discover that she was still in roughly the same spot in the same room. The pain that had assailed her before was quieter now—a dull roar in the back of her head. She rocked her shoulder back twice, shoving off the floor with surprisingly weak arms until she rocked over to land on her left side. She looked down and saw her left leg wrapped from knee to ankle with a clumsy bandage, stained red and soaked through. She felt a distant revulsion at the thought of it, but that was all.

She looked around the room, dazedly, and then it hit her. "I've been drugged."

She didn't realize she'd said that out loud until Martin answered her from the couch, behind her now. "Trust me, you needed it." He sounded as bad as she felt. "You're in bad shape, Katie."

Katie tilted her shoulder down and rolled her weight after it, landing on her back with a thump that sent a shock of pain up her leg and right through the haze clouding her mind. For a moment, everything was just a burst of blinding white light, and then she realized she was screaming. She cut it off with a choked sob.

"I'm sorry, Katie."

She blinked away the tears to look up at Martin, ten feet away on the couch. His eyes were full of tears, too. "I didn't know he had anything like this. He used to be a nice guy."

She sucked air in through her teeth, and then shook her head feebly. "You'd be amazed what nice guys can get up to." She let her eyes fall closed. The pain was receding now, back to the other side of that misty gray shroud. "What's our situation?"

Martin didn't answer right away. When he did, he sounded careful, like he was trying not to frighten a trapped animal. "He's holding us prisoner," Martin said. "He asked me to help him with some code he's working on, after he shot you, and I told him to go to hell. He...he threatened to kill you, but I couldn't help him, Katie. Not after what he did to Janeane."

He was apologizing, misery and heartfelt regret warring in his voice. She summoned the strength to put real force behind her words. "You did the right thing, Martin. Don't give that animal a thing."

"I don't even know that I could," he said. "He's listening to us. He's watching us. There's cameras in here, Katie, with guns on them. He made sure I was paying attention when he programmed the cameras outside the room to shoot us if we tried to flee. We're trapped."

"It's okay," she said, sucking in another breath and wheezing it out. Her voice sounded deeper than usual, odd in her ears. "The FBI is looking for us, remember? Rick will find us. How long have we been here?"

"Twenty hours. Maybe twenty-two."

"Jesus, really?" None of the awe she felt made it into her voice. She sounded sleepy. "Well, that's good. That's real good. He's got to be close by now."

"Katie," he stopped, and she could hear the fear in his voice. She rolled her head to the left so she could look up at him without lifting her neck. His eyes were intense on her face. "You've been in and out of consciousness. I've...I've bandaged your leg several times now. It's...." Tears welled in his eyes, and she smiled at his concern.

"It's okay," she said. "This isn't the first time I've been shot at." It was the first time she'd been hit, but she didn't think that information would comfort him any.

He didn't look comforted, anyway. "Katie, you've lost so much blood. You're dying, and Velez doesn't care. He's been giving us food and water, and I've been helping you drink. I was able to bully him into giving me some painkillers for you, but he won't budge on an ambulance. I told him to drop you in the street outside, a mile away, whatever. I told him you can't get back in here, with the cameras guarding the place. I told him you weren't a threat, but he won't listen." He took a deep breath, and let it all out with a *whuff*. "It's bad, Katie. I'm so sorry."

She waved away his concern, a little flutter of her left hand. "Stop worrying," she said. "I'm awake now. It was smart to get the medicine. It's helping." She nodded, and the world washed around inside her head, but a moment later it steadied again. She took a deep breath. "Don't give up on me just yet."

She let her eyes fall closed, and forgot about the world for some time. When she opened them again, she felt a gnawing queasiness in her stomach, but it wasn't pressing. She pushed herself up on her elbow, looking for Martin, but he wasn't on the couch anymore. She found him sitting at the computer desk, working away while one of Velez's killer cameras watched him from above.

She said, "Hey!" and Martin and the camera both turned to look at her. She shouted at the camera. "My name is Katie Pratt, I'm a Special Agent for the FBI's Ghost Targets department, working for Rick Goodall. Help! Send help, now!" She pushed herself up on her elbows and stated firmly, "Hathor, connect me to Rick."

The door swung open behind her, inches from her head, and she rolled her head backward to look up at Velez's pasty face. His mouth was twisted into a sneer. "Hathor's a whore," he said. "She can't hear you here."

He stepped further into the room and slammed the door closed behind him. "I see Martin was wrong about you dying."

"I'm strong enough to take you down, old man."

He snorted a laugh. "You're pale, girl. And you're slurring your words, even if you can't hear it. You're not long for this mortal coil."

Martin slammed a hand down hard on the desktop, with a smack that brought all eyes to him. "Stop it, Velez! This isn't funny."

Velez considered Martin for a moment, then nodded to the desktop. "Have you made any progress on my program?"

Martin said flatly, "I'm not helping you."

"The girl is dying, whether she knows it or not. Help me out, and maybe we can get her to a hospital in time."

"I don't even know what you're trying to do. I haven't touched core code in twelve years. It was all scripts and clever queries. You're the programmer, Velez. You always were." He gestured helplessly toward the desk. "If you can't do this, I can't."

"There's something I'm missing," Velez said, "and no one else in the world who I would trust to look over this code. You don't have to be a better programmer than me—you just have to spot what I've overlooked. You were always good at that."

Martin shook his head. "It's been too long," he said. "I don't even know what you're trying to do here."

Velez glanced at Katie, measuring, and apparently decided she wasn't a risk to anyone anymore. "I'm trying to take it down." He seemed to think that was answer enough.

Martin didn't get it. "Take what down?"

"The system. Everything. I want to blind Hathor for good."

Martin didn't answer right away. His jaw fell open, and he shook his head. "How could you do that? Why would you do that?"

"We never should have made it, Martin. It was a mistake. I knew that fifteen years ago, and apparently so did you. For a while, I thought it was enough to live outside it, but it's wrong. People are...changing. Everything is different now. There are no secrets. Hathor sees everything—"

"Except us," Martin said. "Except the ghosts. We need to fix *that*. We need to get into Hathor Corp., figure out who's really running it, and change things."

Velez barked a laugh. "There's no fixing it, Martin. From the ground up, it's a spy network that never should have existed. People need privacy, not more perfect surveillance."

"How...it doesn't matter," Martin said, frustrated. "It doesn't matter. You can't take down Hathor. It's too big now."

"Maybe *you* can't take down Hathor, but I can." He frowned. "I just...there's a few things I can't handle. I needed a little help. There's something I'm missing."

Martin shook his head. "I won't help you kill Hathor. Why would you ever think—"

"Because you know as well as I do, we never should have done this." Velez turned away, staring at a painting on the wall. "She's bloodthirsty, Martin. There's never enough. When we started, it was just crucial information, because that's all there was room for in the storage space. When we started, I thought maybe we'd keep a week-long backup on general surveillance, to give us time to parse the feeds and just archive relevant information. A couple years later, storage space was cheaper, faster, and I thought maybe we would save at most a year of history. Yesterday I checked, and I found footage of little Janeane's seventh birthday."

He glanced back over his shoulder, and found Martin grinding his jaw, fists clenched tight and knuckles white, and he shrugged as though he hadn't meant to goad him. "You weren't there. I forgot. It was cute. She got her first full-featured handheld, but she was more interested in the stupid dolls her mom gave her."

"She stopped caring about computers when I went away," Martin said.

Velez nodded. "That makes sense." He sank down onto the couch. "Hathor remembers all of that, Martin. Even though you and I are hidden, Hathor remembers everything. There's this cute girl who works at the *mercado* down the street. I go there from time to time just to catch a glimpse of her. I got curious once, and traced her back through time. I saw her as an eight-year-old playing soccer barefoot with the other poor kids. I saw her as a two-year-old running around naked in her parents' front yard. Hathor sees everything, and she doesn't forget."

Martin shook his head. "That was the point," he said. "It has changed the world."

"She was never supposed to be that powerful. There should have been some control. Just think of the story! You're the one who's always getting all mythological. Hathor, the all-seeing, but she was second to Ra. We should have built a Ra, Martin. We should have *been* Ra." He trailed off. "I can't believe neither of us stuck around to run Hathor."

"It doesn't matter," Martin said. "None of this matters. You can't shut down Hathor. It's too distributed."

"I can," he said, jumping to his feet. "I got it from your story. I looked up Hathor, you know, and in the old legends, they said she turned bloodthirsty. Something went wrong, and instead of watching over hearth and home she started just killing everyone, with this insatiable lust for blood." He glanced involuntarily toward Katie, then shook his head. "The people cried out to Ra, and he made the Nile flood and stained it red like blood. Hathor was confused, and she drank it in until she was finally sated."

Martin said, "The blackout—"

"I'm going to flood the Nile," Velez said. "I'm spoofing the identities Hathor so craves, and I'm going to pour them down her throat until she can't drink anymore." He laughed. "I can't believe it took some stupid African story to give me the idea for a Denial of Service attack—"

"Hathor can withstand DoS," Martin said, and Velez cut him off.

"Well, it's *designed* to." He jabbed a finger at Martin, grinning victoriously. "We wrote it that way. That's why I didn't think of it. But there are ways around that. For us. For me. We left a loophole for creating our one-time IDs to get through identity gates and such, and there's no limit on those. They're made to be built up, used, and discarded in an instant. I just turned off the part that discards them."

Martin thought about Velez's plan. After a while he said, "But if you...oh." He looked at the code on the desktop and scrolled slowly down through it. "Hmm."

Velez watched him work, a hunger in his eyes. "What am I missing, Martin?"

Throughout that conversation Katie fumed from her place on the floor. Her stomach roiled, constantly threatening, and the pain in her leg mumbled ever in the back of her head, distracting even through the drugs. Her mind darted, out of her control. She tried to listen to Velez, to understand his dastardly plan, but mid-monologue she caught herself recalling the shot that had destroyed her calf. She could picture it perfectly, brilliant splash of blood against the wool-white carpet, her own scream the only sound.

She wondered how the weapons worked. Were they single shot? If not, how quickly could they reload and fire? How much ammunition could the spindly camera hold? They used some special equipment mounted on the camera for targeting, she had understood that much from the men's conversation. But could the guns fire blind if the cameras were disabled, or did they depend on those sensors?

The questions crowded into her head one after the other, leaving no time to consider one before the next distracted her. And then something Velez said caught her attention before she had found any answers at all. Martin started talking, and she found herself thinking about the family puppy that had died while she was in elementary school. The drugs were messing with her mind. She pushed sad puppy eyes out of her head and tried to formulate a plan to take down Velez, but they all ended with the words, "Wound the girl," and a splash of red against wool-white carpet, and a scream, and oh, the pain. She let her eyes fall closed and listened to the men talk.

Martin was arguing with animation, "It doesn't matter, anyway. You won't be able to finish the job. Even if you can bring down all the Aggregators in the world, overload every server with garbage data, there's still a backup. The Justice Department uses it for Jurisprudence. It's a full-fidelity copy of the entire Hathor database—"

"I know," Velez said, his voice considerably calmer than Martin's.

"It doesn't run code, Velez. It just duplicates the entries in the main system, on a one-day delay. That means you'd have to run your blackout on a live system for at least twenty-four hours before it even started impacting the backup, and that will only work if nobody notices, which seems unlikely since services around the world will start crashing after the first five minutes, if you do this on the scale you're talking about. That gives the Justice Department twenty-three hours and fifty-five minutes to discover what you're doing and disconnect the backup, and they've got a perfect copy waiting for the days or weeks it takes them to figure out what you've done and stop it. You'll cause some real chaos for a month or two, but the whole system will grind back into motion soon enough."

"I told you," Velez said with condescending patience, "I know all about the Justice Department backup, and I've taken steps to address that. Just the other day I did a test run—"

"Janeane." Martin's voice was cold.

"Yes!" Velez threw his hands up in the air, irritated at the tangent. "Janeane, Janeane, Janeane! The girl's dead, Martin! Man up, get over it, and get your head in the game."

"You son of a bitch—"

"Watch it," Velez said, and cast a meaningful look at Katie that shut Martin up. "I didn't kill your damn niece, Martin. Jesus. I hate killing people. But when it became necessary to ghost the crime, that seemed like as good a place as any to test my new code. And, for your information, it worked."

"Oh, yeah?" Martin was petulant, sarcastic.

Velez took him at face value.

"Like a charm," he said, but then he scowled. "Sort of. I've got something wrong. It bogs down trying to over-saturate a single point, instead of cascading outward like I'd intended. I probably just have a sign backward somewhere, but I need you to—"

"Dammit, Velez, can't you be human for a moment? I'm not going to help you. You just admitted you ghosted the man who killed my niece!"

"And I'm glad I did," Velez said, puffing his chest out. "It got you here, right when I needed you. Talk about providence. That's going to prove more valuable than anything else." He kicked Katie lightly in the side, just below the ribs, to make her open her eyes. "Your other girl here is going to die if you don't figure out what I did wrong. Fix it, and I'll ship her straight to Memorial-o Hospital-o up on the hill. Got it?" He took two long strides to the door, then stopped with his hand on the knob and looked back at Martin.

"She's gone, pal. Let her go and live in the now. I need this done tonight."

14. Goodall

Velez left them alone in the room, and Martin went immediately to Katie's side. He knelt by her side and brushed the hair out of her face with a deep concern in his eyes. "Are you alive, Katie?"

She coughed weakly, but forced a smile. "I'm alive, Martin. Help me sit up."

"I'm not sure you should—"

"I've been lying on the floor like a rag doll. It's undignified and uncomfortable, and I don't want Velez kicking me anymore. Help me up."

"*Up?*"

She nodded to the couch. "It's my turn on the couch," she said. "You can sleep on the floor tonight."

He still looked doubtful, and when she climbed up onto her knees, her whole body tensed hard against the pain. He didn't argue, but ducked under her left arm and wrapped his right arm around her waist, lifting her as he rose. Together they hobbled to the couch, and then she sank down on it gingerly. Once she was settled, he said, "Is that better?"

"No." She spoke through gritted teeth. "It hurts like hell, but at least I'm off the floor." She spent several minutes just breathing, trying to control the pain, and it finally faded into the background again. When she could think again, she looked up to meet Martin's worried eyes.

"I'm fine," she said. "What's your plan to get us out of here?"

"I'm going to fix his code tonight. The way I see it, that's our only shot."

"That's a death sentence, Martin, and you know it. Don't ever trust a man with enough experience to say, 'I hate killing people.' That's a dead giveaway right there."

Martin shook his head. "Katie, I don't know what we can do. I can't just let you—"

"Don't do it, Martin." Her voice was firm. She was starting to feel better, sitting up. Her head seemed like it was finally working again. "I may not be a programmer, but I know enough to understand what Velez is talking about, and I'd rather die than help him accomplish that. Governments are built on Hathor at this point. Society can't survive without it. If he's as close as he says he is, you need to find some way to slow him down. Buy us some time."

"Katie, you don't have time—"

"I know!" She felt bad at the hurt look her retort brought to his face, but she was tired of his concern. "Dammit, Martin, I'm telling you. I'm prepared to make the sacrifice, so let's stop talking about it. I need you to delay Velez long enough for Rick to get here."

Martin frowned, obviously confused, then he shook his head. "Katie, I know you tried to contact him earlier, but these recorders aren't repeating anything out to Hathor." He touched the headset still on his ear. "Velez is capturing any data addressed to Hathor and routing it back into his own system, or I wouldn't still be wearing this. We're in containment here."

It was her turn to shake her head. "I'm not talking about that. Rick was already on our trail. We shook him, but there's no way we lost him. Once he caught his cool, got back to the office with all his agents, all his resources ready to hand, I guarantee you he'll be able to track us. That should lead him right here."

"I don't think so, Katie." The look on Martin's face said he really didn't want to break Katie's hope, but he wasn't prepared to lie to her. "I doubt Rick will have much luck."

"Oh, don't judge him off what I can do," Katie said. "I've only been with the bureau five days. Maybe six now." She frowned. "Maybe seven. I don't know. Rick is the boss. He has tricks I can't dream of."

"Not really," Martin said, and forestalled her argument. "Katie, I've been watching Rick in action for five years now. You might have been green at the start of last week, but if you've been paying any attention at all, I've taught you more in that time than Rick could have taught you in all your years in the service." When her eyes widened in surprise, he shrugged. "That's not pride, it's just the situation. Rick is guessing blind, and I know all the important function calls. Hell, I've stayed off his radar all these years, and I'm just a scripter. If Velez doesn't want to be found, Rick doesn't stand a chance."

Katie fell silent. After a while, a tear leaked from her eye, and he reached up to brush it away. She batted his hand down. "There has to be something—"

"He's holding all the cards, Katie." He lowered his voice to a whisper. "Whatever it is he's missed, it can't be anything major. He'll spot it eventually." He leaned in close, until their heads were almost touching. "He's going to figure it out, no matter what we do. I have a chance to get you help—"

"No," she said. "You don't. I'm FBI, and he knows it. There's no way he lets me out of this alive."

"Don't say that."

She pushed away from him and caught his eyes. "It's true," she said. "You need to understand that. You need to accept it and make your decisions accordingly. No matter what he promises, he's not letting me go."

He caught her hands in his, still trying to comfort her, but something else caught her attention. She said, "I think I have an idea." She hoped the drugs weren't leading her astray again.

He put a finger on her lips, and when her eyes widened he leaned close again, pretending to kiss her, and whispered in her ear, "He can hear everything we say." Before she could mention the pad of paper, he shot down that suggestion, too. "And he could read any notes you wrote me. We're in a cage, here. If you have a plan, if you think it might work...try. But don't say it out loud."

He sat back, and she held his eyes for a moment, trying to think of a way to warn him what she had in mind, but nothing came to her. It might have foiled the plan, anyway. At last she said, "Are you sure?"

He nodded.

She said, "You could get hurt."

He shrugged. "I think it's my turn."

"Then turn around." His eyes narrowed and he frowned, confused, but he turned where he sat, his back to her. She sidled up close to him on the couch and leaned up against him, wrapping her arms around his neck in a hug. Taking a cue from him, she whispered in his ear, "This might not even work."

He chuckled. "Whatever it is, just try it."

She gave him no more warning. It might not have worked if she had. She shifted quickly, forcing her weight onto her right knee. She lifted herself up off the couch, behind him. She shifted her grip around his neck, and bent her right elbow around his throat. It was the same choker hold she'd tried on Velez the day before. She crushed his throat with a squeeze, cutting off his air, and his hands came up instinctively to claw at her arm. "Katie!" he choked. "What are you—"

"Call for help," she said in his ear. She could feel him start to panic in her grip, and she repeated herself more firmly. "Say, 'help.'"

"Help!" It came out a grunt, but clear enough.

"Good," she said. "Now say my name."

"Katie, please—"

"My full name, Martin. Say my name."

"Katie...Katie Pratt." His eyes rolled wildly. He struggled to get a glimpse at her face, to comprehend what was going on. She could feel his pulse pounding, feel the strength going out of his fingers as he scrabbled to pull her forearm off his throat. Another tear escaped her eye, and she said softly in his ear, "I'm sorry, Martin."

A moment before he would have passed out, the door swung open and Velez strode in. As he entered the room he said, "Lock target on the girl." The camera above the door swung to point at her, aiming center mass on her chest, and she could imagine the one above the computer desk pointing at the back of her head. For his part, Velez was carrying a baseball bat, but he was swinging it freely, more like Charlie Chaplin's cane than the deadly club he intended it for. Velez's voice was cool. "Let him go."

She did, and he fell forward off the couch and landed on the floor on his hands and knees, coughing violently. He tilted down until his forehead was on the ground and put a hand to his throat, massaging it lightly. She could just hear him weeping through his gasped breaths.

She looked up to find Velez eying her. "What was that about?" he said. She tilted her chin up, unwilling to answer, and his mouth twisted into a smile. "On your feet." When she didn't respond right away, he looked menacingly toward the camera high on the wall behind her.

She gulped down her fear and gingerly lowered her feet to the floor, then pushed herself up off the couch to stand. Even with all her weight on her right leg, the pain shot up her other leg in waves, crashing thunderously at the base of her skull, and she had to bite back her own whimper. She saw Velez's smile widen.

"You're dangerous, aren't you, Katie?" He looked down to Martin, still collapsed on the floor. "Not to me. You should know that. Here, in my lair, you're no threat at all. All it takes is a word, and you're nothing but a puddle of leaky meat on my floor. I could break your bones or burst your head. Name an organ and I can put a hole through it with surgical precision. My cameras have an amazing grasp of human anatomy." Tears leaked from her eyes, at Martin still helpless on the ground as much as from the pain in her leg, but she made it clear in her expression that she wasn't impressed with Velez's speech.

He rolled his eyes. "Fine," he said. "Look, I heard your conversation. You know that, right? All your precious plotting. You should have listened to Martin. Killing him wouldn't have done you any good, anyway. I *can* figure this out without him. It's just faster with his help." He glanced up at the camera again, and sighed with obvious regret. "And I can get his help more easily if you're about to die than if you're dead. I can't let behavior like that go unpunished, though."

He hefted the bat, and she reacted in fear. "No!" she said, reaching out a hand to him, but he ignored her plea. He stepped into the swing, throwing the bat at her ruined calf. She tried to turn away, but her leg gave under her and she fell. She caught the full impact of the swing on her hip, then an instant later her knee crashed into the floor. The pain that accompanied the dual blows doubled her over with a sob. Her stomach cramped in a dry heave and she fought desperately to catch her breath.

Out of the corner of her eye, she saw Velez's foot fall as he stepped closer. She glanced up and saw the bat coming down. This time she couldn't dodge at all. It slammed into her skull, and the world flickered scarlet. And blinding white. And then totally, blissfully black.

She woke to a pounding. With no windows to let in light from the world, no clocks on the walls and her watch stripped from her, she had no way of knowing how much time had passed. This prison was outside the real world, outside of time and hidden from the eyes of gods and men. A shiver chased down her spine, and she yelped at the pain that accompanied movement. Her head pounded, and the wound in her leg stabbed at her.

It took some time to realize the pounding wasn't only in her head. A steady thunder, muted by distance, broke the silence that otherwise reigned in Velez's subterranean stronghold. She opened her eyes, forced them to focus, and found herself lying on her side once more on the bedroom floor, her face inches away from the door, which stood slightly ajar. She titled her head down to get a good look through the crack, and saw Velez hurrying across from left to right—from his computers to the doorway that led upstairs.

At last she placed the pounding. Someone was knocking on the closet door in the rundown apartment up above. Insistent and strong, the thudding knocks echoed down the spiral stairway and slipped past the closed door downstairs, refusing to be ignored. She could tell from Velez's gait that he was irritated.

He yanked open the door at the bottom of the stairs and shouted up the stairwell, "What?"

A voice answered, muffled by the echo, but Katie thought she heard, "I'm coming down."

Velez stepped back a pace, and a moment later his visitor came through the door. Rick Goodall, her boss, her white knight, her cavalry. Her heart soared, and she bit down a cheer, realizing at the last moment that Velez still didn't know she was awake. His cameras were still armed, too, which meant Rick would have to be careful making his move. She couldn't think of a way to warn him about that without giving away her position.

As Rick stepped into the workshop, his eyes must have fallen on Martin, out of sight to her left, because he froze. His eyes darted to Velez. "What's going on here?"

"Rick, this is Martin Door," Velez said, making polite introductions. She remembered her own arrival in this basement, Velez playing the part of polite host, bragging about his technology until he'd shot her where she stood. He played out the same game with Rick. "He's my old partner in crime. He's here because someone murdered his *niece*. Your girl Katie was working on the case."

"Pratt?" he said. In just the one syllable she heard the disgust in his voice begin to change to comprehension. "They tracked you here—"

"I invited them here," Velez said, condescending. "Because I needed Martin's help with something."

"He's in pretty bad shape for an invited guest," Rick said, irritated now. He towered over Velez, threatening, but Velez turned his back and walked back over to his computer desks. Rick followed him, barking angrily, "Just what do you think you're doing here, Jesus?" He didn't bother with the Spanish pronunciation, but leaned on the long "e," pronouncing it "Jee-zus." He dropped a heavy hand on Velez's shoulder, heavy enough to make the smaller man wince as he pulled away. "What have you done with Pratt?"

Velez said, "The girl is out of the picture."

Katie didn't know what she expected for Rick's answer, but when he just shrugged it broke her heart. "Well, whatever you're up to, I don't have time for this. Dammit, Jesus, I was on my way to meet with the president when you called me down here. He wanted an explanation for the modification I installed on the DoJ mainframe—" He wasn't even there for her.

"All in due time," Velez said, offhand. "The president can wait." They were all outside Katie's vision now, so she quietly eased the door open wider and inched closer, out into the alcove, peeking around a corner to the end of the room where Velez did all his work.

She saw right away what had stopped Rick in his tracks. Martin sat in a chair in the corner, his hands bound behind his back. His face was puffy, purpling with bruises, and one of his eyes already black. A bloody nose and split lip further marred his kindly face, attesting to the violence Velez had inflicted upon him. Katie imagined he had used the bat that lay discarded nearby. A little guy like that couldn't have done so much damage with his bare hands.

Rick stood right behind Velez now, looking over his shoulder as Velez picked through the same page of code he'd been looking at since she arrived. Rick wasn't done chastising Velez.

"You're gonna have to make this right, Jesus. I told you how to get in touch with me. You can't just reroute my plane—"

"I can and I did," Velez said, clearly unafraid of Rick's size. He reached past the younger man to grab a handheld off his other desk and poked at the screen. "Is the DoJ going to revert the changes you made?"

"No," Rick said, frowning. "No, I had full authority. Your change is in place, and I can't think of anyone with both the clearance and the technical knowledge to change it back."

"So—"

Rick bulled over him. "So now it's your turn. I did what you asked me to do, now give me access to direct input." Katie remembered Martin on the train, looking over a list of his own invisible actions to find the record of his conversation with Velez. She remembered something Rick had said on the day she had first met him, too, insisting that was everything he needed to track down all the criminals in the world. And that he was close to getting it.

"I don't think I will," Velez said, and turned to Martin. Even from across the room, Katie could tell that Martin looked dazed, punch drunk. Velez said, "Martin, Martin!" He snapped his fingers to catch his attention. Then he jerked his head toward Rick, towering behind him. "You see this man here? Martin!" Martin finally nodded, dully, and Velez said, "This is your man."

Martin tilted his head, quizzical, clearly not understanding, but Katie figured it out. She didn't yet know why, but she understood. She gasped, horrified, and Rick started to turn toward the sound. Velez hadn't heard her, though. He wanted

Martin to understand, so he leaned down in his face. "This bastard here is the one who killed Janeane."

Rick turned on Velez, and roared, "What!" But Velez ignored him.

"She stumbled across the blackout code right after I uploaded it, and she called the FBI about it. He killed her for being too smart." He said that last like a playground taunt, trying to get a rise out of Martin, but all he got was a moan, and a trickle of tears out of his puffy right eye.

Rick reacted more violently. "You little shit," he said. He drew his gun, and the click of him releasing the safety echoed in the open room. He chambered a round and pointed the gun at Martin's head. "You've got a big mouth, you know that? Now I've got to kill this sad sack."

She couldn't let him do that. She was huddled against the wall now, up on her hip, her legs curled around behind her, most of her weight resting on the wall and just a sliver of the right side of her face peeking around the corner at the three men. She glanced up at the cameras she could see, but the only one with an angle on her hiding place was tracking Rick. She didn't think he knew.

She took a deep breath, desperate to sound authoritative, not like the pathetic, weak girl she was. She forced her voice to a bark, "Don't do it, Rick." She saw him whirl toward her, eyes wide, and instinctively drew back into hiding. She went on, though. "You're in a bad spot right now, whether you realize it or not. Don't make it worse."

He didn't answer right away, and she felt a rising panic that he was stalking straight toward her. She risked a peek around the corner and found that he had turned on Velez instead. "What the hell is this? You told me Pratt was taken care of."

Velez shrugged, still entirely unthreatened by Goodall's menace. Katie could tell that it irked Rick the little man could so easily ignore him. "Pratt is not an issue," he said. "She's as good as dead."

"She is *now*," Rick said, looking toward her corner again. She didn't duck back in time, and when his predator's gaze fell on her she couldn't move, she just cowered in her corner while he stalked toward her. Over his shoulder, he grumbled to Velez. "Dammit, Jesus, I wasn't planning on killing anybody today." He stopped, two paces from Katie, and raised the gun. A thoughtful frown creased his brow, though, and his arm kept moving. He straightened it out to the side, holding the gun out at shoulder level and turning to look back as he pointed right at the back of Velez's head. "Maybe I should just get rid of you while I'm at it."

Velez didn't even look up. He kept typing, working away at his code, but he answered Rick almost distractedly. His voice was that same, infuriating cool. "The girl will sort herself out, and I still need Martin," he said. "I don't need you. Kill Goodall."

Rick didn't have time to pull the trigger. Three of the roving security cameras fired rounds into him—one shot slipped past his spine, smashed through his heart and breastbone and blasted a hole through the door above Katie's right shoulder. Two more tore through his head, exploding it like a melon. The silence of it was eerie, but more so the dispassionate look on Velez's face as he finally looked up from his work to watch a man being obliterated. He frowned at the mess that splashed across his walls, stained his carpet, and then again when his eyes fell on Katie, still alive.

Then he turned to Martin.

"There," he said. "Happy birthday. Janeane is avenged. Will you help me *now*?"

15. Unmasked

As Rick fell, his gun flew from his hand, bouncing once on the carpeted floor and landing enticingly close to the corner where Katie was hiding. She inched forward, pressed her feet painfully against the wall so she could make a good lunge into the room, and just before she moved she glanced up and found Martin's eyes locked on her. She was surprised at the awareness in his eyes now, matched with a blazing intensity as he finally caught her gaze. He shook his head, subtly but enough that she picked it up, then looked up to Velez.

"Yes," he said. He took a deep breath and let it out. "I'll help you. I've seen enough bloodshed."

"Whatever does it for you," Velez said, shrugging. He pointed up to the code, displayed large on the wall. "This is it. The main function is at the bottom, but it mostly just calls other functions that are in roughly chronological order from top to bottom. The big math functions are here," he pointed to a section of code on the display, then scrolled down a couple pages, "and here. It *has* to be a math problem because of the way it's compounding, but I've been over both of these a thousand times. See if you can find something I missed."

"I'll need my hands," Martin said, and Velez nodded and spun Martin's chair around so that he faced the wall opposite Katie. Velez ripped open a drawer on one of his desks and pulled out a pocket knife, and for a moment Katie had a terrible vision of Velez spotting Martin's bluff, and cutting his throat like a butcher. Instead, he dropped to his knee behind Martin's chair, and began sawing at the knots binding Martin's wrists.

Katie inched forward, stretching out a hand in front of her, but something Martin had said earlier swam up in her memory. He had watched Velez program the cameras to prevent them escaping the room. She didn't know what that entailed, exactly, or how it had been overridden to let Martin out. And she still didn't know how many shots a single camera could fire, but three of them had just used up a round each on Rick there. One had shot at her, too, but that had been days ago. Surely it was reloaded by now.

There were two cameras she could see clearly, from her hiding spot, and another just out of sight around the right corner. The three on the near wall were completely hidden from her, but she had a pretty good idea where they were located. For now, her attention was all on the two she could see, swinging lazily back and forth. Lying perfectly still on the floor, she watched the middle one rove in her direction. Her whole body tensed painfully as its dreadful gaze passed over her, but there was no alarm, no silent shot accompanied with screaming pain. The camera moved on, peeking over at the TV on the wall.

The gun was two feet away. She didn't know how much effort she could get out of her damaged leg without passing out, but there would be enough for that lunge. It would also put her well in sight of at least five of the six cameras, though, and for all she knew, motion could be the triggering effect that would leave her in the same messy state Rick was in. She closed her eyes, breathing slow and steady while she summoned the courage to do what had to be done.

Before she found it, Velez spoke up, dashing what hopes she had. "Cameras, forget Goodall. Resume normal operation. Den cameras' primary focus should be on the girl. If she so much as moves—"

He had no chance to give the kill command, though. Martin, hands still bound behind him, heaved his feet up on the edge of the computer desk in front of him and then shoved hard, toppling the chair over on top of Velez. She heard Velez scream, but she didn't waste time worrying what was happening over there. Katie seized her chance and dove forward, fingers closing surely around the grip of the gun, and rolled onto her back in the same motion. Her leg screamed with pain, but she forced it from her mind. The camera directly above her was twisting, contorting to point straight down, and by her estimation it was one of the two that hadn't fired a shot yet. Its lens met her eyes in the same instant that she pulled the trigger. A whisper and a *thonk* told her the camera had fired, too, but her shot ripped the camera loose from the wall and the jostle was enough to make the bullet miss its mark. It buried an inch deep in the subflooring by her left shoulder. She shoved off from the wall and rolled to her left to get an angle on the camera that had shot her before, and it fired on her again as she took it out. The camera's bullet went well astray, exploding through the suede couch and spiderwebbing the surface of the TV before burying itself in the wall. The next camera in her line of sight was one that had shot Rick, and she shattered its main housing with a third shot.

She took out two more cameras with three more rounds, then ducked back into her alcove and hoped the last camera didn't fire on Martin. It was to her right, high up on the wall she was hiding behind, and she'd have to expose herself pretty bad to get a good shot at it. It was loaded, too. She was almost certain it was the last camera that hadn't made a shot.

She checked the clip on Rick's gun, toying with the idea of firing blind, but just then Velez cut through her concentration with a high, thin scream. "Stop it!" She was back in her corner, hiding in the alcove with her back to the wall, and she tried to judge from the scream exactly where Velez was. She could probably roll around the corner and take him out—

Velez interrupted her plans again, and this time his voice was more normal, although still strained. "Drop the gun, Ms. Pratt, or Martin dies." She risked a look around the corner, and saw Velez and Martin both on their feet now. Martin had clearly taken a bad gash to his wrist in that first tumble, because blood soaked his left hand and stained the floor around them. Splashes of it on the toppled chair and both of their clothes showed that they had fought, too, but Velez had clearly been the victor. He stood behind Martin now, his eyes barely peeking past Martin's left shoulder, and the tip of the pocket knife indenting the soft flesh of Martin's neck. Katie's earlier vision swam back up again, and she fought it down.

Martin shouted, "Shoot him, Katie!" and she shook as though he'd hit her.

She yelled back, "Shut up, Martin." She took a deep breath, and then another, trying to calm herself. Her head was starting to spin. Her whole body ached, but this was no time for weakness. She tried to fight past the drunkenness brought on by heavy doses of adrenaline and severe blood loss. She struggled to find some shred of clarity. "Don't hurt him, Velez."

Martin shouted again, and she could hear the stain of heroism in his voice. "Do what must be done, Katie. I'm prepared to make the sacrifice. He's too dangerous—"

"No," she said, hoping the force in her voice would be enough to stay Velez's blade. "Velez, he can still help you. I'm harmless, as you said."

"Then drop the gun, Ms. Pratt."

She held it out at arm's length, in his sight, and let it fall to the floor. She heard him let out an involuntary sigh of relief, and Martin one of disappointment. It didn't matter. There was no reason for Martin to die here.

For a moment it felt like an impasse. She remained hidden, all too aware of the threat of that last remaining camera. The gun was still in range for her to grab, and she knew Velez knew that, but she was at a marked disadvantage until she could reach it. She listened to Velez give new orders to the camera, damning her to death on sight, and wondered how she might possibly get out of it.

As though in answer to the question, Velez spoke up with a cackle. "This place can be your tomb, lady. It's a pretty one. And an expensive one. You can take some consolation from that." Movement caught her attention, and she saw him walk into sight, dragging Martin in front of him as a human shield, the knife's point drawing a bead of blood on his throat. He was crossing toward the door, leaving her here. "If the pain gets too bad," he said, still far too casually for such a topic, "or if somehow you make it past the blood loss and find yourself facing starvation, that could be bad. I'm going upstairs." That last was clearly to his security system, because the steel door at the bottom of the stairs flashed open. "All you have to do is step into the living room to end the pain, Pratt. Remember that, in case it gets too bad."

She ignored his generous offer. Her eyes were past him, locked on the specter looming at the bottom of the stairwell. She couldn't conceal her surprise, the look of hope that bloomed on her face, and Velez responded, but too late. He tried to turn, he even let Martin go to free himself up, but help stood waiting just on the other side of the door. It was Agent Reed, Rick's pretty green-eyed second-in-command, and the slick shadow of Ghoster one step behind him, but Katie only saw a pair of knights in shining armor, there to rescue her. For a moment she mistook Reed for Marshall, her old partner from Brooklyn, and maybe Ghoster looked something like her dad, huge and powerful, and even as Velez started to turn, Reed flashed his right hand up high over his head, and then brought the butt of his gun down hard, catching Velez just below the right ear.

Velez fell like a sack, and Reed's eyes immediately went to the cameras on the wall. Katie remembered the one in the stairwell, and realized her rescuer must have already figured them out. He pointed, cursing, and said, "We've got one more!"

Ghoster never looked up from his handheld. Typing away, he said confidently, "Got it!" Reed hesitated for just a moment, then took a deep breath and stepped into the room. Nothing happened at all. She smiled weakly and let her head fall back against the wall.

And then Reed came to her, the shining armor resolving into jeans and a ragged t-shirt. She blinked, and focused, and recognized him from her few days at the office. He looked almost as tired as she felt. His hair was messy and his eyes bloodshot, and he limped as he came into the room. One step behind him, officers of the Buenos Aires police department flooded into the room. Reed shouted instructions in Spanish, pointing as he crossed the room, and most of the police swarmed on Velez and Martin, hauling them apart. Ghoster moved past them both, fixedly avoiding eye contact with either of his old friends as he headed toward Velez's computers and started searching through the code. Reed's attention swiftly settled on Katie, though, and he didn't stop until he was at her side, kneeling.

"Y'know," he said, reaching delicately to check the bruised knot on the side of her head before he turned his attention to the leg. "I told you you were in over your head."

"Hah!" she said, and it came out almost a cough. She forced a smile anyway. "I solved my case before you solved yours."

"You cheated," he said, playfully severe. "I knew you would get in the way." He finished checking her over, and sank back onto his knees, shaking his head. "We need to get you out of here right away."

She realized he was trying very hard not to look at the corpse right behind him, and she looked down. "Reed." She said, shaking her head quickly. "That's.... Rick was—"

"I know," he said, but he looked away. "I heard it all."

"You what?"

"I heard it all," Reed said. "I'm still not entirely sure how, but about an hour ago Hippocrates got a sudden, massive data injection from an anonymous server, which happened to contain spoken keywords that triggered a red flag Rick had set up—"

She said her name. "Katie Pratt."

"Katie Pratt. And with it an emergency signal on one Martin Door that included not only location, but a real-time audio stream."

She smiled, staring up at the ceiling. "It worked."

"It worked," he said, admiration in his voice. "We heard everything, Katie. And with Ghoster's assistance—" He stopped, eyes suddenly distant as a voice spoke into his headset, and then nodded. "Site secured. Come on down. The paramedics are here, Katie. We're going to take care of you."

She caught at his arm, suddenly worried about Martin. "Reed, Velez is a monster, but Martin Door—"

"It's okay," he said, as a pack of paramedics swarmed into the room behind him, rushing straight to her with a gurney between them. He pulled free of her grasp and stepped back to give them room. "Everything will be okay. I just want you to focus on getting better. We're going to need all the help we can get back at Ghost Targets."

She shook her head, trying to argue. She didn't need his fake encouraging words. This was important. But the paramedics pressed close, and one of them might have given her an injection for the pain, and Reed clearly had more important matters to deal with right then. He turned away, barking at the police officers in Spanish. She tried to fight, to catch his attention, but there was no strength left in her. They hoisted her up onto the gurney, and halfway across the room all the energy she had left fled her at once, and she surrendered to sleep.

16. Goodbye

She woke up in a hospital room, eight hours and two surgeries later. Narrow windows high on the wall still let in a piercing shaft of the bursting dawn, and the light drew her from her sleep. For the first time since she'd been shot, she came to with no feeling of disorientation. Even with the drugs still in her system, she knew immediately where she was, and why. The room was clean. Sterile. White. And the pain that growled angrily through the shroud of her meds guaranteed she knew why she was there.

She had an IV in her right arm, and a breakfast tray set out on a stand at her left hand, but what really caught her attention lay on the bedside table right by her head. A headset and a handheld. Links to the real world. She wondered that the watch wasn't there.

Of course they weren't hers, but she knew immediately whose they were. She recognized the battered, ancient handheld Martin had used. It occurred to her he might be dead, these his last possessions given to her in respect. She shook her head, dismissing the thought, and finally gave in to her desire and grabbed the headset off the table. She slipped it over her ear and turned on the audio.

She heard Reed's voice. Not the sharp, frantic bark of orders he'd been engaged in before, but the quiet, concentrating mutterings of someone deep in thought. It was all very technical, and she couldn't quite hear the other side of the conversation, but she picked up to know it was Ghoster talking things through as the two of them tried to find their way around Velez's computer.

She smiled. "Reed," she said.

"Katie?" She heard the pitch of hope and relief tint his voice, and in an instant whatever he'd been working on was forgotten. "Katie, are you okay?"

"I will be," she said. "I'm a tough one."

"So I've heard."

"Reed, Rick was a killer. He was the ghost in the Little Rock case—"

"I know," Reed said, soothing. "We've been over all that." She blushed, remembering their brief conversation inside Velez's lair.

"I'm sorry," she said. "The drugs—"

He cut her off with a laugh. "You don't owe anybody any apologies," he said. That didn't seem right to her, for him to forgive her so much, so quickly, and she caught herself frowning, several moments into a pregnant silence, when he said, "What is it, Katie?"

She blinked. She shook her head. "How can you know...." She couldn't find the words, but she didn't need to.

"We've known about Rick for a day now," Reed said. "I got a call from DoJ concerning a firearms violation in the metro. He had taken my sidearm, locked in my desk at the office, and used it to fire on you, Katie. HaRRE showed him plain as day, though, and that was enough to clear my name. Rick, though.... We could all tell, looking at the footage, that something was wrong with Rick."

"Did he try to explain it?" Katie said. "What was his justification?"

Reed laughed, bitter. "We never got one. He was gone, Katie. From the moment we lost track of you at Union Station, he disappeared. Rick wasn't taking our calls, you were off-grid with a ghost, and we just had one unholy mess on our hands. So, first things first, I called the Secret Service to warn them we probably weren't going to be able to resolve the assassination case in time."

"Oh no," she said, fearing the worst. "And?"

"And...there was no case." Reed sighed. "There never was. Rick had made it up, I guess as a distraction."

"He didn't trust Velez, then," Katie said. "Or he thought you guys could see through his ghosting."

Reed shrugged it off. "Whatever the reason, he didn't want any of his real agents working the Linson case. Anyway, when I figured out something was going on, I convinced the Secret Service to call Rick in. He took *their* call, even when he wasn't taking mine. They went with a fake summons by the president, which was enough to distract him from his hunt for you. He got on a plane to Toronto, to meet the president at a conference there, while we started trying to figure out what was really going on."

Katie remembered the man's outrage that Velez had summoned him. "He never made it," she said. "His plane turned toward Argentina—"

"We caught a lucky break there," Reed said. "We were running short on personnel and ideas by then, so I'd finally agreed to listen to Ghoster and he was helping us track Rick's flight. Somehow he caught the signal that changed the plane's destination just before it disappeared."

"Disappeared?"

"Velez got to it. Rick, the plane, the pilots—everybody went ghost at once, and we lost all information. Ghoster told us he was headed here, and we got on a jet maybe twenty minutes later. Beat him here, but he got past us at the airport somehow. After that, we had nothing to go on. No leads, nothing. We half suspected the plane had changed routes again after disappearing, and then we got your message."

She smiled again, still proud of that one. "I'm amazed it worked."

"We were close to the right spot, actually, but it took me a while to figure out what was really going on," Reed said. A note of sadness entered his voice. "We probably could have been there right behind Rick, if I'd figured it out sooner."

She said, "How could you have?"

"I know." He took a deep breath, and let it go. "Maybe it's easiest this way, anyway. I couldn't have.... Jeez, Katie. What the hell is with these cameras, anyway?"

"His custom security system," she said. "He built it for the Navy or something. They're wild."

"We battled one in the stairwell," he said. "Took out three men before Ghoster got it locked down. And you got five of them on your own." He whistled. "This whole thing, Katie. This is good police work. Martin's immediate personal history, in the Hippocrates submission, included voice records from his headset. I've had a little time to review it now. You're a hero, Katie."

"No," she protested weakly, but he spoke over her.

"You went deep undercover and took out a real threat to national security. Do you have any idea the catastrophe you prevented?" He sighed. "It would have been...unbelievable. Apocalyptic. You exposed a traitor at the highest level of the FBI, and helped us capture two of the most notorious ghosts in the system. These guys have been a black eye for the bureau for as long as we've been around."

"Reed, Martin isn't—"

"I know he helped you, Katie," he said. "We'll take that into consideration. But we can't just let him go."

"You don't understand," she said.

He sighed heavily. "I do, Katie. But he's too dangerous to be loose. We'll have to do something about him."

"No, Reed—" She stopped as a face appeared in the door window, purple and black, and one eye swollen all the way shut. The other danced, though, with the same grin that twisted Martin's split lip when he saw her. They had done some work on him, but he was still in a terrible state.

Reed spoke in her ear, "We'll deal with Martin later, Katie. I've got to take care of stuff down here. Ghoster's been digging through Velez's system for hours, and it's a labyrinth. You just focus on getting well." He sighed again, and she could hear how tired he was. "We're going to need you to be strong, in the days to come."

She ignored him, though. Her attention was on Martin, who held up a finger to his lips, for her to be quiet, as he slipped through the door and up to her bedside. She saw a police officer, one of the locals, peer in through the door's window as the door fell shut, watching Martin suspiciously. Martin, for his part, kept his body between Katie and her bodyguard as he held out a hand toward her, palm up, asking for his stuff back. His wrists were cuffed together.

Katie muted the headset so Reed couldn't hear them, although she could still hear him trying to work out one of Velez's many mad secrets. She ignored him as she scooped up the handheld from the table and pressed it into Martin's hand. Hesitantly, hating to give up her connection to the world, she reached back up for the headset, but he waved her away. "Keep it," he said.

She sighed. "I'll take care of this," she said, nodding at his handcuffs. "They can't lock you up, not after everything you did."

He smiled back at her, reassuring, and shook his head. "Don't worry about it, Katie. You've done enough." He nodded down at his handheld, and it took her a moment to realize what he meant. He tapped on it for a moment, operating controls, and then nodded as his handcuffs clicked open, and fell uselessly to the floor with a tinny rattle.

Her jaw fell open. "How did you...."

He shrugged. "These have a safeguard that prevents them being used against the federal agents that carry them. I just borrowed your credentials for a moment."

He was going to get himself in real trouble. She shook her head. "Martin, I can take care of this. I'll make sure nothing happens to you. You don't have to do this."

"I do," he said, and reached out to brush the hair from her face. The smile was gone now. "Velez was right, Katie. Mad as a hatter, but he was right. Hathor can't go on ruling the world like a corrupt tyrant. Something must be done. For one, we have to figure out who's really running things."

"I have a guess," Katie said, and Martin smiled knowingly.

"Oh, I do, too," he said. "But if it's true, he has resources far beyond anything we imagined. And he could catch me, even if no one else could. It's going to take someone outside the system, someone with special access, to counteract the threat he poses."

"No," Katie said, suddenly afraid. "Martin, don't. You already tried that, for years, and you regretted it." Tears sprang to her eyes. "You said it was a mistake. You said you never should have gone along, and that you could trust me. Martin, you *can* trust me."

He laid a gentle finger on her lips, and met her eyes with a deep sadness in his. "I know," he said. "I can. But I don't have faith enough that the system will cure itself. I have to do what I can, while I can. Besides, now I have a plan. For the first time, I have a definite purpose." He looked at his handheld for a moment, thinking, and finally said absently, "I have his code. Every line of it, on this. I had to tell them it was yours to get it smuggled out of there. I'm sorry about using you like that."

"Martin, don't go. You can help me, and we'll sort out Hathor together."

"We will," he said, clapping her on the shoulder with a smile. "Don't you worry about that. I won't try to do it all on my own. For now, though—"

She was distracted by the quiet audio in her headset, Reed suddenly shouting something, quick and loud, and immediately behind it the unmistakable, thunder sound of an explosion. Her eyes grew wide, and Martin must have recognized why because he started operating the handheld furiously, and a moment later his eyes grew wide, too. "Katie," he said, "I didn't do that—"

Most of her attention was on the audio, though, and a moment later her heart started again when she heard Reed talking, "I need help here. This is Agent Reed, and I'm trapped in suspect Velez's apartment." His voice was irritated, but he didn't sound panicked. He didn't sound injured. "Some of his computer equipment was rigged, and it exploded when we tried to remove it from the premises. If any friendlies copy, I could use some immediate rescue help here." He paused for a moment, then began to repeat the same message in Spanish. Katie opened her mouth to respond to him, reached up to turn her mic back on, but Martin stopped her with one hand on her wrist and the other laying lightly on her lips, just the fingertips.

"They'll be okay," Martin said. "I had no hand in that, but it's as good a time as any for me to make my exit." He leaned down to kiss her on the forehead, gently, and said, "You're an amazing woman, Katie. I'm glad to have met you."

She tried one last time. "Don't do this, Martin."

But he only shrugged and executed some script he had prepared on his handheld. A voice in her headset announced an emergency downstairs, something in Spanish about a suspect spotted somewhere unexpected, and she heard the officer outside her door respond, and then boots slapping on the floor as he fled his post in search of a phantasmal Martin.

Meanwhile, the real one smiled down at her in her bed. "Don't bother looking for me," he said. "I have work to do. I can see that now." He took two long steps away and pulled the door open, his eyes still locked on hers, and just before he disappeared into the hall he said, "But don't worry. I'll be in touch."

A moment later, he was gone.

THE END

Don't miss out!

Click the button below and you can sign up to receive emails whenever Aaron Pogue publishes a new book. There's no charge and no obligation.

http://books2read.com/r/B-A-E-B

Connecting independent readers to independent writers.

Did you love *Surveillance*? Then you should read *Expectation* by Aaron Pogue!

Eric Barnes put an end to human aging. Now he's paying for it with his life.

FBI Special Agent Katie Pratt returns to the Ghost Targets team to find herself and the rest of the team under investigation for corruption by a government agency. Katie's relationship with Martin Door, one of the creators of the Hathor system and its surveillance of everyone and everything, leaves her especially vulnerable.

The new boss assigns Katie to a case in Boulder, Colorado to save her from ongoing interrogation, but the case quickly steals the Ghost Targets team's full attention. A scientist, violently attacked in his own lab, is in a coma.

The victim leads the research for a drug that could end human aging, extending lifespans to thousands of years. The key to the drug is locked in his slumbering brain, but even in this world where every action is recorded in Hathor, the records of the attack on him are gone. Katie must uncover the truth to protect the miracle drug and regain her own reputation.

Katie's search for answers will force her to scale a mountain of secrets and lies whose summit is the overwhelming power of human expectation.

Expectation is the second book in the Ghost Targets series.

Read more at AaronPogue.com.

Also by Aaron Pogue

A Consortium of Worlds
A Consortium of Worlds No. 1
A Consortium of Worlds No. 2

A Dragonswarm Short Story
Remnant
From Embers

Auric's Valiants
Notes from a Thief
Auric and the Wolf

Ghost Targets
Surveillance
Expectation
Restraint
Camouflage

The Dragonprince's Arrows
A Darkness in the East

The Dragonprince's Legacy
Taming Fire
The Dragonswarm
The Dragonprince's Heir
The Original Dragonprince Trilogy

Unstressed Syllables Presents
Turn Your Story into an eBook: Easy Self-Publishing with Draft2Digital.com

Watch for more at AaronPogue.com.

About the Author

Aaron Pogue is a husband and a father of two who lives in Oklahoma City, OK. Aaron started writing at the age of ten. His first novels were high fantasy set in the rich world of the FirstKing, but he's explored mainstream thrillers, urban fantasy, and several kinds of science fiction. Author of the Dragonprince's Legacy, the Godlanders War, and the Ghost Targets series, Aaron Pogue has sold a quarter of a million books since his debut in 2010.

Aaron has been a Technical Writer with the Federal Aviation Administration and a writing professor at the university level. He holds a Master of Professional Writing degree from the University of Oklahoma. He also serves as the President of Draft2Digital, an ebook formatting, conversion, and distribution service that he helped found in 2012.

Read more at AaronPogue.com.

CPSIA information can be obtained
at www.ICGtesting.com
Printed in the USA
FFOW02n0802091215
19470FF